ENTHRALL

BOOK ONE

VANESSA FEWINGS

This story is a work of fiction. References to real people, events, establishments, organizations, or locales are intended only to provide a sense of authenticity and are used fictitiously. All other characters, and all incidents and dialogue are drawn from the author's imagination and are not to be construed as real.

Cover design by VMK
Cover photo is from Shutterstock—Photographer Phase4Studios
Edited by Louise Bohmer

For Brad

"Pain is the root of knowledge."
Simone Weil, (1910-1943) French Philosopher

CHAPTER ONE

I NEEDED THIS.

More than anything.

On the other side of that long, dark wooden table sat three beautiful women, all unimpressed with the answers I'd given so far. I was blowing this interview.

And sabotaging my future.

Enthrall, L.A.'s most exclusive BDSM club, was hiring a new secretary and by the look of things I wasn't going to be her, and that unbelievably high salary wasn't going to be mine. This moment wasn't about greed, but survival. I was done with eating Ramen noodles, living in a studio, and riding my bicycle around the city's streets to save on gas. Working two jobs was grueling. Monday through Friday I was a salesperson at Willem's art supply store in West Hollywood, where many of the city's creative wannabes hung out, dreaming of making it big. On the weekends, I worked as a server at the Cheesecake Factory. Both jobs I enjoyed, but never having a day off was starting to take a toll.

This interview felt like a lifeline, though somehow my hands were slipping down the rope toward failure.

Two of the women on the panel hadn't even introduced themselves, which I found odd and made this even more awkward. Tara, my best friend's girlfriend, could have warned me about this. Having been their previous secretary for years, she was probably used to all this intensity and thought nothing of this sexual tension that even oozed from the designer red brick walls.

Walls that were closing in around me.

The woman on the right had a Scottish accent and was somewhere in her forties. She wore an expensive Chanel suit and designer spectacles that she peered through to text away on her BlackBerry. The stunning raven-haired woman on the other side, with her model good-looks and head-to-toe black leather, contradicted her colleague's conservative attire. At least the raven-haired interviewer was kind enough to throw me the occasional smile.

"Your resume is very limited," said Mistress Scarlet, the stern brunette in the middle, as she scanned the file.

I questioned why I continued to put myself through this. Five minutes ago, while in the waiting room, one of the other interviewees had burst out of here and given me the thumbs up.

"It went great!" she'd told me, her cleavage doing a happy dance as she sashayed down the hallway.

My black skirt and white blouse felt wrong on so many levels. I'd gone for serious, studious even, trying to look professional. They must have been looking for a sophisticated type, an employee who would easily mingle in. I sat up straighter, unwilling to admit defeat just yet.

The hardwood floors, dim lighting, and low hanging black and white prints of city life gave off an east coast feel, exuding swanky. If this was all put together to intimidate, it succeeded.

"Why do you want to work here?" said Ms. BlackBerry obsessed.

"Well—" I gestured to make my point. "I truly believe this open-minded environment and diverse clientele will help me to grow as a person."

Mistress Scarlet looked amused. "So it's not the salary?"

"The salary is generous," I said, saving my humiliation for later when I'd drown my sorrows with a bottle of wine.

I blushed in response to their fixed gazes. I could swear they saw right through me, catching me wilt with each failure to deliver the answers they seemed to want.

"Where are you from?" said Mistress Scarlet.

"Charlotte," I said.

"Bet you don't miss the humidity," said raven-haired.

"No."

"You're very young," she said.

"Twenty-one."

Mistress Scarlet looked tense. "What do you know about what we do here?"

"You fulfill the exotic needs of special clients." I prided myself on side-stepping that one.

"Please answer the question," said Ms. BlackBerry while texting.

I waited for her to push send. "This is a private club."

Mistress Scarlet's mouth twisted in a half-formed smile.

"S and M," I said.

Mistress Scarlet was giving me a taste of how she made her client's feel.

"Sadism and masochism?" I made it a question.

"Pleasure and pain," said BlackBerry user. "What does your mom think of you working here?"

Understandably I'd not gotten asked that when I'd been interviewed for Stella Willem's art store. "She died years ago. I have a step-mom."

"I'm sorry to hear that." She rested her cell on the table. "Does your step-mom know you're here?"

"Yes, of course," I lied.

Mistress Scarlet steepled her fingers. "We pride ourselves on hearing secrets and keeping them. This is more than a club. It's a society for well-balanced adults who enjoy exploring their predilections in a safe and nurturing environment."

"I have to be honest," said Ms. BlackBerry. "Which we pride ourselves on here, you don't seem comfortable with your sexuality."

I had no answer for that.

Mistress Scarlet continued, "We can't have the receptionist blushing every time a client comes in."

"What Mistress Scarlet is saying," added Ms. BlackBerry, "is we have clients visit from all over the world. Exclusive members. Their contentment is our priority."

"My best friend's gay," I said. "I'm open minded. We shared a dorm."

"Are *you* gay?" said Ms. BlackBerry.

I wriggled uncomfortably. Weren't there rules in interviews?

Mistress Scarlet threw her colleague a look before nodding at me. "Mia?"

"No," I said, blushing.

Raven-haired added, "Mia, we don't abide by rules that you find in other places of employment. Perhaps you'd be more comfortable in that kind of job? We applaud your visit here today. We do."

My stunned silence lingered.

Mistress Scarlet leaned forward. "Self-control, tact, maturity, wisdom, these are all traits we need in our staff."

The room fell quiet.

"I've always been good at putting people at ease," I said softly.

A telephone rang from somewhere down the hallway, breaking the silence but not touching the tension.

"What we need," said Mistress Scarlet, "is a receptionist to facilitate appointments. Sign in our clients. It's an important job. We need an individual who can respect our member's privacy and make them feel welcome. As the senior dominant's secretary, you'll be expected to possess excellent communication and organizational skills."

"I have that," I said.

Raven-haired raised her chin. "Well that's good."

There came another awkward silence.

"Thank you for coming in," said Mistress Scarlet.

I rose and reached into my handbag. "Here are my...um... Victoria's Secret." I placed my lacey underwear on the table before Mistress Scarlet.

Cheeks burning, I backed away and headed for the door.

"Wait a moment, please," said raven-haired, rising to her feet and making her way around the table.

I caught sight of her black leather thigh-high boots. The spiked heels appeared deadly. Elegantly, she closed in. This striking woman was the first dominatrix I'd ever met. She oozed a sexual confidence and her musky perfume of fresh cut flowers and amber wafted over me; the heady scent of Dior's Poison. Yet strangely enough there was something comforting about her. The sense that she could handle pretty much anything. Or anyone.

"What did Tara tell you exactly?" She straightened my collar, which must have been sticking up the entire time.

I glanced over at Mistress Scarlet and Ms. BlackBerry, while fumbling to get my collar under control. "Tara mentioned you'd see this as a gesture of my seriousness to…"

"Go on?" she purred the words like a panther, pretty to look at but ready to pounce; a dominatrix's allure.

"Tara told me it got her the job."

She leaned in closer. "Tara took them off in front of us."

I wondered why Tara had left that out.

She gestured to my skirt. "You have panty lines."

My gaze found the door and I held back a cringe. I'd merely popped into the mall on my way here and picked up a brand new thong and ripped off the tag. Though I'd never have gone pantyless no matter how much I needed this job. I wasn't ready for anything like that.

These women specialized in the darker side of sex. If I wanted to work here I'd have to prove I could handle whatever they threw at me. Studying the faces of my female jury, I'd clearly failed to convince them I could live on the edge. Instead, I balanced precariously on it, ready to fall from the dizzying heights of lasting embarrassment and land squarely on my ass.

"I'm willing to learn." I ran my hand through my hair, conceding it was over. "I want to learn."

Panther peered under her long black lashes at me.

"You never told me your name?" I said.

"Charlotte."

"I'm from Charlotte."

"You told us."

Yes, I had, and now I'd gone and embarrassed myself all over again.

"Call me Lotte," she said.

There was a ping on Ms. BlackBerry's BlackBerry and she peered up. "We'll be in touch."

Lotte lingered close, as though testing my personal boundary. "I'll show you out."

We made our way down a long hallway. The artwork was stunning; dark gothic paintings lined the walls on both sides and I wished there was more time to look at them. Whatever hung in the air in that room had taken on a life of its own. Perhaps it had been the combination of their richly textured perfumes, the kind I could never afford, mingling with the warrior confidence of these women.

I wondered how they'd all ended up here. What had driven them to this lifestyle choice of black leather and getting up to goodness knows what in dark, sexually charged dungeons. The kind they apparently had here on the lowest level. There was something so wicked about this whole punishment and pleasure thing, and I was fascinated by what really went on.

After we went out another door, back the way I'd come, we headed toward the elevator. Lotte punched the down button to call the elevator. Upon her neck twinkled the largest diamond I'd ever seen.

She twirled her fingers around the delicate chain. "From a very naughty client."

My eyebrows rose before I could stop them. "What did you do before this?"

"I was a pharmacist."

"This pays better?"

Lotte burned a look through me. "I don't do this for the money." Her gaze drifted over to the other elevator. The one right behind the secretary's desk. "I'm a healer."

"Where does that lead?"

"That's where we take our clients," she said huskily.

My spine tingled with anticipation. I discreetly took in her attire. Those thigh high boots and her fitted leather corset that creaked seductively when she moved; the way her pale cleavage rose above the delicate lace edging. The spicy scent of incense wafted through the air and music flowed out of hidden speakers; a deep, foreign chanting that was so soothing, so enticing, it made my stomach quiver. It was all so forbidden.

Slowly, she curled a strand of my long hair around her fingertip. "Are you a natural blonde?"

"Yes."

"Beautiful," she said. "You look like you've stepped right out of a William-Adolphe Bouguereau."

"Um..."

"A painter." She smiled softly. "He knew how to portray the soul of a woman. He'd have perfectly captured your delicate frame, those deep blue eyes and your rosebud lips." She leaned in closer. "Only the old masters could have painted your innocence."

An awkwardness followed.

After stepping into the elevator, I held my breath until the doors closed. Mistress Lotte oozed a sensuality I'd only ever read about. Those last few minutes left my head spinning, as if I awoke from a dream. I took in the expensive full length mirrors, plush carpet, and state-of-the-art buttons. I glanced around for a camera but couldn't see one.

My Mini-Cooper was parked between a silver BMW and black Jaguar. I moaned when I saw oil trailing from beneath my car, staining the concrete. I hoped my Mini would at least start and I'd not bring unwanted attention by having to rev the engine to get it going.

Lingering for a few minutes in the fresh air, I took in all that grandness. This Hollywood Hills club even intimidated from the out-side with its chic brickwork design, an ornate facade rising up as a majestic statement of privilege. Had I really believed a girl like me could ever get to work in such an elegant place like Enthrall?

What the hell had I been thinking?

CHAPTER TWO

A NEW DEGREE OF HUMILIATION HAD FOUND ME.
Apparently I'd discovered original ways to embarrass myself. I sat at my studio apartment kitchen counter, replaying the hellish interview over and over.

I buried my face in my hands.

That dream of a one bedroom apartment would have to wait. When I'd first moved into this studio it had felt like a palace with more space then I'd ever had to myself. Though now I'd outgrown it, and all this secondhand furniture made me feel like a failure. That old couch in the corner with its strategically positioned pillows to hide the stains left by its previous owner. That rickety old fridge that woke me up each night as it shuddered away, trying to spit out cubes of ice from its freezer long broken.

This glass of Sauvignon Blanc did nothing to soothe my disappointment. My anger at myself for blowing such a great opportunity wouldn't let up. The idea I'd not prepared properly and had allowed the chance to earn some real money to slip through my fingers brought waves of regret.

Had I really handed over a pair of underwear during an interview? Placed those lacey Victoria's Secret before Mistress Scarlet as a hint I wasn't wearing any? What were they meant to do with them anyway?

Tara had let me down in the worst kind of way and I tried to wrap my head around why she'd want to sabotage me. She'd dated Bailey, my best friend, for over a year now and I'd always liked her, very often going out with them on the weekends and never feeling like a third wheel. Not once had Tara shown any sign of jealousy, even though Bailey and I had a long history of friendship, having grown up together in Charlotte. Tara and Bailey's relationship had been a little strained lately but that had nothing to do with me. Tara had been threatening to fly off to Australia to join her brother who lived there. I'd hated seeing how much stress this caused Bailey, even though all she wanted was for Tara to be happy.

Bailey's positive reaction to me applying for this new job had been surprising considering how old fashioned she was, but she'd seen every bit of bad luck that had come my way. She knew firsthand how shitty life had been for me.

Was Tara's jealousy rearing its ugly head for the first time? I'd gone into that interview unprepared, looking overly innocent, all blonde curls and caught in the headlight eyes.

Tara knew how much I needed this money, how important it was for me to get my life back on track and ease up on drowning. My step-mother, Lorraine, had more medical bills piling up and I'd promised to take care of them. Lift some of that stress she was under. Still, Lorraine was in remission now due to all that chemo and that was an answered prayer. Having taken me in after my dad died, Lorraine had saved me from life on the streets, and now it was my turn to save her.

I sighed deeply, realizing I'd been so close to pulling it off.

That last look Mistress Lotte had given me still haunted, and coming from a dominatrix only made it worse. Those glares of disapproval from the other two women achieved their desired effect, leaving me feeling insignificant. More disturbing still, my banal answers failed to let them see my upbeat personality, my joie de vive attitude, and my ability to approach everything with an open heart and mind. I'd looked like a scared schoolgirl. I'd blown the whole thing.

Reverently, I picked up the small rectangle plastic sleeve containing the mint condition 1952 Mickey Mantle baseball card. I'd just retrieved it from that metal box I kept hidden in the cupboard. I got it out for moments like this. A lifeline to my past and I found it comforting to look at. It reminded me of my father. I'd managed to salvage it from a footlocker he had left after he died. His widow, Lorraine, had sold off everything else at a Rose Bowl swap meet. We needed the money. She'd not seen me rummage through his stuff and take it out. I felt guilty as hell as it would fetch around ten thousand dollars, maybe even more, which was a small fortune to me. I'd gotten the card valued once when hunger had pushed me to it, but when it came to letting it go I'd not been able to part with it. This Mickey Mantle card was my only reminder of him.

If I couldn't get this job I was going to have to sell it.

The wine tasted bitter. Having gone for the cheapest bottle, I now suffered the consequences of drinking the overly fermented white; an acerbic twang lingered. Still, its promise of numbing this ache in my chest kept me sipping away.

To think I'd spent hours mulling over whether I felt ready to work in a fetish club. I'd self-explored with surprising results and come to terms with the idea of a place like Enthrall. I'd reassured myself I'd merely be working as their secretary. Not that it mattered now.

There lingered a curiosity for what went on in those dungeons. A fascination with Mistress Lotte who, according to Tara, was one of L.A.'s most renowned dominatrixes. Her BDSM world of black leather and whips lay a million miles away from my own.

I braved another sip and smacked my lips together to soften the sharp tang attacking my tongue.

My iPhone rang and I nudged it away. I didn't care who was calling. I wasn't going to answer. My hand betrayed me and I glanced at the number. Wasn't that the area code for Santa Monica? Or even Hollywood Hills?

I took a gulp of wine.

CHAPTER THREE

BAILEY HAD COME THROUGH FOR ME YET AGAIN.

She'd leant me all of her black dresses until I could afford to go out and buy my own. Black being the dress code for Enthrall. My head was still spinning that I'd actually gotten this job. Talk about reading people wrong. Those three vixens had actually liked me. What a mind fuck.

There was a simple design to my desk, with its elegant glass front panel that was perfect for showing off my new boots. The flat screen computer was easy to navigate and Lotte had provided me with Enthrall's diary in which I'd be making all their appointments.

Wearing this Elie Tahari Estelle dress, I hoped to make the best impression on my first day. Along with my Calvin Klein black high-heeled boots, which was the only item I'd been able to afford to buy brand new in a Macy's sale.

I already missed my friends from the art store and promised them I'd stay in touch, just as I had with my Cheesecake pals who'd made those long evenings of waiting tables all the more bearable. I'd told them my new job was as a hostess in a nightclub, not sure quite what they would think of me if I shared the truth. I still had to break it to Lorraine.

Breathing in the fresh scent of incense, I marveled at how quickly this had all happened. My life had taken what felt like a 180 degree turn. A sense of order found me for the first time in years. My fear of having crashed and burned at my interview was now replaced with a sense of pride that I'd pulled it off. My one chance to let them see my potential had gone way better then I'd thought. Excitement swelled in my chest as I took everything in.

Behind that main doorway to my left, where clients were not allowed to venture, were three lavishly decorated offices. Next came the luxurious well-stocked coffee room, and they even had a staff changing room that doubled as a spa. It reminded me of one of those high-end places where you spend a fortune at to get pampered on your birthday, with its heavenly scent of sandalwood and the Buddha head resting upon an elegant waterfall pushed up against the far wall. A wooden bench sat facing it for staff needing to Zen-out. There was even a Jacuzzi and a sauna in there; the lemon ice-water drinking fountain made a nice touch. I'd been giddy with excitement when Lotte had invited me to use the facilities.

Enthrall's other elevator sat behind me. It's old fashioned crisscrossed golden gate providing a dramatic entryway into the lowest level. Lotte had given strict orders that under no circumstances were any guests allowed to venture down there without prior consent. She'd gone on to advise me I was also forbidden. Though being banned from the dungeon was fine by me.

The reception area was all dark wood and dim-lighting. A familiar theme it seemed. The burgundy, velvet sofa looked cozy. The hardwood floor provided a loft-like feel, though the deep red walls of the entryway gave off a disquieting aura. There was a perfection here that made me unsettled. Would I ever get used to it?

There came a ping from the front elevator.

Preparing to meet the first client of the day, I ran through my mind how I'd greet them and what kind of words I might draw on to soften what must be an embarrassing ordeal of needing to visit this place. Opening Enthrall's appointment diary and scanning today's page, I couldn't see any appointments scheduled earlier than 2:00 P.M.

The elevator doors parted and a tall, dashing, twenty-something man strolled out, his short sandy-blond hair windswept, the strap to his satchel lying flat across his chest. He headed fast toward me with his hand cupping his right eye.

"Hi." He waved at me and headed for the staff door.

I flew from my seat and edged my way between him and the door. "I'm sorry, sir, but that's staff only," I said, proud of the authority in my voice.

I was sandwiched between him and the door.

He peered down at me with his noble, intelligent face. The kind that hints at good breeding, as though both his parents had been stunners. Like he'd stepped off the cover of a yachting magazine, all suntan and privilege. Yes, beautiful, that was it, and rugged at the same time. An hypnotic combo.

"My contact lens is boring its way into my iris." He scrunched up his face. "Please, get out of my way."

"Sir, I'm going have to ask you to take a seat."

"What temp agency are you from?" he said.

"I'm not a temp. I work here full-time."

"No you don't." He seethed, grabbing the handle and opening the door. He nudged me aside and bolted down the hallway.

Annoyed by his arrogance, I ran to my desk and pushed the panic button.

Nothing.

What good was an alarm if no one responded? I opened the door and peeked down the hallway. At least I'd warned them we had an intruder.

Mistress Lotte appeared, taking her time to reset the alarm on what looked like an air con panel on the wall. "Mia," she said, "everything's fine."

"You know him?" My gaze moved over her shoulder and rested on the young man who'd barged in.

Oh shit.

He fixed on me with a glaring intensity, his midnight blue eyes burning through me. Chiseled features worn so well on a proud face. An edgy confidence. He wore round rimmed glasses, having taken out his contacts, and that five o'clock shadow I'd failed to notice when he'd first appeared oozed *don't mess with me*. Yet he dressed preppy, his white shirt open at the collar and his black jacket now removed.

Lotte motioned toward him. "Mia, this is Richard Booth. Your new boss." She turned around. "Master Richard, I'm delighted to introduce you to your new secretary, Ms. Lauren."

My blood pressure spiked and my legs wobbled as I realized this strikingly handsome man, this apparent dominant, was my boss.

I steadied my breathing.

"Mia's well trained," said Lotte. "See, even we can't get in." She made it a joke.

"Why didn't I get to interview her?" he said icily.

"We have the director's approval," said Lotte. "He wants you to know this is non-negotiable."

"When is anything negotiable with him?" said Richard.

"Say hello," Lotte whispered to him.

Her domineering demeanor had its expected effect upon him.

He conceded with a nod. "Ms. Lauren, I like my coffee white with one sugar. My office, five minutes."

"Please," I said.

Lotte threw me a look of surprise.

"Please," he said with a frown.

"Call me Mia," I said, remembering Tara telling me to act self-assured. "May I call you Richard?"

He turned on his heel and headed off through the door.

"Beam that sweet smile of yours," said Lotte. "He's bound to come round."

A little disconcerted he'd not known about me being hired, I headed past Lotte and into the kitchen.

I inhaled the fresh scent of the finest coffee beans. They were costly too, based on the price tag on the packet. Musing how the smell was always nicer than it tasted, I added milk from the carton I found in the stainless-steel fridge, grabbed a sweet and low and a white sugar sachet, and headed out. Pausing before Richard's door I stole a moment to raise my guard, preparing to feign nonchalance. Richard was a little scary.

He chatted away on the phone and gestured where I could place his mug, pointing to a silver coaster on his desk. Careful not to spill any, I rested it on the coaster and stepped back. Richard oozed intensity even when he wasn't looking at you. I was happy to head out of there.

"Mia?" he called after me, his hand covering the receiver. "One moment, please."

I neared his desk again.

He rifled through a beige folder lying open on his desk. "I have his file here," he told the caller. "What happened?"

This had to be the swankiest office I'd ever been in with its wooden paneled walls and an even darker bookcase. Instead of books, it housed several ornaments: a Buddha on the lowest shelf continuing the theme from the changing room, a sailing yacht rested upon the uppermost shelf, and just beneath that, tucked inside another alcove, lay a medieval thumb screw. That really clashed with the Buddha.

Along the back far left wall rested a luxury leather studded sofa. I imagined him stretching out those long legs of his and taking a nap during his lunch break.

To the right hung three black framed photographs. A single man had been captured in each one, performing some kind of daredevil stunt. In the first, the man literally hung from a sheer rock face, the shot taken from a helicopter; the man wasn't wearing a safety harness. The middle photo had caught a man jumping off the top of the Eiffel Tower, a thin parachute strapped to his back. In the third photo, and easily the most extreme of all three, a man reached out beyond the confines of an underwater cage toward a shark.

I looked away and wondered if Tara had decided to go to Australia yet, though hoped for Bailey's sake she'd change her mind.

"Absolutely, revoke his membership," said Richard. "Refund him." He peered up at me.

I snapped my head away from the shark photo. Somehow the thing had drawn me back.

"No, I completely agree," added Richard. "Dominic, thank you for taking care of that. I'll see you later." He hung up and his gaze followed mine.

"Those men are crazy," I said, though the one trying to pat the shark was certifiable.

"He pulled his arm in before the great white came any closer," said Richard. "Pretty cowardly if you ask me."

I gave him the frown that deserved.

He took a sip of coffee and pulled a face.

"Oh." I opened my palm. "I wasn't sure if you wanted sweet and low or—"

He pointed. "The real stuff."

I ripped open the sachet and poured white crystals into his coffee, stirring it with the wooden stick before throwing it into the trash bin beneath his desk.

Richard took another sip. "Better." His gaze lowered. "Nice boots."

"They're new." I suppressed a cringe at my embarrassing answer.

"I like them."

This was the hint of kindness I needed to see from the man I'd be working for and it felt nice to catch a glimpse of his thoughtfulness.

He took another sip. "Lotte's been over everything with you?"

"She has."

He swiveled in his high-backed chair. "You completely understand what it is we do here and you're one hundred percent on board with it?"

"Oh yes," I said, hoping he didn't ask for specifics.

"Every day you'll arrive half an hour before me. Check my emails and tell me which ones are urgent. Do not answer them on my behalf. Ever." He leaned forward. "First thing, we'll go over the day's appointments. Not all of them are reserved for Enthrall." He waved that off. "We can go over that later."

"Thank you for this opportunity," I said. "I'm very grateful."

He looked surprised. "I didn't hire you. The director did."

"Oh."

He leaned back and that icy-stare lingered on me for a little too long.

"Another coffee?" I said.

"Haven't finished this one." His stare refused to let up.

There came a flitter in my solar plexus, a foreign feeling I couldn't quite place.

Richard slid open a side drawer and reached in.

He held his palm out to me. "Here."

I stepped forward and took the key out of his hand and his touch made my fingers tingle. He snapped his hand back.

"It's for the elevator gate to the dungeon," he said. "It's your job to open the gate for guests and their escorts. Keep this hidden. Don't take it home." He narrowed his gaze. "Don't go down there without my permission. Am I clear?"

I gave a nod.

"That'll be all for now."

I headed for the door.

"Make our clients happy," he said. "That's all we ask of you. Be polite. Patient. Kind."

"Of course," I said, turning back to face him. "What else would I be?"

His keen stare found me again. "Buddha Nine."

"Sorry?"

"The password to my Gmail account."

"Got it." I closed the door behind me.

In the kitchen I poured myself a coffee from what was left over and returned to my desk. Within minutes I'd used Richard's code to access his emails. Nervous he'd know I'd rummaged through the old ones, which I really wanted to do, I resisted.

Other than a new email from a Cameron Cole, confirming meeting Richard later this evening at some place called Soho House, nothing else came in for several hours. This gave me time to rearrange my desk. The office supplies were all over the place so it took me a little over an hour to get organized.

The elevator pinged and I knew to expect Monsieur Trourville. His name had been neatly written in Enthrall's diary for a 2:00 P.M.

Lotte had explained that clients were uncomfortable with their names being stored on any kind of database, therefore all appointments were written in pencil and erased by the secretary when the client presented. I wondered how they kept track for billing and tax purposes, but wasn't going to mention that in case she handed that aspect of Enthrall's administration over to me. Hanging out here at reception, transferring the occasional call, typing up the odd letter for Richard, as well as welcoming guests, had a nice feel to it. After trying to hold down two jobs I was grateful for the break. And just this for the amazing salary of seventy-five thousand dollars a year showed I'd landed on my feet for once.

Monsieur Trourville strolled down the hall. I rose to greet him. His name made him sound old, but he was in his thirties. His air of superiority broke when he smiled. He looked so formal in his three-piece suit and waistcoat. A kind face and regal arched nose would have said European even if his name hadn't.

"Monsieur Trourville," I said, "May I get you a drink?"

"No, but thank you," he said. "You must be Enthrall's new secretary? Mistress Lotte told me a new girl would be here when I came in."

I went to shake his hand. "I'm Mia."

Aghast, he glared at my hand. "I don't…"

Lotte burst through the staff doorway. "Monsieur." Her usual kindness was gone, her demeanor domineering. "Sir, you're late. This is unacceptable."

The wall clock proved he was in fact right on time. Yet he accepted this accusation and bowed his head in shame.

"I see you've met our new secretary." She turned to me. "Unlock the gate please, Ms. Lauren."

Relieved Lotte's sternness wasn't directed at me, I removed my well hidden key from the second drawer down. I eased it into the lock of the golden crisscrossed gate. It turned smoothly. On Lotte's nod, I slid it open and called the elevator with a push of a button. The doors parted and Monsieur Trourville and Lotte stepped inside.

"Lock it," said Lotte.

The doors closed on them.

I hoped they had another means of escape should one be needed. Though to be honest, the way Lotte had Monsieur Trourville under her control that was the least of his worries.

Lotte carried a whip.

CHAPTER FOUR

A FTER A WEEK I REALLY FELT I'D GOTTEN THE HANG OF THIS. Richard had stayed out of my way, hardly giving me any work to do, and I'd actually gotten to hang out in the coffee room with Lotte, Scarlet, and the former Ms. BlackBerry, now known as Lady Penny. Though Penny only worked some of the time at Enthrall, apparently.

I felt grateful when they welcomed me into their clique, offering words of encouragement and sharing their wisdom about all the life lessons they'd learned on work, love, and as Scarlet put it, most importantly, shopping. All of this while sharing crumbling homemade cookies that Lotte had brought in. They may have looked menacing in their dominatrix outfits but they were kind to me.

I took pleasure making them coffee every morning and ensuring they had everything they needed, running errands for them, making visits to the post office, dry cleaners, and even picking up the occasional grocery item.

The highlight of my day was eating my catered lunch outside the back of the club in the private garden overlooking the koi pond. Watching those orange and silver fish swim around had a soothing effect, and I wondered why no one else took advantage of this setting.

Back at my desk, with half an hour to go before Monsieur

Trouville's next appointment, I opened my pocketbook and spent half an hour or so calculating where I was financially and estimating I'd be able to pay off my step-mom's medical bills in about two years. That was, of course, if I stayed on track with my spending. Light shimmered at the end of this dark tunnel, though it hardly compared to the blackest years of my life. That award went to losing my real mom after she'd overdosed on cocaine, right after my fourteenth birthday, and a few years later my dad crashed his motorcycle in a fatal accident.

With a shiver, I buried those thoughts where they belonged, far away from where they could touch me or hurt me anymore. They had no right to infringe on my new life and cast a dark cloud over what promised to be a better future. My hands clutched the edge of the desk.

The entryway elevator pinged.

I pushed myself to my feet. This time I remained behind the desk. Trourville didn't want to be touched, according to Lotte.

"Unless it's the extremes of pleasure or pain," she'd told me.

I wondered what terrible things might have happened to him to make him like that. On the outside he seemed so calm, so normal.

Monsieur Trourville strolled out carrying a briefcase. A subtle nod let him know he had my empathy. With a glance at the clock, I estimated he was at least ten minutes early and guessed he must be compensating for being late last time.

"Good morning, sir," I greeted him.

He lingered before my desk. "You were kind to me when we first met. I want to thank you for that."

"Of course," I said. "It's my pleasure." I hoped my kindness might balance out Lotte's sternness. "Can I get you anything?"

He rested his briefcase on the desk and clicked it open. "I have a gift for you." He presented the hand sized silver and red wrapped box. "I was hoping you'd wear these next time I come in?"

"I'd love to." Remembering the blinding diamond he'd given Lotte, I took it from him, careful not to touch his hand. Was he hinting these were earrings?

"It would mean the world to me."

"Then it'll be my pleasure." I wondered how long I could keep the gift before re-selling it. If these diamonds were half as big as Lotte's I'd pay off my debt in a heartbeat.

He lowered his gaze. "If you really do wear them I'll see you get a bonus."

"Of course I'll wear them," I said, amazed at his generosity.

Lotte burst through the staff door.

Where I'd expected to see her pleased that Monsieur Trourville had arrived early, instead she looked annoyed. Her gaze shifted to the box. I clutched it to my chest.

"You may keep it," said Lotte, pointing her whip at Trourville. "Are you expecting leniency for this?"

"Never, Mistress," he said.

I pounced for the key.

"Ms. Lauren, we'll open your gift together," she said sternly.

"Yes, Mistress Lotte," I said, beaming a smile at Monsieur Trourville.

I set the box next to the computer.

They disappeared into the forbidden zone and I closed the gate behind them.

There was still time to continue my research on the kind of things they did here. I opened the browser, typed in S & M, and disappeared into cyberspace...

I couldn't understand why anyone would want to be bound and gagged like that. Not to mention where they were shoving those sex toys. And what the hell was that expression on their faces? Bliss? It didn't fit.

This fleeting escape left me baffled.

I rested back, not quite sure what I'd been looking at and wondering if they did any of those things here. Perhaps I'd gone to the wrong websites. Hardcore images of men dressed in leather using all kind of accruements on naked women left me stunned and yet strangely aroused. Richard didn't seem the type to dabble in anything like this.

He always had his head in a book, like something by Chaucer last week and more recently Thomas Hardy's *Jude the Obscure*.

Squeezing my legs together, I tried to shake off these feelings stirring between my thighs. My imagination ran wild with thoughts of Richard doing those things to me in their dungeon. The one I was banned from. Which made it all the more mysterious. All the more forbidden.

My thoughts raced…

Richard spanking me. Richard kissing me. Richard's hands trailing over my breasts and tweaking my nipples. Did he ever use nipple clamps like the ones in the photos? Didn't they hurt? After a session, could you snuggle into him for a hug? I'd breathe him in, that delicious scent of ocean and something else, something expensive.

A flutter of excitement. The nicest tingle below…

Richard's kiss lowering, settling between my thighs, his tongue tracing between that delicate cleft, circling there, flicking—

A ping of the elevator.

I went for the mouse and shrank the browser, feigning being busy.

Richard strolled out. "How's your morning going?"

Averting my eyes from his, I said, "Good, thank you."

"Any calls?"

"No calls. Monsieur Trourville's just arrived. Lotte's with him." I glanced back at the gate.

"Everything okay, Mia?"

"Yes," I said, suppressing a blush.

The way he said my name caused a shiver and I found it hard to look at him. Not after the trip my imagination had just taken with him in that room of pain. His narrowed gaze locked on mine.

"How is your day going?" I said.

"Just got here." His stare was on my unwrapped gift. "Did Monsieur Trouville give you that?"

"Yes. Haven't opened it yet," I stated the obvious. "Lotte wants me to wait for her." I swallowed hard. "Mistress Lotte."

"Ah."

"Coffee's brewing."

"Perfect. Go put one on my desk, please."

A shiver ran up my spine and I froze, feeling guilty over my cyber-probing.

Richard leaned over to peer at my computer screen. "You need a new background for your desktop." He came round my side and gestured for me to get up.

He sat in my chair and grabbed the mouse, shaking it to awaken the screen. Mentally, I backtracked over whether I'd closed the browser from the last website. Richard's hand was poised on the mouse and his stare was still on mine.

"I'll get your coffee." I headed off.

The fear of him catching my internet search with one click made my cheeks burn. Leaning against the kitchen counter, I buried my face in my hands. I could only imagine how useless I'd be if he really touched me down there. Trying to re-focus on something else, I worked on making Richard's coffee, adding sugar and milk to his beverage and making my way to his office as I tried to calm my still thundering heart.

I placed a mug of hot coffee on his desk. Everything on it had been perfectly organized. Even the pencils were aligned and set apart with precision, as was the collection of luxury pens. His iMac computer looked expensive with its sleek design and the elegant arched mouse resting before it.

Richard startled me when he came in.

"I heard you like the koi pond?" he said, throwing his satchel on the leather sofa. From his unfazed expression, it seemed he'd not caught my web browsing. Or the effect he had on me.

"It's relaxing." I shrugged. "You should go down there during your break too."

"I do. I use the fire escape."

I wondered what kind of exit they had in the dungeon, though didn't feel ready to discuss that with him yet in case the conversation veered off to what he did down there.

"Do you need something?" he said.

"Um, no."

He raised his eyebrows in amusement.

On my way out I felt his stare.

Back at my desk, I was grateful for the distance between my work station and his office. He'd set my background to the image of a Japanese garden with a koi pond. The vision of the soothing photo made my shoulders relax and it made me smile that he'd taken the time to do this for me. Maybe he liked me after all. I reassured myself I'd clicked away all evidence of my viewing long before Richard had a chance to catch sight of it. I'd worried myself over nothing.

My gift wrapped box was gone.

Checking each drawer, I wondered if Richard had tucked it away safely.

The phone buzzed. "Can you come in here please, Mia," Richard's voice rose out of the speakerphone.

Unhappy to leave my search unfinished, I hopped out of my chair and grabbed my note pad and pen.

Waiting for him to look up from scribbling something, I lingered before his desk. My gift sat next to his phone.

"I'm low on ink." He passed me a post-it note. "Usually we order this in but my last secretary was a little distracted." He smiled. "She had exams and it addled her brain. Can you pick this up for me at Office Depot?"

"Sure."

Richard rested his hand on the gift. "Hope you don't mind. I thought it best to return this."

"Why?"

"It has nothing to do with what your role is." He sat back. "I'll explain it to Monsieur Trouville." Richard thinned his lips in a *thank you that'll be all* kind of way.

"Mistress Lotte kept her gift from him."

"She's his Domina." He took a sip of coffee. "Anyway, different kind of gift." He shooed me out. "Thank you, Mia."

"Can I see what it is?"

He leaned back and caressed his forehead. "Later."

Unwilling to give it up so easily, I stood my ground.

"Something tells me you won't like it," he said.

"You know what it is?"

"I can guess."

"How can I not like it?"

He threw his hands up in defeat.

Suppressing my excitement, I reached for the box.

"Come on. Let's open it in the coffee room." He rose and led the way. "It's best we do this with women present."

Was that an indication this really was a diamond?

Mistress Scarlet smiled at us when we entered. Her gaze fell on the gift.

Lady Penny raised the coffee pot. "Want a top up?"

"Sure," said Richard, offering his half empty mug to be filled.

Penny poured coffee into it. "Want one, Mia?"

"No thank you." I tore off the wrapping. The black box within had two hinges and I eased them open. Inside were two delicate silver balls attached with a thin thread.

"Who gave you that?" said Penny, glaring at Richard.

"As if." He rolled his eyes. "Monsieur Trourville."

"What is it?" I tried to hide my disappointment.

Richard took a sip. "What do you think it is?"

I twisted my mouth thoughtfully. "Paperweight?"

He coughed and suppressed a grin. Penny and Scarlet shared a wary glance with each other.

"You sure you don't know?" said Penny.

I blushed wildly, wondering if it represented some part of the male anatomy. "This is so not going on my desk."

Richard offered a sympathetic gesture. "I did try to save you from this."

"They're Venus balls," said Scarlet.

I frowned down at the box.

"Mia, they're sex balls," said Penny.

My jaw dropped. "You mean you put it in your...?"

"Yes," said Scarlet.

I placed the box on the table. "It's bad enough having to put a tampon up there let alone something like this."

Silence reined and I read nothing but surprise on their faces.

"Okay then," said Richard and he headed out with his coffee.

I waited for him to leave. "Monsieur Trourville asked me to put this in each time he visited. I thought they were earrings."

Penny laughed. "You crack me up, Mia."

My cheeks burned. "Oh no, I told him I'd be happy to."

"What did he promise you?" said Penny.

"A bonus."

"Tell Monsieur Trourville you've got them in," said Scarlet.

"He'll know." Penny took the seat beside her. "He'll look at her pupils."

I sat beside Penny and rested my head on my hands. "To see if I'm lying?"

She shook her head. "Aroused."

"Don't they hurt?"

"They vibrate," said Scarlet. "It's a pleasant tease, actually."

I stared at the box, hating my big mouth for talking Richard into letting me open it and wondering how I'd ever face him again. I wished I'd waited for Lotte.

The door opened.

In strolled a dashing, thirty-something man dressed in a snappy suit and waistcoat. His short, neatly styled dark-brown hair looked ruffled to perfection and he oozed class. The kind of man who was not only out of my league but everyone else's too. Even a supermodel would have to work extra hard at nabbing this one, with his perfect bone structure and that ridiculous well-toned body which even his expensive suit didn't hide. It was the way he moved, demure and yet masculine. He reminded me of one of those photo-journalists you see on TV reporting from the middle-east, with bullets flying over their heads and yet the person gives not so much as a blink. Sophisticated and earthy all at the same time.

His chestnut gaze settled on me with an unnerving scrutiny. There was something sensually alluring about him too. Dangerous. As though he knew of his effect and could turn it up a notch just to amuse himself.

Penny and Scarlet rose and I followed their lead.

"Sit," he said, and it kind of sounded like an order.

He came closer, walking with the confidence of a man who could handle anything. Or anyone. From the way Penny and Scarlet reacted they'd picked up on this too. For the first time, they looked nervous. I hoped we hadn't been caught doing something wrong, like enjoying one too many coffee breaks.

"You must be Mia," he said, his tone low, his voice cultured.

A thrill of excitement shot up my spine. The kind that has no right to happen, the kind that threatens to embarrass me.

Oh no.

Those damn balls were still on the table.

"Mia, this is Cameron Cole," said Mistress Scarlet.

He gave a nod of approval and his attention fell on the Venus balls.

"They're mine," Penny told him.

He looked unfazed and his vivid brown gaze found me again.

Penny stood. "Sir, let me get you a drink."

"Sit," he said. "I'll get it."

I flushed wildly at the way he'd spoken to her. Penny merely sat back down and twirled her gold pinky ring.

Cameron poured himself a drink, added a shake of coffee mate, and stirred. I wondered about his connection to Enthrall. He couldn't be a client, could he? They weren't allowed back here. Penny threw me a wink of encouragement and I returned a gesture of gratitude for her lying about the box. These women really knew how to have your back.

Cameron turned around. "Mia, sit."

I realized Scarlet had also taken her seat again and I dropped into mine.

"How's your first week going?" he said.

"Second week," I said.

"It's her second week," said Penny at the same time.

He wasn't just making me jumpy.

"It's going great, thank you." I wished I'd agreed to a coffee so I could peer into a mug rather than having to hold his fiery gaze. I wondered if it was possible to run out of blushes. This day was turning into an ordeal of epic proportions.

"FMBs." He looked down at my feet. "I approve."

"He likes your boots," said Scarlet.

"Thank you," I said.

He loosened his tie and a silver cufflink caught the light.

Licking my dry lips, I tried not to hold his stare. It was severe. As though any minute he'd scold me for something I'd done wrong.

Not letting up, he blew onto his drink.

"Can I get you anything?" said Penny.

"No, thank you. How's the boss?" he said, thankfully turning away from me and toward Penny and Scarlet.

"Fine," said Scarlet. "Busy but good."

"Glad to hear it," he said. "How does he like his new secretary?" His lips curled into a smile.

Something fluttered inside my chest and I tried to suppress another threatening blush.

Richard appeared in the doorway. "Hey, buddy, perfect timing." He seemed to purposefully ignore me. "Cameron, my office please." Richard disappeared again.

Cameron snapped his head back toward Penny. "How long has he been like this?"

Penny twisted her mouth into a frown.

"Really?" said Cameron, unable to hide his satisfaction, and he flitted a final glance at me before he headed after Richard.

Penny and Scarlet shared a look, but it was hard to read it.

"What was that about?" I said.

"Nothing to concern yourself over, Mia," said Penny.

"Who is he?" I whispered.

"A good friend of Richard's," said Scarlet.

"Are they lovers?" I braved to ask. After all, we'd bonded over these Venus thingies.

"No," Scarlet answered pleasantly. "Just good friends. They go way back."

"Is Richard okay?" I asked.

"Never better," said Scarlet.

"Try not to engage with Cameron," said Penny.

"Oh, all right," I said. "Why?"

"He's… bossy." Scarlet slid her chair back and went over to top up her coffee.

Penny gave a nod as though warning me not to push the subject. Was I in trouble for the way I'd spoken to him? It wouldn't surprise me with all these strange rules.

"Stay off Cameron's radar and you'll do fine," said Scarlet.

"I can do that." I rose and headed toward the door, turning before heading out. "Can you give those back to Richard?" I said. "I'm too embarrassed."

"Sure thing, Mia." Penny smiled. "We'll re-gift them."

I gave a wave of thanks, assuming she'd have plenty of people to choose from amongst her kinky circle of friends. Grieving for those diamonds that never were, I made it halfway down the hall. Richard's voice rose from behind his closed office door.

Cameron's voice rose over his. "Because I know what you need and you need this."

Glancing both ways, I checked to see the hallway was empty and neared his door.

"Back off, Cameron," it was Richard's voice.

"Let's talk," said Cameron.

"There's nothing to talk about. I want her gone."

"Keep your voice down," snapped Cameron.

I cringed, hating to hear such tension between two people who were meant to be friends, and feeling for the poor person they were talking about.

"Don't make any decisions until we've had a session, understand?" said Cameron.

"There's nothing to talk about." Richard slammed a cabinet drawer. "Did you even read her resume? She has no experience. She's at risk here."

"Protect her. That's what you do best," Cameron's tone sounded soothing.

"For fuck sake," said Richard. "She doesn't even know what Venus balls are."

I jolted back.

CHAPTER FIVE

W IPING TEARS AWAY, I TRIED TO WORK OUT IF I'D BE ABLE to drive.

Richard had fired me. Although nicely and with two week's pay, after reassuring me this generous offer came as an apology for their error in hiring an inappropriate candidate.

I cursed my ineptitude for not Googling sex toys before. Those pesky Venus love balls had given away my lack of knowledge. Anyway, didn't Google record everything you searched for, holding it back and waiting until you married a governor before they revealed the documented proof to the world? *Why yes, you are a kinky bitch and your husband's run for the presidency is now dashed because of your twisted fuckery.*

More tears fell. My inability to impress my boss had lost me my job. I shoved my Mini Cooper into reverse and backed out—

After jolting forward, there came an awful grinding of metal and my foot slammed on the brake. I spun around to see an open topped silver sports car stuck to the back of my Mini.

Oh no…

My moan filled the space around me. I pulled forward, heart racing. It threatened to burst out of my chest and render me unconscious.

I buried my face in my hands. "Grrrr."

I climbed out, psyching myself up to face the other driver and what damage I'd done to their car. Brave their wrath.

Oh shit.

Cameron Cole swept his hand over the large dent in his front side door. He tilted his head when he saw me, his expression lacking any anger, which I found strange considering his car was the most amazing thing on wheels I'd ever seen.

A wave of panic hit me. "I'm so sorry. I'll pay for it."

He narrowed his gaze as he took in the back of my car. Unable to stop my tears, my aching chest threatened to burst wide open and I sucked in a sob.

"Are you hurt?" he said.

"No. Are you?"

"Of course not," he said calmly. "Are you insured?"

"Yes."

"Well then." He shrugged. "Though don't be surprised if your insurance broker cries too when you tell him you hit a Porsche Spyder."

Although I had no idea what kind of car that might be, his vehicle looked even more expensive close up. I broke my gaze from it as though the car might spring to life and chastise me. With a trembling hand I reached into my bag and felt for my wallet.

"This really has been a horrible day for you," he said, "hasn't it?"

I looked up at him.

"Richard told me." Cameron neared the back of my Mini to examine the damage. "You'll need a new bumper." He peered around toward the front. "Is your oil leaking?"

Unable to wipe the tears away fast enough, I started to shake.

"You can't be in shock," he said. "It's a bump. The body shop will knock that out in less than an hour."

"I could have killed you."

"I'm sure your insurance would have covered that too."

That was bad enough, but my mind spiraled and I wailed with the thought it could have been a woman with children.

"Where do you live?" he said.

"Studio City."

"You can't drive in this state. Let me take you home."

"No." I shot my hand up.

"Well at least let me buy you some tea to calm your nerves." He pointed to the Coffee Bean across the street.

He hopped inside his Porsche and parked it beside mine. My Mini looked tiny next to his car. Although I insisted this wasn't necessary, secretly needing to get home and cry in private, Cameron wouldn't take no for an answer. Within minutes he'd led me across the sidewalk and opened the door to the cafe for me. He ordered two Earl Greys and found us a table by the window.

Mistress Scarlet warned me to stay out of Cameron's way, or as she'd put it, off his radar, and yet here he was being nice. I wondered why she'd given the warning. I braced myself for when he'd realize what I'd done to his car. Maybe he was in shock too. More than likely a chastisement was brewing as well as the tea. There was no question I deserved it.

"Better?" said Cameron, his face full of concern.

I bit my lip; my way of bringing this punishment on quicker. I hated the tension of waiting for it.

"Please don't bite your lip." He let out a long sigh. "It's distracting."

Caressing the ache out of my lip with a fingertip, I wondered what he meant. Cameron broke my gaze and shook his head, amused by something.

It was hard to pull my stare away from him. His features were striking, and from the looks the other customers gave us they thought so too. Cameron gave a kind smile as though aware of all this attention and not in the least bit thrown.

The taste and aroma of the Early Grey soothed. I wondered why I'd never tried it before.

"I'm so sorry," I said.

"You're very hirable." He dipped his teabag a final time before resting it on his upturned lid.

"I meant about your car."

"It's only a car. What happened with Richard?"

"I spell checked that letter twice," I said. "I really did."

"Did Richard fire you over a misspelling?"

"Yes. The letter was for a senior client. Apparently they're particular about that." I gave a shrug. "Who knew the British spell differently."

"Richard made you type a letter to an English client using English spelling?"

"Yes. But he's British, not English."

Cameron narrowed his stare. "Same thing, Mia."

I frowned at him.

"If you're British you could come from Wales, Scotland, Ireland or England. If you're English, you come from England. Kind of a fun fact. Not that anyone cares. No one can understand what they're saying half the time anyway."

"Have you ever been?"

"Yes." He took a sip.

"What's it like?"

"Cold." He smiled. "Though they have striking architecture and a fascinating history." He shook his head. "I'm sorry Richard is such a Mr. Grumpy pants."

"I don't know what I'm going to do," I said, tears flowing again.

Cameron reached for a napkin. "Sorry. It's a bit scratchy." He stared at me under long, black lashes. "Here."

I took it from him and dapped my face, scrunching it up and holding onto it in case I couldn't suppress these tears.

Cameron handed me another napkin. "I want you to know that I talked with Richard."

"What did he say?"

"He feels heroic about you."

"What does that mean?"

"Richard's not sure you're quite ready to work at Enthrall."

"I so wanted to make it work. There's no other job that pays as much." There, I'd admitted why I took the job, kind of.

"Minimum wage sucks."

"And I need the benefits," I said. "All the other places I applied for didn't pay benefits until you'd been there for at least three months."

"Corporate America." He twisted his mouth. "It can be pretty tough on the middle class and verging on cruel to the lower."

Cameron probably watched a little too much CNN, by the sound of things.

"Are you a member of Enthrall?" I said.

"Not exactly a member."

"What do you do?"

"I'm a psychiatrist."

"A doctor?"

"They generally are, yes."

"Oh."

His gaze settled on my mouth. "Please don't go and clam up on me. I've not finished analyzing you."

I must have looked horrified.

"I'm kidding," he said.

I wondered what Cameron had been doing at Enthrall if he wasn't a client. From the way he'd argued with Richard they seemed close. My tea tasted nice and it made me realize Cameron knew a thing about calming people.

"Did you study medicine at UCLA?" I said.

"Harvard."

It was too late to pull back on impressed.

"That's where I met Richard," he said.

"What did he study?"

"I'll let him tell you that." He sat back. "He's very private."

"If I worked in a sex club so would I be."

"I thought you wanted your job back? Enthrall isn't a sex club."

"Don't people have sex there?"

"That would be illegal."

I squinted at him, wondering if he'd dodged the truth.

"So you're from Charlotte?" he said, and on my reaction added. "Lotte told me."

"Yes."

"Is your family there?"

"I have some cousins and a few other relatives."

"So everyone else is here?"

"Um, my dad died in a motorcycle accident. My mom died a few years before." I rested my hand on my chest to let him know I was fine with it all. "My step-mom's here."

"That's pretty rough."

"Not really. There are people worse off."

"Like who?"

"Those people dying in the Sudan."

He broke my gaze, his frown deepening.

"This is delicious." I took another sip. "Thank you."

His attention drifted to a customer at the register who argued with one of the young baristas about his wrong order. Cameron glowered at him and when the man caught it he shut up, took his drink, and left.

I blinked at Cameron, marveling at his ability to intimidate with merely a look.

"Where were we?" he said.

"Do you think Richard's still angry with me?"

"No."

A Chihuahua barked at us from the other side of the window. His owner threw us an apologetic wave and tried to get the mutt under control. Cameron chuckled and shared an amused smirk with me.

"Where do you live?" I said.

"Venice Beach." He shrugged. "For now. I enjoy the hustle and bustle of the place but it's pretty loud at night."

"I have a friend who surfs in Venice."

"It's great for surfing." He peered out of the window at the dog. "I take a board out there in the mornings."

Cameron reminded me of Richard in a way. They both shared an unwavering confidence. Something they'd picked up at Harvard, no doubt. Though Richard did seem more guarded. I wondered

how long they'd been friends. They'd certainly look striking out together. Women-magnets for sure. You'd have to be pretty confident
to approach these two with romance in mind. Anyway, they seemed
more the hunting and trapping of perfect female specimens kind, and
would very likely get anyone they set their sights on. They'd probably
mastered the one-night-stand thing, leaving a bunch of heartbroken
lovers behind them.

Maybe that was why Scarlet had told me to stay away from him?
She feared I'd start crushing on this unobtainable sex god.

As if.

"Please talk to Richard again," I said. "I have to stay employed. It's
life or death."

"Let me see what I can do." He gave a nod. "I'll tell you what,
write the most amazing letter to Richard. I'll get you in the room with
him tomorrow evening." He pointed a finger at me. "Write something
compelling."

"I can do that," I said, knowing full well I couldn't.

"Let's meet back at Enthrall tomorrow at six. I'll stay in the room
with you and cheer you on." Cameron smiled. "Let's see if we can get
you your job back."

I let out a long sigh of relief that hope had returned.

Cameron glanced at his watch. "I'm meeting Richard for tennis in
an hour. I'll loosen him up for you."

"Thank you so much." My tears fell again.

"No tears tomorrow. You need to be confident."

"Confident," I said. "I can do that."

He squeezed my hand. "You'll do great. I can feel it."

Through the window I watched him head off back across the
street and realized I'd not given Cameron my insurance information.
I'd have to give it to him tomorrow.

With my cup of Earl Grey in hand, I made my way along the cross-
walk and took another look at my car. I would need a new bumper.-
Cameron had been right about that. Mulling over whether I'd had my
fair share of bad luck, I hoped Cameron might persuade Richard to

give me my job back. He certainly seemed to think he could convince him. After what I'd done to his car, he'd shown exceptional kindness. Though after what Mistress Scarlet had told me about him I was still wary.

Traffic south made the ride home to Studio City grueling, though it gave me more time to think. This job was worth fighting for. If I was going to stand any chance of convincing Richard, I'd need help with that letter. Instead of going home I headed to Bailey's apartment, which was only ten minutes away from mine.

She answered the door in her silk P.J.s.

"Sorry to visit unannounced," I said.

"Don't be ridiculous." She bounced back into her living room.

What with me balancing two jobs and now starting a new one, and her nursing shifts at UCLA, we'd hardly seen each other lately. Bailey didn't seem fazed by it. She was all flowing long titian hair, big white smile and easy breezy attitude.

I followed her into her two-bedroom apartment with its spacious living room decorated warmly with Pier One furniture, and a few pieces of Z-Gallery thrown in care of Tara. Out those double doors, straight ahead, led to an enormous balcony which overlooked a large pool. No one ever seemed to swim in it, which seemed strange. I'd be in that pool every day if I lived here. There certainly were benefits to sharing the rent.

Up against the hallway wall leading to the bedroom rested Tara's faded mermaid surfboard. Bailey's birthday was coming up and I'd hoped to buy a board for her. Though my financial future looked shaky again.

"Want one?" said Bailey, holding up a bottle of Chardonnay.

I leaned my elbows on the kitchen counter. "Sure."

"I'm celebrating," she said."Tara isn't going to Australia now. She told me this morning."

"Yay." I waved my hands in a cheer.

"I know right." Bailey glugged wine into a fresh glass.

"Is she enjoying nursing school?"

"Loves it." She handed me the drink. "Stay here on the sofa tonight."

My lumpy bed certainly wouldn't be missed.

"How's your mom doing?" she asked.

"Better."

She rested her hands on her hips. "She lost her hair yet?"

"Not yet."

"She's always been particular about—"

"Her looks. I know. She's coping okay. I chatted with her last night on the phone and she seemed fine."

Over the last couple of weeks, color had returned to Lorraine's cheeks and she gotten some of her energy back. I'd managed to wrangle time off work to sit with her during her chemo, hold her hand, and even read to her when she'd stopped throwing up long enough. Lorraine was obsessed with all things celebrity and took great pleasure from watching TMZ. She couldn't understand my lack of enthusiasm for wanting to watch B-actors walking in and out of airports, filmed on shaky cameras, and rarely saying anything interesting. Still, it made her happy and took her mind off the beeping machines and endless rounds of meds. If anyone could survive this, she could.

"How are you holding up?" asked Bailey, shaking me from my daydreaming.

"Good. Where's Tara?"

"The gym."

That's right, this place also sported its own gym. Again I reflected how bad I had it in my studio. Still, it was home and I'd managed to decorate it with odd items I'd found at thrift stores. My carved brass headboard being an amazing find. Even if it did squeak each time I rolled over.

"I don't think I'll stay," I said.

"Sure you don't want a girl's night?"

"Wouldn't Tara mind?"

"Of course not. How's the new job?"

"Great."

"Seriously?" She threw me a knowing look and led me back into the living room.

We plopped down on her golden chenille couch.

I ran my hand over the fabric, coveting this piece of furniture as always. "I got fired."

"What?"

I set the glass down on the coffee table. "I made a mistake on a letter. A typo—"

"Oh Mia, I'm so sorry," she said. "Maybe it's for the best."

"I'm only the secretary, Bailey."

"Still."

"Tara worked there."

"Not anymore."

I gave her a look. "It's not all bad. Cameron, a friend of my boss's, told me to write a letter to express why I believe I'm a great fit. I'm going to literally beg for my position back tomorrow evening."

"Well that's hopeful," she said. "Want help with the letter?"

"American's Top Artist is on tonight. Don't want to ruin your evening."

"I'll record it." She jumped up and went for her remote.

A few clicks of the buttons later and she'd recorded her show. Bailey grabbed a notebook from her bookshelf and sat back down.

"How does this sound?" I began, gesturing for her to write. "Dear Mr. Booth."

"Too formal. Call him Richard. People respond to their own names."

"Yes, good. Richard—" I stood up and faced Bailey. "I may not have the experience you believe you need." I shook my head. "I need." I motioned to erase that. "What I do have is honesty. I'm able to put people at ease—"

"That's good." Bailey scribbled away.

"Your clients need to feel comfortable. Safe. I can do that." I took a swig of wine and placed my glass back on the table.

"One more sip and you're staying," she said.

"I'll stay."

"I'll get you a blanket and pillow."

"Thank you." I raised my hands to gesture my next thought.

A key turned in the lock and Tara came in. Despite being drenched in sweat she still looked fresh. Her tall, lithe body appeared ridiculously fit in her workout gear.

Tara's Indian mother, Mrs. Razor, was a talented violinist who'd been discovered in Calcutta by her father, a famous conductor. He'd married her and brought her back to live with him in L.A. Tara had inherited her mother's exotic complexion and her father's forthrightness; a captivating mixture of east meets west.

Bailey had fallen head over heels with Tara on their first date. It really did seem mutual. That's why all this talk of Australia was a surprise. Tara hadn't come out to her parents yet. A sore point between her and Bailey.

"Hey babe." Bailey greeted her.

"Hi." Tara dropped her workout gear by the door and came over to kiss Bailey's cheek. "I can't wait to hear all about your job, Mia. How are the Mistresses? Isn't Richard dreamy?"

"Hey," Bailey chastised her.

"As if." Tara rolled her eyes. "Well?"

"They kind of fired me," I said.

Her face fell and she sunk to the floor in front of us and crossed her legs.

"She misspelled a word in a letter." Bailey told her.

"Weird. Did it change the nature of the letter?" said Tara.

"No. Anyway, Cameron told me he'd have a word with him," I said. "He thinks he can change Richard's mind."

There was no way I'd tell either of them about the Venus balls and Richard hinting at this as the real grounds for firing me. This whole thing felt too embarrassing as it was.

Tara held Bailey's gaze. "I'll grab my laptop and we'll take a look on Craigslist."

Bailey held up the notebook. "She's got a second chance. She has to come up with a good reason why they should rehire her." She gestured to the kitchen. "Pour yourself a glass and help us out."

"I need to re-hydrate." Tara turned to face me. "Richard's an old soul. He's also stubborn. I hate to tell you this but he's not likely to change his mind."

I felt sick, though despite this I reached for my glass and gulped it.

Bailey raised the notebook. "Then why would Cameron have her write this?"

"Can you talk to him?" I said.

"We got on great," said Tara. "But he's still upset with me that I left. He hasn't returned any of my texts." She peered over at Bailey. "I've checked on him a couple of times."

"He should be happy for you," said Bailey.

"Richard's complex." She sat back down and gestured to my wine. I handed it over.

Tara took a sip. "So much for re-hydrating."

"What are you not telling us?" said Bailey.

"This is absolutely private," said Tara. "Not to be repeated under any circumstances."

I gestured for my wine back.

Tara took another gulp and handed it over. "About a month ago Cameron and Richard disappeared into the dungeon for well over an hour."

"Gay?" said Bailey.

"No." Tara shot her a look. "Listen. When they came back up I noticed blood stains on the back of Richard's shirt. Cameron had done something nasty to him."

"Cameron's a psychiatrist," I said. "That doesn't sound right."

Tara rummaged through her rucksack and withdrew a bottle of water. "I'm just telling you what I saw."

"You told me those dungeon walls are all painted red," said Bailey. "Maybe they'd been repainted and he leaned back on it?"

"Did you ever go down there?" I said, needing to hear more.

"Once." Tara unscrewed the cap and took a swing of spring water. She used the bottle to motion to us. "The blood was beneath his shirt." She raised her gaze to the ceiling. "Paint."

"That guy's messed up." Bailey turned to me. "I think it's best you're out of there."

"Cameron's actually kind of cool," said Tara. "So is Richard. Did he really fire you over a misspelling? That's so strange."

I broke her gaze.

"What really happened?" said Bailey.

I slumped back. "A client gave me Venus balls as a gift."

"I don't see the problem," said Tara. "Unless…"

"You didn't know what they were," said Bailey.

My cheeks burned with embarrassment.

"Richard realized how inexperienced she is," said Tara, cringing.

"You don't get it," I said, despair threatening to eat me alive. "I have to come up with an extra $600.00 a month. The billing department at Cedars have threatened to cut off my step-mom's treatment otherwise."

"They can't do that," said Tara. "Can they?"

"I don't want to find out," I said. "It's the best place for her."

"Maybe they'd transfer her care to a city hospital?" said Bailey.

Tara gave me a look of sympathy.

"I have no choice but to get that job back," I said. "Nowhere else pays the same."

"Well," said Tara, thoughtfully. "There is something you can do." She shook her head. "You're not going to like it though."

"She's not becoming a stripper," snapped Bailey.

Tara threw her an amused glance and zeroed in on me. "Richard's into extremes. Do something that will be so unexpected you'll blow his mind."

"His mind and not him, right?" Bailey's stare jumped between us.

"Show yourself to him." Tara tilted her head. "Elegantly, of course."

"You mean tell him how bad things have been for me lately?" I said.

Tara frowned. "No, I mean *show* yourself to him." She pointed between my legs.

"What?" said Bailey. "We are talking about Mia Lauren, the girl who hates even looking down there."

I cringed when that revelation came out.

"Really?" said Tara. "We've got to get you a toy."

I gulped more wine, not sure we were on the same page.

"I know this man," said Tara. "Richard's into risk taking. Do this and you'll get his attention and you'll prove you're more than capable of working there."

"What do you have in mind?" Bailey sounded suspicious.

"Put the notebook away," said Tara. "What I'm about to tell you to do will be easy to remember. And it'll guarantee you'll get your job back."

I downed the rest of the wine.

CHAPTER SIX

"READY?"

Asked Cameron. He arrived at Enthrall right after me and buzzed me in.

Hands shaking, heart pounding, I forced a smile. "Absolutely."

"You'll do great." He led me into the elevator.

Cameron looked clean cut and had effortlessly dressed in blue jeans and a white shirt. He couldn't even make that look casual. Despite his confident posture offering some reassurance, his close proximity made me nervous as his gaze swept up and down my short trenchcoat. His focus never wavered and it made me wonder if he ever took a day off from studying people. Stepping out, I tried to keep up with his determined pace.

"You never gave me your car insurance yesterday," I said.

"I'll put it on mine," he said. "After careful consideration, I realized it was my fault."

"Um…no, I think I backed into you."

"We'll agree to disagree. How about that?" He glanced at his watch. "I know a great body shop. I'll have them check out your Mini while they're working on mine. We'll get them to fix that oil leak too. How does that sound?" He gave a nod to confirm he liked this plan and opened the door to the staff hallway, gesturing for me to go ahead.

Taken aback by his kindness, my spirit lifted and I almost forgot what I'd come here for.

Was I really going through with this?

As I passed the reception desk, it felt eerie to see no one there. That should be you sitting there, I mused, trying to distract myself from having to face Richard again and the impending drama I was about summon. Excitement mixed with trepidation spiraled tingles in my chest.

"I must warn you." Cameron paused outside Richard's office. "He doesn't know about this."

"At tennis yesterday, you didn't mention it?"

"He wasn't really in the mood. And you know what I thought? Hell, why not just surprise him."

"What if he's angry I'm back?" I covered my face with my hands.

"Something tells me he'll be happy to see you." Cameron reached for the handle.

I grabbed his wrist and stopped him.

He glanced at my hands. "Where's your letter? Leave it on his desk afterwards."

"I saw Tara last night," I said. "She was Enthrall's secretary before me."

"I know Tara."

"She told me the letter wouldn't be enough."

"It's worth a try." He faced the door. "Speak from your heart."

The door flew open and Richard's stern demeanor met us.

"Hey Richard." Cameron took my hand and guided me past him.

Richard turned to face us. "What's going on?"

"Please, sit down," said Cameron.

Richard didn't look happy and ignored his friend's invitation to sit.

You can do this, I told myself, rallying my courage.

What was the worst that could happen? It's not like he could fire me. He'd already done that. Tara seemed pretty convinced this would work and she was the one to get me the job in the first place.

"Mia has something she wants to say to you," said Cameron.

Richard strolled back to his desk and spun around to face us, leaning against it, his expression taut. He folded his arms across his chest.

Cameron frowned at him and tilted his head toward me. Richard gave Cameron a *what the hell* kind of look.

Back in Bailey's apartment, going over the plan with her and Tara, this had felt doable. Madness, yes, but possible. Yet here, now, standing opposite Richard and his fierceness made me question my ability to pull this off. This had to be how it felt when a tanker truck hit your car in one of those freak accidents you see replaying on the news. The kind you think will never happen to you. Very comparable.

Cameron moved closer. "Mia, whenever you're ready." He gave an assured gesture to Richard. "Give her a second."

Bailey's words found me again. *"Jump in, like you're at a cold swimming pool and you know that once you're swimming you'll love it."*

"Or drown," I think I'd answered her; how apt that was.

My mind wandered further, as though trying to locate the courage I'd left back in their apartment.

"These guys get up to all kinds of things, trust me," Tara had told me. *"Nothing shocks them. Think of this as speaking their language."*

"Mia," said Cameron, shaking me from my daydream.

I rummaged inside my handbag and brought out an iPod. "Put this on, please." I handed it over Cameron and dropped my bag onto the chair.

"Sure thing." Cameron beamed at Richard and headed over to the sound system at the back of the room.

Masked Ball by Jocelyn Pook burst out of the surround sound speakers and filled the room with a deep bass rhythm. I unbuttoned my trenchcoat, slipped if off my shoulders, and threw it over the back of one of the leather armchairs. My short tartan skirt may have looked out of place for autumn but neither Richard or Cameron seemed to notice. Despite the coolness of the room, my boots held some warmth and gave me just enough of the edgy confidence I needed to pull this off.

My heart pounded so hard inside my chest; my breathing was just short of panicked.

Standing in the center, I steadied myself. "Richard I do belong here. You know it and I know it."

His gaze locked on mine with an unmatched fervor.

"And I can prove it." I glanced over at Cameron to let him know I was ready.

Cameron smiled back.

Biting my lip, I lifted my skirt, tugging it around my waist and holding it there, revealing my black stockings and lace garter belt. From Richard's face, he'd noticed I wasn't wearing any panties.

Richard swapped a glance with Cameron.

Cameron paused, appearing intrigued.

"Master Richard, I want to apologize." My fingers scrunched my skirt. "For that spelling mistake." My other hand moved, ready to stroke myself just as Tara had told me to, but something flipped inside my chest and I froze. I'd come too far to go back and yet couldn't proceed any further either. Trapped in some sensual halfway land, my cheeks burned and my breathing stifled. Aroused and yet...

Richard's frown deepened.

Cameron neared me. "Show Richard how you're going to do that." Seamlessly Cameron saw where I'd planned on taking this and softened the moment with reassurance.

"Cole, let's talk outside," whispered Richard.

Cameron slid behind me and wrapped his left arm around my waist, hugging me back towards him. "Mia, let me touch you."

"Yes, please," I said, trying to control my shaking hands, grateful he'd come to my rescue, giddy with the feel of his strong arm squeezing me back into him, against his firm chest.

Cameron moved his other hand down over my belly, and lower. "Part your legs a little."

Feeling safe in his arms, I adjusted my footing, though when his fingers found me, sliding over that delicate cleft, I held my breath. Glancing down, he'd parted my nether lips to expose me further.

Holding still for what felt like a lifetime, my heart quickening, my legs weakening, I let out the longest sigh.

This wasn't the plan.

"This is merely a gesture," said Cameron as he placed two fingers against my clit, sending a jolt of pleasure.

It throbbed beneath his touch. With my mouth gaping, my fingernails dug into his left arm. Having never before been touched by a man down there, my mind tried to grasp these feelings, these sensations, this thrill causing spasms throughout my belly. His caressing brought waves of hypnotic pleasure.

Richard's expression hadn't changed; his critical stare roamed over me.

Say something.

Cameron broke the silence. "This is an apology from Mia to prove how sorry she is."

My eyelids fluttered and I strained to keep my gaze upon Richard's.

Richard leaned back farther, his focus still upon Cameron's fingertips moving over my sex. Richard's gaze rose to meet mine only to return once again to his friend's hand bringing me closer. This man really knew how to touch a woman.

Something told me Richard would too.

Tell me this pleases you; but I didn't dare say it.

"Mia, relax," cooed Cameron.

And I did, leaning back into him, concentrating hard on keeping this pout that Tara had instructed me to hold. Though back in her two bedroom it had sounded doable. Now however, with Cameron's fingers masterfully stroking, circling, maintaining these stunning sensations I'd only ever read about, my lips trembled with emotion; a mixture of desire and exhilaration.

"Do you want me to stop, Mia?" said Cameron.

"No," I managed faintly, breathlessly. "Don't stop. Please." My moan filled the room.

Cameron's fingers reached farther, though they didn't enter me.

They merely dipped into that moisture, using it to wet my arousal more, these tingles intensifying blissfully against his touch. I tried not to gape in ecstasy but Cameron's expert flicking sped up and stole my breath away...

Yes...

His fingers cherished that part of me I'd never felt comfortable with until now. Feeling lightheaded, I rested my head back against his chest and surrendered, my eyelids straining to remain open, my mouth parted and desiring a kiss I knew would never find me, my gaze on Richard. Here, now, feeling more loved than I ever had I feared when this would end, never wanting Cameron to cease.

"Oh, please." I moaned again and a sob escaped.

These two unobtainable men were sharing this exquisite moment.

Surreal. Exotic. Mine.

Swept away, touched so gently, so firmly, yet my innocence remained, my purity endured. Richard gave a ghost of a smile and his expression reminded me of a painting where the subject glimpses a miracle or even beyond the veil.

Was he in awe?

I knew I was.

Electricity danced between us, this flirting with pleasure so intense I longed to share it with Richard as it unfolded. Silently, I tried to convey these feelings.

This wanting...

"Richard will tell you when you may come, Mia," whispered Cameron.

I gave a nod, feeling too ravaged by pleasure.

The music's cadence unfolded dramatically, and I was so lost I failed to tell who led who. Perhaps the notes were guiding me on or maybe it was the other way around, as though through the bass they found their way inside me.

"Richard," said Cameron, breaking his friend's trance.

Richard blinked with surprise and he tilted his head as though he too wanted this scene to play out forever, his expression full of wonder.

"Mia." Richard gave a simple gesture. "You may come."

Holding his stare, I conveyed without words that I came for him, my breathing ragged, my thighs shaking, my gasps transforming into groans of ecstasy. As though Cameron had delivered on an unspoken promise, he continued guiding me to that place of bliss, holding me suspended there, and I finally stepped over the threshold of surrendering and came hard, hoping somehow, someway, I'd found a place in their world. My eyelids squeezed shut as I went within, trembling all over. All sights and sounds dissipated, and my only awareness was this blinding heat of pleasure pulsing beneath his touch.

When I braved to look again, it was to meet Richard's reassuring expression.

"Well, that was articulated well," he said with a dangerous softness.

Still riding the wave, ready for whatever happened next, my legs weakened. I was relieved it was over and yet tormented with a fear it may never happen again.

Cameron tugged down my skirt and stepped back. I turned, relieved to see him smiling, his nod letting me know everything was fine.

A wave of dizziness hit me again.

Cameron stepped forward and took me in his arms, guiding me across the room. When we reached the studded couch, he eased me down to sit and I sank into the leather. He settled beside me, rubbing my back with affection. When I finally braved to look up, Richard had gone.

Pressing my hands against my chest, I willed these palpitations to slow, hoping to remember how to take deep breaths again and make it look easy.

Lotte entered and made a beeline for us. In her hand she carried a beige folder. She joined us on the couch, sitting beside me.

She tucked a stray hair behind my ear. "How's my darling Mia?"

"Oh, fine." Eyeing that beige folder suspiciously, I hoped it didn't contain my official marching orders.

Not now, not after having tasted the sweetest forbidden fruit.

Cameron straightened my skirt, his fingers easing my hem towards my knees, his touch firm and comforting.

Lotte handed me the file. "Type these up, please, and have them on Richard's desk by tomorrow."

My gaze shot up to meet Cameron's.

"Well done," he said. "Ms. Lauren, well done."

Lotte squeezed my arm. "Mia, your boss wants you to check his emails one final time and then you're permitted to head home early."

I gave a nod and tried to make it to the door without tripping. I couldn't bear to look back and have them see me flustered. I'd already shared more of myself in these last moments than I ever had, exposed my heart as well as my most private of places, shocking myself into silence.

Outside, I took a moment to steady my nerves, pressing my forehead against the wall, trying to catch my breath and calm my shaking hands. Those stunning tingles of pleasure still lingering between my thighs and made me ache for more; an indescribable longing. I willed these unfamiliar thoughts away before they rendered me useless.

Vaguely, I became aware that Mistress Scarlet had appeared out of nowhere. She closed the gap between us.

"Mia," she said. "You have color in your cheeks. I don't think I've ever seen you look so lovely."

"I understand now," I told her. "This place." I felt silly for saying it, my mind so consumed, my heart still racing.

She smiled. "Cameron?"

My cheeks blushed wildly and I averted my gaze.

"No one understands the delicate blossoming of a bud more than Cameron." She stroked my cheek with curled fingers. "My sweet butterfly, draw in your wings when near Richard. He has a penchant for singeing them."

She headed off down the hallway, showing remarkable poise in nine inch heels.

Hadn't she warned me off Cameron? A trace of his touch still lingered low in my belly; the shadow of his grip.

All for Richard's approval.

Clutching that beige folder, I made my way toward the reception desk, grateful it was mine again, and tried to grasp Scarlet's words.

CHAPTER SEVEN

"How are we this morning?" said Richard.

He lingered on the other side of my desk, oozing his usual sexual confidence and looking ridiculously dashing in a suit. This whole pretty boy mixed with rugged explorer was distracting. I'd been so busy shoving invitations into envelopes for Chrysalis's party I'd almost forgotten yesterday's breathtaking event of getting my job back, with what Cameron had assured me was panache. What would usually be considered tartsville behavior was all so normal here.

"Mia?" he said.

Ravaged by the memories, I blushed wildly. "Fine, thank you." I slid a blank post-it note inside a beige file trying to look busy. "How are you?"

"Fine, thank you," he echoed. "Are you sure?"

I glanced up. "Why wouldn't I be?"

"We could perhaps talk about yesterday?"

"Oh, no thank you." I waved it off while subduing this threatening blush.

As though still trying to extract more, his eyebrows drew together. "Do you want to meet me there?"

My blush brightened. "Where?"

"Our three o'clock. Brentwood."

I dragged the diary across the desk and opened it. "Our?"

He leaned forward and rested his fingertip on the page. "The Sullivan's."

I hoped to read the answer from his face.

He shrugged. "Or we can go together if you're uncomfortable with finding the place."

"We can go together," I said, my gaze finding the Sullivan's name and wondering what we'd be doing there.

"It's their interview. They feel ready for a stay at Chrysalis." He narrowed his stare. "You know about Chrysalis, right?"

"Of course," I fibbed, and used a pencil to underline their name.

"What you did yesterday was impressive. You know how to take your boss's breath away."

A flutter of nerves tingled in my chest and I wondered if underlining a name ten times might look strange.

"Mia?"

Braving a look up, I let go of the pencil.

"Do you regret it?" he said.

"No." And I didn't. Not really. It was merely this embarrassment of having to face him again.

He sat on the edge of the desk. "That will never be expected of you again. Or anything sexual for that matter."

"Thank goodness," I said, and in response to his look of surprise added, "Thank you for giving me my job back."

"We're happy to have you back. I think you're going to like it here."

"Me too."

He stood there, staring for far too long. "Five minutes sound good to you?"

I tried not to look nervous.

He knitted his brow. "Until we leave."

"That's fine." I cringed inside.

Richard headed to his office.

It felt good to clear the air. He was a hard man to read, and although

I'd glimpsed his ability to show kindness he still scared the hell out of me. Maybe it was his east coast demeanor. That well-educated elitism that he'd never shaken. Yesterday had broken down some of that wall between us. Still, I sensed we had a long way to go before I felt relaxed around him. You'd have thought that after my erotic shenanigans there would be less tension. It was hard to tell if he was looking down on me because I obviously lacked his Ivy league background or whether I was just as much a conundrum to him. My first impression of Richard having a privileged upbringing had been right. I imagined him and Cameron both drinking expensive foreign wine in some dark cornered Massachusetts bar, while discussing philosophy and other pretentious subjects. I wondered if they'd ever been members of a secret society while at Harvard, like the Skull and Bones, or was that Yale? Anyway, I made a mental note to ask him when we'd gotten to know each other better. As well as the most intriguing question of all: how he ended up here.

My iPhone buzzed and I reached into my handbag and read the text.

Bailey: "*How did it go?*"

Mia: "*Mission accomplished. Have job back.*"

Bailey: "*Did you use new super sexy ninja moves?*"

Mia: "*Yes, kind of.*"

Bailey:"*OMG. Call me.*"

Richard stood in the doorway. "Am I interrupting?"

"Um, no."

"Boyfriend?"

"No. My friend, Bailey."

"Please don't use your phone in front of clients."

I gave a nod and shoved my iPhone back into my bag, hoping he didn't ask to look at what I'd texted.

The phone vibrated with a new message.

Richard came closer and leaned forward on the desk. "You're itching to see what it says aren't you?"

I assumed it was Bailey again asking for all the rude details of yesterday. Of course we could have discussed this last night, but she was at her yoga class. I'd rented a documentary on Netflix, some penguin film

I'd found hard to concentrate on as my mind kept dragging me back to when I'd flashed my boss.

"Well?" Richard's face changed and he stood tall. "Ready?"

I rose and grabbed my bag. "I'm looking forward to it."

"You have no idea what the appointment's for, do you?"

I ignored that question and with a flick of my mouse sent my computer to sleep. "It's nice to get out," was all I could think of.

"This is certainly going to be interesting." He led the way to the elevator.

Inside the chauffer driven Lincoln town car, Richard worked on his iPad, pausing now and again to check his BlackBerry.

Sitting quietly beside him, nudged up in the corner of the back left seat, I marveled at his ability not to get car sick. He took a phone call and it was reassuring to see him loosen up, crossing his legs casually and laughing. Something told me the caller was Cameron.

After turning off the main road and heading up what appeared to be a private lane, I was grateful Richard and I were travelling together. I doubted I'd have found this place on my own.

White pillars rose high, emphasizing the grand entrance to an enormous mansion. The architecture mingled Italian and French styles and oozed billionaire. Lush landscaping wrapped around the estate and an ornate dolphin fountain welcomed guests at the front of the house. The lavish outside of the estate equaled the inside, with sumptuous furnishings evidently decorated by an eccentric stylist. It made me wonder if the residents had been too polite to pull the designer back and tame the leopard print theme.

The fifty-something uniformed housekeeper led Richard and I into a living room.

Though I wanted to keep my sunglasses on to ward off the brightness of mismatched golds and reds, Richard reached over and removed them off my face.

"We pay danger money," he said, arching a brow.

I tucked my glasses into my bag and shoved it beside my feet. Perched on the end of a light blue sofa, I was nervous of causing a crease. Seriously, this was the richest house I'd ever been in. The enormous pink marble fireplace must have cost a fortune and the two ornamental dogs sitting on either side of the mantel gave it a regal air. All the furniture in here seemed overly decadent, garish even. I wondered what kind of people the Sullivan's were and how they made their money.

Richard seemed relaxed, leaning back casually on an over-stuffed cushion. "Well?" he said, sweeping his hand wide. "What do you think?"

"This is the biggest house I've ever been in," I admitted.

"What about the decor?"

"Not really my taste."

"What is your taste?"

I wondered if I'd overstepped the mark by being honest. "Simple."

"You mean cheap?"

I threw him an annoyed glare.

"I'm hungry," he said grouchily.

"Maybe they have cookies."

"How old are you?" He frowned. "I mean really?"

"From now on I'll bring a snack in my handbag for you."

"Initiative too. We've outdone ourselves."

"Why are we here?" I said, trying to ignore his attempt to rile me up. If he wanted to get a reaction out of me so he could find another excuse to fire me, he wasn't getting one.

"The Sullivan's need to sign some forms so they're set for next week," he said.

"You can't send them in the post?"

"Tell me what you know about Chrysalis?"

"Well…um…"

A bark pulled our attention toward the door. A Pomeranian snarled at us. The dog's owner appeared, a woman dressed elegantly in a cream suit, her blonde hair up in a chignon. She looked about twenty-five but dressed older.

"Master Richard Booth," she said with a strong Texan lilt, holding her hands out to greet him. She flushed brightly and giggled.

The dog yapped at Richard's feet. He ignored it and rose to greet his highly perfumed friend. Her scent reminded me of a flower shop.

"And who is this adorable young lady?" she said breathlessly.

"Mia, my new secretary," said Richard. "How are you, Constance?" He kissed both her cheeks, and her hands still held in his.

Constance beamed at me. "I'm fine. Bill will be right with us. He's finishing up on a call. Why Mia, do sit and tell me all about you."

Richard sat beside me. "We're not here to talk about us, Constance. This day is all about you and Bill."

She took the armchair opposite. "We are just thrilled you could make it. The driveway can be tricky."

"It's a road," jested Richard.

"Bill gave you directions though, didn't he? He's good at that kind of thing. Me, well if it wasn't for my GPS I'd be back in Texas every time I went to Beverly Hills." She let out a nervous laugh.

"We'll take it slow," said Richard.

Which was kind of strange but it seemed to appease her. She took a long, deep breath and calmed a little.

"Can I get you refreshments?" she said. "Lemonade?"

"Your housekeeper already offered," he said. "We're fine."

She leaned forward. "I am ready for this? Right Richard?"

"Absolutely," he said. "It's only natural to be a little nervous." He opened the envelope. "Once these are signed you'll be all set."

"I wish you guys did a one week thing. A month seems such a long time." She swallowed hard.

Richard leaned back and blinked his answer.

"I am ready," she said. "Really I am. I know I don't sound it."

Richard looked thoughtful.

"They call it emersion, apparently." Constance turned to me. "That's why it goes on for so long. That's what Bill tells me anyway."

Richard motioned he agreed.

Constance continued, "Bill's done it twice before and he says he's a new man when he comes out of there."

The dog yapped toward the door.

A handsome middle-aged man appeared. "Did I hear my name being mentioned?" he spoke with the same Texan lilt.

Constance rose and so did Richard. I followed their lead and stood too.

The man's stare fixed on me. "Why, Richard, you shouldn't have."

"Terrance." Richard looked amused and proffered his hand. "How have you been?"

"Good," he said, "and you?"

"Wonderful." Richard patted his arm with affection. "You've been working out, Terrance."

"Constance's personal trainer." He cringed. "I hate the bastard."

Richard laughed with them.

We all took our seats again and Terrance sat in the other armchair, close to his wife's. Terrance's stare found me again.

I felt Constance looking at me too and yet she wasn't in the least effected by her husband's glaring. Over the last few weeks I'd mastered the art of hiding my reaction and prided myself on even hiding my discomfort from Richard.

"Those for me?" Terrance held his hand out.

Richard gave him the papers. "We have your NDA, the form for your doctor to sign off, and of course your special request form."

I'd signed Enthrall's non-disclosure agreement on my first day. I wondered if Chrysalis's might be the same.

Terrance looked surprised. "Special requests. That's new." He placed them on the coffee table.

I tried to get in a discreet peek at them only to feel Richard's disapproving glare.

"This is Mia," said Constance. "She's Richard's new secretary."

"Well done," said Terrance.

Richard gestured. "Mr. Sullivan has been a member of Enthrall for six years."

"Coming up for seven," said Terrance.

"Now." Richard looked serious. "Constance, I want to make sure you've given Chrysalis a great deal of thought. It's not Enthrall. I'm sure the director's been over everything with you, but once you sign these…"

Constance shifted in her seat. "I feel it's one of those things I'll regret if I don't do it."

"I've told her my first wife loved it," said Terrance.

My jaw almost hit the floor.

"She did," said Constance with a nod. "I bumped into her last week in Neimen Marcus. We caught up."

"Ellen loved it too. My second wife," said Terrance.

How many x-wives did this man have?

"Do you like spending time in Chrysalis?" Constance asked me.

I looked to Richard for help with that one.

He merely stared at me, waiting for an answer which he knew I wouldn't have.

"I've never actually been," I said.

"Oh," said Constance. "Why not?"

"Sweetheart," said Richard. "She's staff. Not a member." He looked sad for me.

Constance shot a sympathetic look my way. "Well maybe we could offer to gift her membership?"

Terrance laughed. "My wife's unending generosity."

"Shall we begin?" said Richard, gesturing to the door, evidently wanting to move on with the proceedings.

I wondered what this part might be.

Constance took a deep breath. "How long do you watch for?"

"It's a formality. Ticks in the right boxes. That kind of thing. Five minutes. How does that sound?" He lowered his gaze. "I'll discreetly slip away and the next time you'll see me will be at Chrysalis."

"Where's best?" said Constance.

"Bedroom's fine," said Richard.

"Well I'm ready." Terrance rose and headed for the door, quickly followed by Constance.

"Stay here," Richard warned me.

"She's not coming with us?" said Constance.

Richard gestured for me to sit. "No."

Constance came back and knelt at my feet. "Do you like puppies, Mia?"

"I love puppies," I said, beaming at Richard.

He rolled his eyes.

Constance peered down at her Pomeranian. "Tilley has puppies." She scratched her dog's head. "Want to see them?"

"Yes, please."

Constance sashayed towards the glass double doorway and opened it and I followed her. A sprawling green lawn spread out before us and beyond that an enormous blue pool. I'd certainly gotten the fun end of the deal and wondered where they were all going. Probably to sign the papers. Surely the office would be more appropriate?

Constance turned to face me. "They're in the guest house." She pouted. "Terrance has banned them from the house."

"They shit everywhere," he told Richard.

"We'll be right back," said Constance. "Mia, maybe you'd like to come back and play with me and the puppies sometime?" She flashed Richard a shy look. "If she's allowed."

Maybe we could swim too, I thought.

My gaze shot back to her then I looked at Richard.

"I keep Mia busy back at the office," he said, gesturing. "Shall we?"

Had Constance just hit on me? She had. She'd frickin hit on me.

I watched them go.

My intrigue got the better of me. I headed off after them, making sure the housekeeper wasn't around. Jolting to a stop at the foot of the sweeping stairway, I looked up to see Richard at the top of the stairs, glaring down.

He'd been waiting for me.

No words came out of my gaping mouth. I merely gestured to let him know I was puppy bound. I could have sworn he looked like he'd gleaned pleasure from my embarrassment. So I turned on my heel and went back the way I'd come.

Sitting crossed legged in the guest house, I played with one of the

Pomeranian pup's in my lap. Inside the velvet lined box, the other five tumbled around, crying for equal affection. I reached in, trying to placate them.

I cringed at my awkwardness and tried to take my mind off it, focusing instead on the puppy. It was certainly interesting to observe Richard interact with the Sullivan's. He didn't seem intimidated in the least by all this grandeur. I wondered if he'd grown up in a house like this.

"Have you had your puppy fix yet?" said Richard, leaning on the doorjamb.

Wondering how long he'd been there, I lowered the puppy back in with his siblings and climbed to my feet.

I headed after Richard. "Did it go all right?"

"Did what go all right?" He led me across the lawn and along the left side of the house.

"Signing the papers?"

"They haven't signed them yet."

"I thought that's where you were going." I broke his gaze and stared back up at the front of the house.

"Get in," he said.

Our driver held the passenger door open for us.

I settled into the corner and reached for my seatbelt. "Do you travel everywhere with a driver?"

"That would be tedious," said Richard, reaching for my seatbelt strap and tugging it across my chest.

"Why today?"

"Showmanship."

The car glided out of the driveway.

I looked back up at the mansion. "But they didn't see us arrive."

"You know this for sure?"

Of course there may have been some truth in that. If it had been me I would have watched from a window in anticipation of Richard's arrival.

"You made quite an impression," he said. "Constance took a shine to you."

"I think she hit on me," I whispered, not wanting the driver to overhear.

Richard peered out of the window. "I'd take it as a compliment."

This visit had been nothing but weird and I actually looked forward to returning to Enthrall. Within minutes we were back on the main road.

"Where did you go with them?" I said.

He gave a ghost of a smile. "To watch them fuck."

"No really?"

His expression remained unchanged.

"It didn't last long," I said, my blush rising.

"I didn't stay for the whole thing. Trust me, my hand twitched the entire time for my cell."

I tried to wrap my head around what he'd revealed. "They didn't mind?"

"It's part of a one hundred year old tradition."

"Tradition?"

"Our meeting today is to confirm they're ready." He turned to face me. "You have no idea what Chrysalis is do you?"

"I'm not sure I want to either."

"You lied to me. You told me you knew."

"You put me on the spot."

His expression turned to disappointment. As though on cue, he reached into his pocket and removed his BlackBerry then ignored me.

Tension hung heavy and despite the air con it felt stuffy. I reached for the button to buzz down my window, but Richard's wide-eyed reaction made me withdraw my hand and rest it in my lap.

"Sorry," I whispered.

"Pull up here, please," Richard ordered the chauffeur.

The car parked alongside the curb.

Richard stared dead-ahead as though deep in thought. After a minute or two he exited the car. I clicked off my seatbelt and slid along the seat to follow him out.

I deserved to be treated better than this. "Well, who are you going to watch doing it now?"

Richard looked amused. "Care for some?"

I frowned at him.

He tilted his head and gestured to Loard's ice-cream store.

"Oh, yes please." Maybe he wasn't angry with me after-all.

A burst of cold air hit us on the way in. Line upon line of flavors rested in their multi-colored tubs secured behind a long glass window, promising no end of bliss.

"Vanilla cone, please." Richard handed over his credit card. "And a coffee."

He'd chosen for me and I tried to hide that it bothered me. Richard reached for the antiseptic gel and squirted some into his palm.

He motioned for me to hold my hands out. "Puppies are filthy."

"They were cute."

"Bacteria ridden fur balls." He rubbed the gel into my hands, caressing them. He took his time massaging and my fingers tingled against his touch, the sensation relaxing.

The shop girl reached over with a cone. "Sir, there you go." She handed him his coffee and card back.

The way she blushed made me realize it wasn't only me he affected like this. Even Constance had acted like a school-girl right up until her husband appeared. I found that strangely comforting.

Richard handed me the ice-cream and led the way to a private booth. Sitting opposite, I waited for him to start talking, curious now more than ever about Chrysalis and why anyone would want to lock themselves away in there.

Richard eased off his coffee lid and took a sip. "Not bad."

"Want some?" I offered my ice-cream.

He shook his head and leaned back, resting his arms on either side of his seat.

Despite wanting mint, vanilla tasted good. This mom and pop store, though small, had a homemade coziness to it. They still had their Halloween decorations up.

"What does the word Chrysalis mean to you?" said Richard.

"As in butterfly?" I licked away.

"Yes."

"Well, it's like when a caterpillar is ready to become a butterfly it breaks out of its chrysalis."

"And that is why our founder named our house in California, Chrysalis." He picked up his cup. "It's important to point out everything we do is with consenting adults."

"So it's like Enthrall, only people are doing it all the time. They live there?"

"They immerse themselves as either dominants or submissives, yes."

"Why?"

"It's complex."

"Do they hate themselves?"

"No." He looked serious. "By the time they come out they're... refreshed. Revitalized. Renewed." He held my gaze. "Reborn."

I took a moment to consider his words, wondering if I'd ever understand them, or even understand anyone wanting that.

A flicker of a reaction from Richard showed he'd caught the gist of my thoughts.

"Is Constance going to be a submissive?" I said.

Richard pulled more napkins out of the silver holder and handed them to me. "Yes."

I wiped the trail of cream trickling down my hand toward my wrist.

He pointed to his chin, mirroring mine. "Here."

I wiped it off and got a nod of approval.

"And Terrance?" I said.

"Sub too."

"I don't think Constance is ready."

He placed his lid back on.

I dabbed my mouth. "She's doing it to placate her husband."

"A psychiatrist with a laser-sharp perception has profiled them both. They're ready."

It was too much of a coincidence for Cameron not to be that man. "Maybe the psychiatrist's wrong."

Richard looked surprised and blinked several times at me.

"You told them you'd see them later?" I said.

"I visit there, yes."

"Will I have to go there?"

"Do you bring in an annual income of at least 1.5 million dollars?"

"You know I don't."

"Then no. You'll never see inside Chrysalis."

I sat back. "So you do?"

"Did you just ask me how much I earn?"

I licked the cold creamy softness. "Maybe."

His gaze fixed on me and he let out a sigh.

"Is everything all right?" I said.

"It really is."

"What did you do before you worked at Enthrall?"

"Why?"

"I'm interested."

"I was a stockbroker. I'm from New York."

"Why did you come to L.A?"

"So I could breathe again."

I twisted my mouth. "I thought there's more smog here."

"Cameron was here."

"You're really good friends, aren't you?"

"The best." He pushed his cup away. "Cameron gets me."

"Where does he work?"

Richard caressed his brow. "Don't take this the wrong way, but I'm not so sure you're a good fit for us at Enthrall."

I lowered my ice-cream.

"The staff like you," he said. "But that's not the point."

"I'm sorry about that typo—"

"You misunderstand."

"You underestimate me."

He let out another long sigh. "I see your future and it looks—" He took the ice-cream from me and licked it. "Mmmm, vanilla." He handed it back.

"I know what that means."

"Well?"

"You're telling me my life will be ordinary."

"Actually, I was referring to your sex life."

"Why do you say that?"

"You're naive."

"I'm not."

"You are, Mia. I've sat here for the last ten minutes watching you with that ice-cream and you have no idea how arousing it is."

Half in a daze and half to spite him I licked the ice-cream again. "You're a pervert. You all are."

"Oh Mia." He beamed at me. "You have no idea."

CHAPTER EIGHT

AVING ADDRESSED EACH INVITATION BY HAND FOR Chrysalis's entire client list, I set about placing stamps on each one. This project would have been a lot easier had I been able to use a label maker. It had been an arduous task with over three hundred members receiving one. Richard had insisted this method ensured privacy as he'd handed over the gold embossed invites. When I finally looked up to take a breather, stretching my aching hand, I almost yelped.

Cameron stood a few feet away, that dark gaze of his burning a hole through me.

"Didn't dare disturb you," he said.

"Hey, Dr. Cole." I tried to shake off this uneasiness, having not seen him enter the building.

"Please, call me Cameron."

"Cameron." I smiled. "Richard's gone home."

He twisted his mouth in disappointment. "I should have called first."

My face burned up and I broke his gaze, reaching for my mouse and feigning something on the screen needed my attention. The last time I'd seen him had been three days ago when our strange ménage a trois of sorts had played out in Richard's office. The life changing event that made me giddy when I thought of it. For goodness sake, this man had touched me intimately and yet now we were both being so formal with each other. Like nothing had ever happened.

He was still staring.

"How are you?" I said, trying to appear busy.

"More importantly, how are you?"

Please don't want to talk about what you did to me.

"I'm fine," I said. "Thank you so much for taking care of my car." There, I'd parlayed an embarrassing moment into one that took the focus off me and placed it firmly on an inanimate object.

"That was my pleasure, Mia." He moved closer and casually tucked his hands into his pockets.

I wondered if his patients fantasized about him getting into their pants as well as their minds. There was something so perfect about Cameron. He'd be a hard man to open up to for fear of disappointing him. Was he the psychiatrist who'd profiled the Sullivans? If so, I wondered how he concluded a person was ready for a stay at Chrysalis. Shouldn't he be advising them to seek some form of treatment instead? Pop a pill. A round of therapy.

"Please don't ask me what I'm thinking," I said firmly.

"Why, what are you thinking?"

"That you want to talk to me about the other day."

"Do you want to talk about the other day?"

"No, thank you."

He lowered his gaze. "How are you settling in?"

"Great. I like it here."

"Is your boss treating you well?"

"Yes, Richard's very nice."

"Nice?" He seemed to mull over the word. "Well that's good to hear."

I held up the list. "I was just finishing off with these invites."

"You going?"

I placed the list back in their folder. "Richard told me it was probably best I didn't." I scrunched up my nose. "I don't mind. Apparently things get pretty wild."

"They kind of do," he mouthed dramatically.

The way he'd said it made me smile. "I'm going to pop this back in his office." I headed toward the door, file in hand, grateful Cameron had let me off the hook about discussing our recent tete-a-tete.

I was even thinking in French now, like a European hussy right out of a burlesque show. I hoped this shyness might soon pass. I needed to act normal and not let him see how he affected me. Still, from the way Penny and Scarlet acted when he was in the room they too were intimidated. I managed to make it past Cameron without looking at him.

"I can talk to Richard about letting you go to the party," he said. "As long as you don't go alone you'll be fine."

I paused by the door. "Richard was pretty insistent."

He leaned against the desk and lowered his gaze. "He's probably right."

I forced another smile and headed through the door, making my way into Richard's office. I secured the file safely away in his cabinet, locked it, and dropped the key back into his pen holder.

When I returned to my desk, Cameron had gone. It didn't take me long to secure the invites into the lowest drawer, power down my computer, shred the post-it notes I'd scribbled on, and restock my printer paper. I went to grab my handbag and a wave of terror hit me. The gate to the elevator was wide open.

With a quick glance I confirmed my key to the elevator was still taped to the top of the lowest drawer. Whoever had gone down there hadn't used mine. Though someone could have used it and placed it back during the time I'd been gone. I reached into my bag and pulled out my cell and texted Richard.

And waited.

Five minutes later and there was still no response from him. I wondered how he'd react to me visiting Enthrall's forbidden zone to check for intruders. There was a lingering intrigue I'd not been able to shake. This out of bounds area had taken on a life of its own inside my imagination. Still, no way was I going down there.

Cameron reappeared from the staff hallway.

"I thought you'd gone," I said, relieved to see him.

"Just left a note on Richard's desk."

"Why don't you text him?"

"Not answering." He glanced at his watch. "He's probably out on a run."

"Look." I pointed to the gate.

"I thought we were the last ones here."

"So did I." I stared at the elevator as though this alone would cause it to spill its secrets.

"Let's check it out."

"I'm not allowed." I raised my hand to let him know I had no intention of going anywhere near there.

"Don't be ridiculous," he said, calling the elevator. "You're with me."

The doors parted and we stared into an open elevator.

Cameron strolled on in and gestured for me to join him. "It's safer. I don't want to leave you up here alone."

"What do you mean?"

"If someone did break in they may be up here now."

I leaped in and with a push of a button we descended.

"Shouldn't we call the police?" I said.

"They have a knack for spoiling all the fun."

"Do you really think someone has broken in?"

"No."

"Oh."

He shrugged.

"Will you explain this to Richard for me," I said.

"Of course."

"I'm actually kind of intrigued." I felt a jolt of excitement.

Tara had been right about the deep red walls. Soft lighting fell upon the five pieces of furniture, if you could call them that. More appropriately they were beautifully carved, dark stained contraptions. A table positioned in the middle had reams of fine silver chains hanging over it, reaching all the way to the floor. To its right stood a crisscrossed wooden panel with leather handcuffs on either side to stretch out the victim's arms. Upon the wall hung an assortment of equipment, including paddles, whips, and blindfolds. A chest pushed up against the far wall hid what was probably more torturous accruements. I resisted the urge to take a peek.

What looked like a stock out of the Middle Ages was easily countered by the elegant throne, a velvet cushion before it. To its right hung an enormous steel cage, and farther along more contraptions rested on shelves: silver-link chains, ropes, blindfolds, gags, and what looked like a black pair of gloves with spiked fingertips.

This place set medieval devices against modern in the most startling way. No wonder Richard didn't want me down here. He probably assumed I'd have bolted on my first day. Yet the soft scent of sandalwood and the womblike aura felt surprisingly calming. My lightheadedness muddled my brain. This risqué decor stirred feelings that had lain dormant, the thrill of delicious intrigue, a throb low in my belly that had no right to make me believe any of this was okay.

A door at the end of the room promised to lead off to more rooms of pain. There was no getting over this was a dangerous place to be in, and how anyone would voluntarily want to be strapped into any of these baffled me.

I turned to see Mistress Scarlet step out of the shadows. Her dominatrix outfit was a mixture of leather and latex. Her gothic-styled eyeliner and mascara highlighting her eyes, and her rouged lips, sharp cheekbones and hair worn back accentuated her commanding presence.

"Hi Scarlet," I said, hoping that glare of hers wasn't anger at me for being down here.

"Mia," she said, tapping the whip in her other hand. "Cameron."

There came an unsettling feeling she'd been waiting for us. I glanced back at the elevator, wishing I'd brought my cell. Richard might have texted back by now. Though the reception down here might be sketchy. We were way underground.

"We were concerned someone came down here." Cameron arched an eyebrow.

Scarlet's gaze slid over to me. "It's just us."

Cameron gestured. "Come here, Mia."

I took the few, short steps toward him, though my gaze stayed on Scarlet, wondering about that whip.

"Come look at this," he said. "Have you ever seen one of these?"

"What's it for?" The ornately carved crisscrossed post felt smooth beneath my touch.

He placed his hand over mine. "Want to see?"

Cameron looked fierce. The change in him so surprised me I didn't struggle when he took hold of my shoulders and eased me back against the bar.

"You stand here." He tilted his head. "Well, the client does."

I almost lost my balance as he stretched out my left arm to the side. He used his weight to keep me there, his body pressed against mine as he secured my wrist inside a leather strap; tight. A thrill shot from my chest to my groin and I caught my breath. There came a waft of Cameron's light cologne; a balmy scent stirring my senses.

"I don't like it," I lied, unsure of these sensations awakening in my chest and shooting downwards, reaching that place where he'd touched me not so long ago. My lips trembled as my gaze fell upon his mouth.

"You're quite safe." Cameron tugged the straps. "It's good to have a feel for what our clients go through, right?" He secured my right wrist.

I resisted, though his strength overwhelmed mine. He tugged my wrist tight in its buckle.

A throb in my chest lulled me. Scared me. "Scarlet?" I looked to her.

She gave a nod of encouragement.

The elevator shuddered and began its ascent.

"Let's pretend she's not here." Cameron pulled a thicker strap across my waist, buckled and yanked it. "In most sessions it would only be us two." He held his hand against my chest. "You're breathing way too fast. I don't want you to faint."

Mouth dry and thirsting, I tried to slow it down. "I have to get back to work."

"Thought you were finished for the day." He reached for my shirt button and undid it. His fingers moving fast on the others.

I screamed and he stepped back and laughed. "Not the shirt then."

"Not the shirt."

"Screams echo down here," he said. "We get that a lot."

Oh no...

His hand returned to my chest, pressing against it, his body close, his gaze boring into my mine with a fierce intensity. "What are you feeling?"

My eyelids fluttered shut, my heart beat way too fast. This desire intensified an ache sending spasms low and deep inside; a building pleasure. My nipples pushed against my bra, the hardened buds betraying me through my blouse.

"Very good." He leaned toward my ear and whispered, "That's what this one's for."

Another thrill of excitement shot between my thighs and I hated the fact he could tell. His fingertip brushed along my right forearm, pressing beneath the crux of my arm, sending a shiver up my spine.

"Cameron." I shuddered in response and twisted my wrists in their straps. "I can't breathe."

"Relax." He caressed my bottom lip.

I nipped at his thumb, my tongue tracing the tip.

His eyelids became heavy, his teeth clenched, his jaw tensing. "You are exquisite."

The elevator purred, getting louder, pulling his attention away for a second.

His dark stare found me again. "Has anyone ever told you that?"

"No."

He looked surprised. "Let me show you just how exquisite you are."

Cameron pressed his lips against my mine, bruising them, opening my mouth with his, daring me, capturing me with ferociousness. His erection pressed against my belly, and the pleasure and pain it would bring became all too real. Unable to push him off, I had no choice but to surrender, opening my mouth and going with him, drowning in the lightheadedness caused by his embrace.

This man was way out of my league, and yet he was here with me, seducing me, his velvety tongue tangling with mine. He'd called me exquisite. Made me believe it. This dreamlike moment was an impossible fantasy. A slow, steady throb of pleasure built as my moan entered his mouth, my tongue battling his, lost in this craving.

He pulled back slightly and held my gaze. "How do you feel?"

"Nice," I murmured, hating myself for saying it.

"Aroused?"

I gave a nod.

"Is your pussy nice and wet?"

I bit my lip, hard.

"Good girl." He gave an impressed smile.

"Cameron," snapped Richard.

I jolted back into the room.

Richard stood ten or so feet away, his face unreadable. Cameron glanced his way.

"Untie her," said Richard.

"We were exploring." Cameron found my gaze again. "Weren't we, Mia?"

"Now," said Richard.

Leaving me strapped in, Cameron stepped back. "Mia's been a *very* naughty girl."

"So I see," said Richard.

Cameron headed toward Richard and tapped his arm as he past. "See you later at Skybar."

Richard ignored him, keeping his glare on me.

The elevator doors closed on Cameron and Scarlet. A fuming Richard and I were alone. Within seconds he'd freed me. I sidestepped away from the board and away from him. I felt like I'd broken from a dream, my cheeks blushing wildly.

"I'd ask you what you're doing down here," Richard gestured to the crisscrossed board. "But it's quite clear."

"I texted you," I said breathlessly. "I waited for you to get back to me."

"You're forbidden from coming down here."

"But Cameron—"

"You take your orders from me."

"But—"

"Are you really this naive?"

I rubbed my wrists to sooth the sting. "I didn't expect this."

"Have you opened your eyes to your environment?"

"I should never have come down here."

"That's the first intelligent remark you've made."

"Cameron's been so good to me—"

"Looks like the intelligent streak is over."

I resisted the urge to glare at him. "You're both so…" I searched for the words that would make my point and not get me fired.

His face darkened and he dropped his hands to his side. "I may well be the flame but Cameron's the one who loves to watch you burn."

Silence. The uncomfortable kind.

My gaze flittered to the crisscrossed board.

"You liked that?" he said.

No.

"Speak up."

"No…well…yes. Kind of."

Whoever had a session here could be interrupted by someone arriving in that elevator, removing all hope of privacy. My mind searched for another distraction.

"Was it the board or Cameron or both that turned you on?" he said.

Breathing way too fast, I hoped he'd read from me what I dared not say.

He was mesmerizing.

Richard flipped me forward over the central table so fast he stole my breath away. My hands were out in front of me, trying to grip the wood, and yet all I grasped were chains. My vulnerable bottom jutted out. He held me there, still, unable to move. My skirt hiked up around my waist. He ripped off my thong.

My darkest fantasy with him was being realized...

"It's best if you don't resist." His hand pressed down on my spine, forcing me to arch my back. "Don't ever come down here again." The strike of his hand came down hard on my buttocks. "Understand?"

"Yes." I bit my hand to muffle my scream, fearing I'd alert Cameron and Scarlet and they'd return and see this.

"Yes, what?"

"Yes, sir."

"Good. Both hands on the table. Now!"

Another strike, only this one more vicious.

"Richard," I begged, my thighs shaking.

"You do not speak." He struck again. "Unless permitted."

This was too much. The pain lasted seconds but the pleasure pulsed into my clit. Time itself seduced me, stealing my thoughts and owning my dignity. I gritted my teeth, a soft moan escaping.

"Shush," soothed Richard, as his left hand slipped to my abdomen, lowering farther to cup between my thighs, his fingertips stroking along my cleft. "Well we know you like this, don't we?"

Yes.

A spasm of pleasure made me gasp.

"This doesn't lie, Mia. You're wet," he purred the words, his other hand bestowing a punishment of continued slaps I didn't deserve.

"Oh, yes." I pushed back into his hand, grinding against it.

"Be still," he ordered.

I was being attacked by both pain and pleasure and it made my head spin. I splayed my fingers farther, trying to better my balance as well as placate him. My thighs trembled as I became lost in a sea of sensations, trying to remain calm, fearing I'd pass out with the thrill of having Richard master me like this.

I yanked at the chains.

He waged his sensual war against me, his fingertips massaging with firm strokes, making me moan and I moved against his hand again, wanting, needing more, needing to come. This was wrong, but it felt so right. The tingling desire burned within, causing sensuous spasms that made me trance out. Another hard slap brought me back into the present, the sting sending shockwaves of heat through me. My thighs shuddered, rebelling against this position he had me in as I climbed higher, reaching the point of no return, pouting my way to climax.

Richard let go, denying my bliss.

The pleasure slipped away, leaving a low thrum where his fingers had been. He stepped back and gave me some space. I tried to steady myself, raising my hand against another sensual attack; it was hard to think straight.

He spun me around and lifted me up and sat me on the edge.

His hand swept wide. "Anything else you found you liked in here?" His tone was firm, scolding.

"We only tried that one."

Richard glared. "How long has it been going on?"

"What?"

"You heard me. How long have you and Cameron been fucking?"

"We've never…"

He ran his hand through his hair, his face full of concern.

My gaze shot to the crisscrossed board and I realized why he thought that. "We've never done anything."

"I deserve to know the truth."

My mind raced with what he must have thought he'd seen.

"Damn it, tell me," he said.

"I've never done it. Ever."

"What are you saying?" Richard jolted back. "Are you saying… Mia, are you saying you're still a virgin?"

"Yes."

He looked horrified.

"I have no idea what's going on," I said. "I'd almost finished addressing your invites and was about to head home when Cameron brought me down here."

"For God's sake, Mia." Richard's eyes widened. "I just nearly fucked you on this thing."

CHAPTER NINE

RICHARD'S RUBICON WRANGLER VIRTUALLY FLEW UP THE 101.

With the top down it felt like we were going faster than the 85 miles an hour I'd caught on the odometer. This losing battle with my hair blowing into my face was getting annoying.

"What if you get a ticket?" I shouted over to Richard.

"I'll pay it." He fell silent again.

He'd insisted on taking me home.

I too fell quiet after receiving yet another snippety answer. The tension of tonight looked like it was far from letting up.

And I wasn't wearing any frickin panties. He'd ripped them off in that dungeon to get better access to my butt. My left hand clutched at my skirt, holding it down. He and Cameron were rogues. My face threatened to burst into flames from the memory of what they had done to me in that dungeon. My groin throbbed with the thought of it and I rested my head back, reeling.

Although I'd had some idea of where my career may lead, this was way off. I never imagined I'd end up in some crazy work environment where the usual boundaries were not so much lacking as nonexistent.

Richard slid the Jeep into fifth gear. I wondered why he'd not bought the automatic version. My gaze rested upon his hands, those strong fingers of his clutching the wheel, having not so long ago held me in the grip of pleasure. I wondered if he ever would again.

I let out a slow soothing breath.

I'd left my car back at Enthrall and was now terrified he'd drop me home and fire me, leaving me stranded tomorrow. Maybe Bailey could drive me down to pick up my Mini? The view fell away fast, along with the hypnotic headlights on the other side heading south.

Richard changed the radio station to a talk show. The host chatted away in an east coast accent about a building in New York. After a few minutes he changed it again.

Even off the freeway Richard drove the Jeep hard, turning sharp onto Ventura and navigating his way through Studio City like he knew the place. Having handed over my address on my application, I could only assume that's where he'd gotten it from. Richard hadn't asked for it and yet that's where we were headed. The familiarity of the stores and restaurants brought some comfort. We soon passed my local Coffee Bean, as well as that upscale boutique I could never afford to shop in and my neighborhood Ralphs.

We pulled up outside my building and Richard parked. With his seatbelt off, he turned to look at me, casually resting his head against his palm, his elbow on the headrest.

"I felt fine to drive," I said, though it was a mute point now.

"How are you feeling?"

"Fine. You?"

"Never better." He arched a brow. "I want to apologize."

"No need."

"I'd give you the name of a good lawyer I know…but he's so good you'd win your case against me."

"Is that your attempt at humor?"

"Yes."

"You might want to work on that. Please don't fire me."

"May I come in?" He glanced over my shoulder.

I wasn't expecting that.

"I don't have any coffee," I said.

"I promise you what happened back at Enthrall will never happen again." He nodded to make his point.

I mirrored his nod, not quite sure what to say.

"Scarlet used to live in Studio City." He removed the keys from the ignition. "You'd never get her out of Santa Monica now." He opened the door and came round to my side.

My hand barely released my seatbelt when he'd opened the door for me.

"Where do you live?" I said, grateful for his hand helping me down.

"Malibu."

"In an apartment?"

"I bought a house a few years ago."

"Do you live alone?"

His gaze locked with mine. "No."

A wave of disappointment hit me.

I wondered if he had a wife waiting for him, and if so would he go over his day with her like a normal couple. Perhaps he'd explain how the last few hours of this evening had unfolded with Cameron, Scarlet, and me in Enthrall's playroom. She'd have to be more than open minded to cope with hearing about any of that. Being married to him she probably needed as much therapy as he did.

Maybe I should have taken that job in Best Buy, though the pay wouldn't have come close to what Enthrall paid. It was exciting to hang out with Richard, even if he did seem overly confident. It was his worldliness, his charisma, that made him fun to be around. And he'd just spanked me in the playroom I was banned from, rounding out my education into his lifestyle.

My legs weakened and I wondered if I'd ever be able to tell Bailey.

Within a minute or two we'd made it to the front door of my ground floor apartment, and I made a mental run through of how I'd left the place. Tidy, as far as I could remember.

"Next time choose a second floor apartment," he said. "It's safer."

He frowned towards my left neighbor's front door; gunshots from a television poured into the courtyard.

We stepped inside my place and the noise dimmed.

"This is a studio." His horrified stare roamed the bedroom, sweeping over to the bathroom door.

"Yes." I strolled over to the kitchen, wondering how long he was thinking of staying and hating the idea of him judging me.

"I thought we were paying you well?"

"You are."

"Do you have tea?" he said. "Caffeine free?"

"I can make you coffee."

He looked amused. "Thought you didn't have any?"

Didn't he know the *I have no coffee code*?

He followed. "Is it decaf?"

"No." I opened a cupboard and reached for the Nescafe jar.

"Oh, instant. Yum." He stared at it. "Just water for me then." He leaned back against the counter.

With a twist of the tap I poured him a glass of water from the faucet.

"You haven't lived in L.A. long have you?" he said.

"How do you know?" I offered him the glass.

With a wave, he declined it. "You can't drink the tap water here."

"Why?"

"Tastes nasty. Amongst other things. Do you have any bottled water?" He widened his gaze. "Not that that's any safer."

"How do mean?"

"The plastic's absorbed into the water." He shrugged, and his steady gaze studied my fridge. "How old is that thing?"

"My best friend gave it to me."

He opened the freezer door, reached in, and removed one of the low fat meals.

"Would you like one?" I said.

He shoved it back. "It would certainly serve as a reasonable punishment for what happened to you tonight."

"Oh."

"Why are you eating low fat? You're tiny."

"Kind of grabbed them quickly."

"You live here alone? Do you have a boyfriend?"

"I live alone. No boyfriend."

"Hence being a virgin."

I blushed. "Are you married?"

He hesitated before answering. "No."

"Do you live with someone?"

"Yes. Winston."

And yet Mistress Scarlet had told me Richard wasn't gay. Maybe Winston was his son.

"He's British and quite dashing." Richard gave a roguish smile. "I am of course biased."

Richard had managed to keep this secret from the girls.

"He's a British Bulldog," he said.

"You don't bring him to work?" I tried to save my embarrassment from Richard's all-seeing stare.

"Sometimes. But he loves the garden." He neared me and took the glass of water out of my hand, tipping it down the sink. "I'm worried you'll drink it."

Something past between us and it caused a wave of giddiness.

"Listen, Mia," he began, his tone soft and coaxing. "Tonight was a dreadful mistake and I can't apologize more."

"Already forgotten."

"I'd like to offer you two weeks pay—"

"You can't fire me now." I panicked. "I'm fine, really. Please Richard, I love working at Enthrall and I get on great with all the staff."

"And they all adore you, Mia. Only…"

"I have to pee," I said, and scurried off to the restroom.

Inside, I stared at my reflection, trying to come up with the words I needed to persuade him not to fire me. I reached for my brush and ran it through my knotted hair, trying to ease out the windblown clumps. Richard's open top adventure had left its mark.

That was the word, adventure. Yes, these people had a funny way of living and working, but it certainly beat the day to day drudgery of being a Wal-Mart employee, which was where I might be headed if I couldn't convince Richard tonight had no effect on me.

It was strange, in that dungeon he'd acted so masterful, kind of pissed off actually, but in my apartment he seemed so normal. So regular. Well, as regular as a hot guy oozing enough sexual energy to power a major city can be. Caressing my lips with a fingertip, my mind wandered, taking me back to that blood red room and Richard's touch…down there. I pushed thoughts of his slaps away and focused on how he'd stirred pleasure. It would be easy to get used to that kind of attention. Addicted to it in fact.

Obsessed.

If I trespassed into that dungeon again would I be treated to the same punishment? The temptation to stray once more into that dark, red room was seductive.

Wanting to look pretty for Richard, I applied a quick touch-up of lipstick and a dab of mascara and felt ready to face him again. Halfway out of the restroom I realized I hadn't flushed the toilet, having not actually gone. I had two choices: hope Richard hadn't noticed or go back in and risk looking odd.

From here, I could see Richard holding a piece of paper. He had in his hand one of the bills I'd left on the counter.

A look of worry flashed over his face. "Mia, are you sick?"

"No." I walked over and snatched it from him. "This is personal."

"This medical bill is for twenty-five thousand dollars."

"My step-mom's not well," I said. "She lost her job along with her medical insurance."

"I'm sorry." He glanced back at the stack of bills.

"That's why I need this job," I said. "The billing department have threatened to cut off her medicine if I don't pay them."

"Why are you paying this? Where's your father?"

"He died in a motorcycle accident. Lorraine took me in soon after. She's an actress."

"You mean waitress?" he said, unaffected. "Let me guess, Denny's?"

"That's not very nice."

"Well I imagine SAG would have covered this." He glanced at the bill. "I'm sorry, Mia. I had no idea."

"So you can't fire me," I said. "Tell me you won't."

"Do you want to be an actress?"

"No." I put the bill back with the others.

"That's lucky for you. Your nervous rash would have its own SAG card." He laughed at his joke. "Do I really make you nervous?"

I slid the bills out of his line of sight.

"I don't mean to."

"Then don't be so…"

"My therapist tells me it's all part of my death wish." His face fell. "Still, at least no one would be left grieving."

"Why do you say that?"

"If everyone loathes you they'll be glad you're gone."

That didn't make any sense. "The girls think highly of you."

"I'm sure they'd like being referred to as 'the girls.'"

"Anyway, they seem more scared of Cameron."

"Most people are."

Hoping he'd say more, I tried to read his face.

He scanned the room.

"What's your place like?" I said.

"Bigger." His gaze settled on my bed in the corner.

Bailey had told me to buy a room divider and right now I wished I had.

He looked over at my television. "You need a flat screen."

"It was a gift."

"Bailey?"

"Yes."

"Awkward bringing boys here."

I chewed my lip. "Do you have a girlfriend?"

"Why?"

"Just wondering."

"Not right now, no." He tilted his head. "So, this Bailey?"

"She's gay but we're just friends. I mean we don't…you know."

He rolled his eyes in feigned shock. "Have sex?"

I twisted my mouth to hide my frown.

He gave a shake of his head. "Poor Bailey."

"Why do you say that?"

"She gave you a fridge and a TV and you still have no idea how much she's in love with you."

"We're not like that."

"Bit defensive."

"We're not. We've known each other since fifth grade."

"Oh well then, she can't possibly want to sleep with you."

"She's has integrity." I held my head high.

"Those two things aren't mutually exclusive." He folded his arms. "I'm only like this with friends I care about." He arched an eyebrow, seemingly surprised with his admission. "I imagine all your friends are smitten. You're quite the prize. But you don't think that do you?"

"Why are you here?"

"We need to talk about what's lurking in your fridge." He leaned back against the counter. "Or we can choose to discuss something a little less scary."

My chest constricted and I broke his gaze.

"Thursday evening, when you came into my office with Cameron and asked, if we can call it that, for your job back."

I blinked up at him, nervous of where he might take this.

"To be honest, your brave move had Cameron and I both convinced you were sexually experienced before ever working at Enthrall." He paused. "I know this is difficult for you, but it's important we get this out of the way. May I go on?"

I gave a nod, my voice evading me.

"During the time you showed yourself to me, Cameron first asked your permission to touch you. Do you remember?"

"Yes."

"You understood what he was asking you?

"Yes."

His frown lifted. "He also asked if you wanted him to stop. Remember that?"

"Yes."

"Why didn't you tell him to stop?"

"I didn't want him to." My words came out faint, nervous.

"You liked it?"

"Yes," I muttered.

"It was a highly charged sexual experience. Do you regret it?"

I blushed. "No."

He looked pleasantly surprised. "The thing is Mia, the brain's sexuality is wired in a certain way. A delicate way. The majority of people never get to explore, or want to, what it is we do at Enthrall. It's an unusual lifestyle choice, but one—" He paused. "It's a very mature and well thought out decision only a well adjusted and—"

"I understand," I said. "You're trying to say that environment might not be good for me."

"Or worse. I'd never forgive myself if this experience caused you distress. You are my concern." He shrugged. "Just because a few of us choose to live life in a decadent fashion..." He looked for words again. "You don't strike me as someone who'd normally do something like that. And I'm sorry you felt the need to."

I suspected what Richard's next words were and my heart sank.

"Would you like to comment on anything I've said?" he asked.

My gaze made a passing sweep of the bills. "Tara's seen your dungeon too."

A look of confusion passed over him. "You know Tara?" Richard blinked. "That's how you knew about the job." Another revelation swept over him. "Tara set you up to perform in my office? It wasn't your idea was it?" He caressed his forehead.

"The music was my idea."

He gave a kind smile. "Are you sure you want to be around people like us?"

"More than anything."

He shoved his hands into his pockets and his gaze lingered upon me. "How would you like to be my executive assistant? It'll entail pretty much what you're doing now. Of course the new position comes with a pay rise."

"Richard, I don't need your charity. I'm more than capable of taking care of myself and those." I pointed to the stack of bills.

"I don't doubt it."

"You were going to fire me weren't you?"

"I can't remember now. Listen, if you ever want to leave, if you're ever uncomfortable with anything you see or hear, you must come to me and we'll discuss it. Understand?"

I gave a nod. "That thing you told me in the dungeon about Cameron wanting to see me burn?"

"I was angry with him for taking you down there. I wanted to be the one to do it when I deemed you ready. Just show you around. Nothing kinky. Cameron's always trying to save someone. His methods are a little dark I'll admit, but so is our lifestyle." He reached into his pocket and removed his BlackBerry. "Talk of the devil. He wants to meet me for a drink." Richard texted Cameron back.

Taking advantage of having him distracted, I studied his sticking up blond locks and the way he chewed his lip when deep in thought, and that dreamy way his eyes crinkled into a smile.

He looked up. "Cameron wants to know if I've damaged you."

"What did you tell him?"

"To mind his own business. Of which he has plenty." Richard tucked his phone away. "Mia, would you do something for me?"

I held my frown.

"If Cameron so much as looks at you," he said. "If he talks to you, if he breathes in the same room as you, text me immediately."

I gave a nod, actually grateful Richard was doing something right for a change.

"I have to go." He fished out his phone again and read a text.

"How am I going to face him again?"

"Well you faced me," he said. "And I did a lot worse to you."

"But you're not him."

Richard's gaze left his BlackBerry and shot up to meet mine.

CHAPTER TEN

CROSSED LEGGED, I SAT ON THE FLOOR IN FRONT OF MY TV. The remote was playing up again and I opened the back of the controller and tried my trick of removing the batteries and putting them back in. I pushed the button and nothing happened. "Grrrr."

The doorbell rang.

Easing the blinds back and peeking out the side of the front window, I almost stopped breathing permanently when I saw Cameron. It was too late to pretend to be out. He'd seen me. Dressed in my PJs, I was hardly ready for company. What the hell was he doing here?

Seriously, couldn't he have called first?

I opened the door. "Hi."

"Hey Mia." He gave the biggest smile. "You don't answer your phone?"

"Didn't hear it." I glanced down at the Saks Fifth Avenue paper bag in his hand. There was another bag behind that one.

Cameron eased past me and came in, uninvited. I waited for him to react like Richard had when he realized I lived in a studio.

He didn't. "How are you?" he said.

"Everything all right?" I made it polite, despite still being annoyed with him for tricking me into that dungeon. That kiss. He'd played with me like a pet. I couldn't understand why he was here.

As though sensing my nervousness he stepped back, putting some distance between us. Richard wanted me to contact him next time Cameron spoke to me, yet I wondered how I'd make that call with him right in front of me. Richard wouldn't be happy about him being in my apartment, I knew that.

Cameron's gaze rested on my sketch pad on the floor. He made his way toward it. "These are good, Mia." He looked up at me. "You drew these?"

I gathered them up. "Just playing around with a few ideas."

He watched me like a hawk as I hid them behind a pillow. I'd never shown anyone my artwork, not even Bailey. These fashion designs still needed a lot of work and I didn't feel confident to show them to anyone yet.

"Are you an aspiring fashion designer?" said Cameron.

"Can I get you a drink?"

"No, thank you." He stared in horror at the kitchen counter "What the hell is that?"

"What?"

"That." He strolled over and picked up my Pot Noodle.

"It's my dinner."

"Not on my watch." He flipped open the trash bin with his foot and dramatically threw it in.

"Hey!"

"How often are you eating like that?"

"Um…every night, kind of."

"I feel like I've just stepped into a William Burroughs' novel."

"A what?"

"Naked Lunch," he said and on my reaction added, "It's a book. Adapted for film." He waved his hand as though bored with explaining.

"Why are you here?"

"We have a VIP client who arrived in from Sicily earlier today." Cameron shook his head in frustration. "Senator Marcello DeLuca."

I tried to work out why he'd want to share this with me.

"Richard's not answering his phone either," he said.

"I'll text him." I made my way across the room and reached into my bag.

Cameron took my phone out of my hand. "He's probably busy."

"He won't mind." I reached for it.

He hid it behind his back. "I have a present for you." He raised the bags with his other hand.

Annoyed he thought I'd be distracted with shopping bags, I reached for my phone again and caught sight of the Manolo Blahniks insignia on the other one.

"These are for you," he said.

"Me?" I stepped back.

"How would you like to earn some overtime?"

"I can't tonight, sorry."

"I'll make it double time." He frowned at my PJs. "Like you have other plans." He tucked my phone back into my handbag. "Come to dinner. Help me entertain the Senator."

"Have you tried Scarlet?"

"She's in Vegas."

"Lotte?"

"My client's conservative."

"What does that mean?"

"Lotte's not his type."

I pulled a face. "Penny?"

"She's at a movie premier with a client. A film producer." He held out the bags. "I'm one step ahead of you." He handed them to me.

Peering inside at the little black dress, I wondered how he knew my size. Inside the other bag was a shoe box.

He glanced at my feet. "Seven?" Cameron reached inside the golden paper bag and eased out a Manolo Blahniks shoe box. He opened the lid, revealing the most elegant pair of strappy high heels I'd ever seen. I wondered how much all of this cost.

"You get to keep them afterwards." He waved it off like it was nothing.

These were the kind of shoes I'd never be able to afford in a lifetime. I was all but drooling, damn it, and from his obvious amusement he could tell.

"Are you prostituting me out!"

His laughter filled the room. "No. It's dinner. Then home." He held up his hands. "Seriously, Mia." He shook his head to chastise me.

"Why can't you go alone?"

"Let down the client? Richard would be furious with us." He gave a nod. "Shall I tell him you refused?"

"Let me text him."

He placed his hand over my handbag to block me.

"You owe me an apology," I said.

"I do?"

"For taking me into the dungeon. You knew it would make Richard angry. He spanked me for it, for goodness sake."

"He did?"

"You're best friends. You tell each other everything." I folded my arms.

"As far as I could tell, you liked it. Besides, you told me in the elevator you were intrigued with what went on down there."

"With what it looked like. Not what you do down there."

"You should have been clearer."

I pointed at him. "I know what you do for Chrysalis."

He looked impressed.

"You're the club's shrink. You assess people to see if they're ready to be members."

"Impressive. Other than calling me a shrink. Please don't."

He'd turned up the intimidation.

"I know you personally assessed the Sullivans," I said. "I don't think Constance is ready."

"If hesitancy is what you observed that's normal."

"She's terrified."

"That's your professional opinion?"

"I don't need a certificate to work that out." I neared him. "And sometimes you're wrong."

His expression changed to fascination.

"On my first day at Enthrall," I said, "I overheard Richard telling someone called Dominic to revoke a client's membership."

"Ah."

"So whoever you profiled had to have their membership cancelled."

His face softened thoughtfully.

"Well, what happened there?" I said.

"I offered a flawless profile. What I had no way of foreseeing was the alcohol they snuck into Chrysalis. When his personal items were searched, a silver flask was discovered." Cameron shrugged. "Both Enthrall and Chrysalis are dry. Drug free. Everyone is clearly briefed on this. We have booze at the party once a year but that's a one drink maximum. We're very strict, in more ways you could ever imagine."

"Oh."

"Next question?" he said flatly.

"You shouldn't have taken me into that dungeon."

"That wasn't a question."

"I know you're smarter than me. But please don't manipulate me ever again."

He narrowed his stare. "Please don't talk to me like that ever again."

I cursed myself for letting him in.

"Remember, you begged me to help you get your job back," he said. "Which I did."

"I'm still grateful. As well as the car thing."

He stepped closer. "What directive did Richard give you on your first day?"

"Make the clients happy."

He glanced at his watch. "The Senator's arriving at a restaurant in forty-five minutes. You're making us late."

"I'm not sure—"

"One of Richard's top clients."

And to think I'd planned a nice evening of watching TV, sipping spring water, and maybe even sketching. My gaze drifted to the drawings I'd hidden and hoped Cameron had forgotten he'd seen them.

"You draw great by the way," he said. "You have a real talent."

Yet again Cameron had reminded me of his laser-sharp perception that Richard had told me about.

"Name your price." He shrugged. "Enthrall can afford it."

"A thousand dollars." I rested my hands on my hips, knowing full well he'd scoff.

"Sounds reasonable."

I chewed my lip, wondering if I should have gone higher.

"Yeah, I see what you're doing there, Missy. Go get dressed."

A thousand dollars. He had to be bluffing.

"Not unless Richard signs off on it," I tried again.

"We'll call him from the car. That way we won't lose any more precious time."

I squinted at him. "You had time to go shopping."

"We actually bought this for you so you can go to the party."

"Lotte told me the women wear bodices and stockings."

"You have to wear something *to* the party." He gave a thin smile. "Richard knows you're great with clients and that's why you were the first person we wanted for tonight." He held up his hands again. "I tried the others to be fair to you. Please hurry up."

"Are you sure Richard won't be annoyed?"

He gently ripped the tag from the dress. "Trust me, as soon as he hears about our dinner he'll be right over to join us."

Reluctantly I took the dress from him. Feeling his all-seeing eyes following me across the room, I opened the drawer to my dresser and removed a thong as discreetly as possible, as well as a matching bra. Doing my best to hide them from him, I headed into the bathroom.

Within minutes I'd put on the little black dress, marveling at how Cameron had guessed my size. It fit perfectly, though showed off my curves a little too much. I tried to pull it down but it wouldn't give.

Short dresses were in but this was way more daring than I'd have ever chosen. The shoes slid on easily, and despite being strappy heels they felt comfy. There was no question this outfit had cost Cameron a small fortune.

After applying some make-up, which didn't take long as I preferred a natural look, I pulled a brush through my hair and tussled it; blonde curls cascaded over my shoulders and down my back. A dab of soft pink lip gloss and I was ready.

I took a second to rally my courage. What if Cameron didn't like the way I looked? Maybe he'd not judged the length of hem right. Vixen versus slut? It was hard to tell having never shopped at Saks. Two deep breaths later and I made an entrance.

Cameron blinked several times at me.

"You don't like it?" I said, though at the same time relieved he might change his mind and not take me now.

"Okay. Wow," he said, standing straighter. "You look um…"

"Too short, isn't it?" I nodded in reply to my own question.

"You're perfect. I mean the dress is perfect." He grabbed my handbag and thought better of it. "You don't need that." He looked addled.

"I have a clutch purse." I walked the short distance over to my bedroom cupboard. I found my mini black purse that went great with my dress. Then I headed over to the kitchen counter where Cameron had set down my handbag and withdrew my iPhone, a spare lipstick, and my wallet, placing them all inside the purse. "You're sure Richard will be fine with this?"

He nodded, though this time remained silent and merely gestured toward the door, hurrying us both out into the night. He held my hand a little too tight. Cameron led me over to a stretch limousine where a uniformed chauffeur waited.

"We're going in that?" I said.

"Yes," said Cameron.

Lorraine would freak out. I went for the door handle and Cameron snapped me back. The chauffer opened the back door for us and I realized my mistake. Inside the car was a bar. Having already embarrassed myself by gushing over our transport, I held back on my excitement.

The driver threw me a polite smile in the rearview mirror and navigated the car onto Ventura. After passing a few green lights and only one red, we turned onto the 101 and headed south.

Something so last minute seemed so well planned.

"Should I have worn stockings?" I whispered, feeling decidedly naked showing off my bare legs.

"Sorry?" said Cameron.

"Should I have worn stockings?"

He gave me the longest glare. "No."

His reaction seemed kind of strange.

He gazed out of his window.

I wondered how often Cameron treated himself to a chauffeur and how much he cost for the night. Though I imagined this would all be going on Enthrall's tab. Remembering I was meant to call Richard, I opened my purse and reached for my phone.

"Not now." Cameron's hand rested on mine and he glanced at the driver to make his point.

"I'll text him," I said.

"At the restaurant." Cameron returned his attention to the passing scenery.

I hoped Cameron wouldn't catch me texting. He leaned over, took my phone off me, eased it back into my purse, and snapped the clasp shut. We drove the rest of the way in silence. I pondered on where we were going and what kind of food they served. Surely if we were going to be entertaining a VIP it would be a high-end restaurant.

My guess was right. The driver pulled curbside outside Chez Polidor.

"I'll do all the talking," said Cameron. "Enjoy your meal and sip your wine. Think about how you're going to enjoy your bonus."

"I'm doing this as a favor."

"Remember who you're talking to."

"Still."

"Still," he said. "Do what I say and when. Understand?"

This is just dinner, right? I frowned, sensing a shift in his demeanor.

Gone was the playful, persuasive Cameron from my apartment and in his place was Mr. Domineering. He made me nervous. The driver opened my door and I slid out and quickly joined Cameron on the pavement.

His hand glided down my spine toward the lower arch of my back and rested there. "Mia, I understand your motivations better than you realize."

"My step-mom?"

"Apparently you're living in a studio so you can afford to keep her alive."

Richard must have shared my personal story. I wasn't sure how I felt about that.

Cameron perused the restaurant front glass window. "You're a very special young lady." He nudged me back into the doorway, right beneath the awning of the interior design store next door. "When you're ready to talk about your personal life I'm here for you."

"Thank you, Cameron."

After all that had happened between us, there came a sense I could trust him. It felt nice to have the softer, kinder Cameron back.

He made a gesture with his thumb and index finger. "Will you do me one small favor?"

I narrowed my gaze.

"Turn around," he said.

I twisted my mouth, not sure about this.

Clutching my shoulders, he eased me around so that my back faced him. "Hold still." His fingers caressed my scalp, tickling as they went. He parted my hair down the middle, forming two ponytails. I felt him securing each one with a hair band. He'd had them in his pocket this entire time.

I spun around, my cheeks flushed. "Is your client a pervert?"

He cringed. "Maybe a tad."

I went to pull them out.

He grabbed my hand and stopped me. "Mia, there's something you need to know." He yanked me from under the awning and pulled me toward the restaurant door.

"What?" I tried to escape his grip.

"They have the finest veal scallopini and linguini with clam sauce here." He laughed and opened the door.

Well-dressed diners chatted away at pristine white clothed tables. Dim lighting bestowed an ambience of decadence. The decor gave the place a homey yet expensive look. Pictures were crammed throughout, heightening the coziness with arty chaos.

"You're a bastard," I whispered, and gave the maitre d' the sweetest nod.

Cameron scanned the room. "You flatter me."

"Dr. Cole, we're expecting you, sir," said the maitre d'. "You're joining Senator DeLuca?"

"We are, thank you, Charles," said Cameron.

"Ma'am," said Charles, turning sharp on his heel and leading us off.

We were guided across the full restaurant, navigating tables and chairs. Staring dead ahead, I didn't want to catch any critical glances from the other guests or even the waiters. My confidence was already shaky and I didn't need any encouragement to descend into panic.

A man rose to greet us. Senator DeLuca, I assumed. He wore the smartest blue pin-striped suit and his bow tie made him look super rich. He beamed at Cameron and reacted with delight when he caught sight of me. He looked around forty-ish and was unexpectedly dashing with his jet-black hair and olive complexion. Though the way he ate me up sent chills down my spine. I cursed Cameron for dressing me so slutty and these ponytails only made things worse.

This, I'd learned, was a subconscious alarm I should have listened to.

Why change a habit of a lifetime and listen to my intuition?

We joined Senator DeLuca in the booth. The high-backed wooden seat gave the illusion of privacy, though the leather padding was at least comfortable on my bare legs. I sat opposite the senator.

Beside Cameron, I watched him navigate the social pleasantries, introducing us to each other and even ordering a bottle of Dom Perignon with the confidence I'd come to know him for.

Oh, champagne. This might even be fun.

Cameron peered at the menu. "For the lady —" He twisted his mouth thoughtfully - "Magret de Canard Sauce Cerises." He handed the menu to the waiter.

I prodded his thigh. "I don't like cherries."

"Someone reads French." Cameron narrowed his gaze. "What other secrets are you keeping from us?"

"Can I order my own?" I whispered self-consciously.

Senator DeLuca and the waiter had fixed their attention upon me.

"Senator?" said Cameron.

"She'll have the sesame seared Ahi tuna?" Senator DeLuca told the waiter.

"Good choice," said Cameron.

If the server thought this exchange was odd, he certainly didn't show it as he scribbled it down. He went on to take Cameron's order of New York cut sirloin steak with asparagus and Senator DeLuca's pan seared brook trout.

The waiter scurried away to the kitchen.

Not quite sure what had happened there, I resisted the urge to speak up, reminded of when Richard had chosen my ice-cream. These men really had control issues. Still, I wasn't here to eat but merely follow through on our agreement and make small talk with Cameron's guest, and make him happy. I hoped this was something I could pull off. There might even be a bonus if Cameron went through on his promise. From all he'd splurged on so far it looked promising. I'd be able to pay off my step-mother's radiology bill, I thought, reaching for my champagne.

My bubbly tasted dry and cold and I took what I hoped were several discreet gulps to calm myself. If Cameron so much as hinted more might be expected I'd merely excuse myself, telling him I needed to use the restroom, and bolt. Even if he had bought me these amazing shoes. My plan helped me relax.

That was until Cameron slid his hand up my dress and along my thigh and rested it there. I glared at him, trying to send a discreet message I wanted him to remove it.

Cameron ignored me, keeping his focus on Senator DeLuca. "How is your family?"

"Well, and yours?" he said.

"All good. I hear our sisters had lunch in New York last month?" said Cameron.

"Yes. They had fun."

"They ate at Vai," said Cameron.

"Yes, have you dinned there?"

"Not yet, but I plan to. Love the Upper West Side."

My attention spiked with the intelligence I was gathering on Cameron and I wondered what else I'd learn.

Cameron sensed a shift in my demeanor and his hand slid up farther. I tried to nudge it off but his grip tightened and his thumb caressed. I tried to squirm free but the senator's scolding glare made me freeze.

The conversation between them flowed, their casual dialogue revealing a friendship that went way back. This easiness they shared gave away they knew each other well.

Senator DeLuca's BlackBerry pinged.

"I have to get this." He offered an apology and slipped away.

Richard had told me off for using my phone at work, and here was our guest using his at dinner. Still, the rich always had concessions, just like the assumed right Cameron seemed to think he had with my thigh. With my thumb and index finger I eased up his pinky, gaining leverage.

Cameron offered the senator a friendly nod and watched him walk away. He snapped his head round to look at me. "You do realize I'm into pain?"

I reached for my glass and took a few sips. This would all be a lot more bearable if I got tipsy.

"Mia, hold your glass by the stem," said Cameron.

"Why?"

He picked up his glass to show me. "Otherwise you warm the champagne."

I was devastated to be schooled like this. "He's probably gone off to arrange a hit on someone."

"Stereotyping?" Cameron shot me a look. "Something tells me you're quite the expert."

Scrunching up my nose, I regretted my outburst. It was actually kind of fun to hang out with someone so prestigious. "Sorry. I'm a bit nervous."

"You're doing great." Cameron took a sip of champagne.

I held my glass by the stem."I'm not saying anything."

"Exactly."

"You're like Richard only craftier."

"I'm in no way like Richard. He's got the biggest heart I know. Pity someone had to go and eviscerate it."

"A lover?"

"You get over a lover."

The waiter reappeared and placed our meals in front of us, having memorized who'd ordered what. The server had annoyingly interrupted, and once he headed off I waited for Cameron to continue talking about Richard. He merely leaned back and sipped champagne.

"Why didn't you let me order my own dinner?" I said.

"To let you know who's in charge."

"You know there is such a thing as women's rights."

Cameron turned in his seat to better look at me. "Care to elaborate."

"Women have died for the right to speak and for equality."

"Can you be more specific?"

"Suffragettes in the late 19th and 20th century." I raised my chin high. "Emily Davison."

He looked amused. "Are you using as an example a woman who

died whilst making a point at the Epsom Derby, trying to throw a banner over King George's horse in 1913?"

"Yes."

"You probably think the king was riding it."

"That's mean."

"How about picking something more topical." He shrugged. "More twenty-first century."

"How about you not being such an ass."

"You're only here to look pretty." He smirked. "I expect more from my submissive."

"I'm not your submissive."

"Tonight you are."

"I'm Richard's." My words stunned me.

"Well, well," said Cameron.

"Well I'm his secretary, which is the same thing." I rolled my eyes.

"Trust me, it's not. Did you just roll your eyes at me?"

Half-distracted, I glanced down at the table not quite sure why I'd told him that.

"Did you just glance at your knife?" he said.

"No."

"Yes you did. Please don't stab me during dinner." He arched an eyebrow. "And please don't use a blunt dinner knife."

"Have you ever seen a therapist? Other than yourself, I mean?"

"You're adorable. I can't get enough of you."

"I have to go to the restroom." I grabbed my purse and gave his arm a nudge. "Please let me out."

He stood, his stare lowered, and I was terrified he'd confiscate my phone.

"Now would be a good time to call Richard," he said.

Relieved I could appease Richard and let him know I was out with Cameron, I eased out. With a polite smile, I strolled past Senator DeLuca, who chatted on his cell in Italian.

I didn't want the money now. Somehow the thought of it left a sour taste in my mouth.

Inside the restroom, I scrolled through my contacts until I'd reached Richard's number. I speed-dialed and waited for him to answer. My stomach sank when I got his answer service.

"Hey Richard," I said, "It's Mia. I'm in—" *Oh shit where was I again?*

"Chez Polidor," said a woman hidden away in a stall.

"Thank you," I called out to her and whispered, "Richard, I'm in this restaurant called Chez Polidor. It's in West Hollywood. Cameron brought me here. Um…we're with this client from you know where. His name's DeLuca—"

The call dropped.

"Nooooo…" I re-dialed and failed to get another signal.

I raised my phone in the air like an idiot, trying to pick up a signal; I was desperate.

Returning my cell to my bag, I stole a few more seconds to fluff my hair in the mirror. A younger version of me gazed back. I looked ridiculous in ponytails and went to take them out and thought better of it. The last thing I needed was an angry Cameron.

Back at the table, I waited for him to ease out and allow me to rejoin them. I tried to pretend the senator wasn't gaping at my legs. They were both eating. I was glad they'd not waited on me. Drawing unwanted attention wasn't something I was in the mood for.

Savoring the way the champagne softened the edge, I finished off my glass. Despite there being only a tiny portion of seared Ahi tuna on my plate, it was all I felt for. I glanced over at Cameron's steak and asparagus, wondering if he'd have to grab a burger on the way home. I felt sure the driver wouldn't mind.

The senator motioned to the waiter for him to fill his glass. His attention fell back on me.

"So you're from Sicily?" I said.

The senator looked surprised.

Cameron's hand found its way to my thigh again. "How's your Ahi tuna?" He shot me a subtle glare to shut up.

"Delicious," I said. "How's your steak?"

He lifted his hand from my thigh and returned it to his fork. "Rare."

"Maybe they'll cook it some more for you?" I said.

"I like it rare."

"Wasn't the Godfather from Sicily?" I asked.

Cameron's ironclad grip shot to my thigh. My breath caught in my throat as his fingers squeezed all the blood from my flesh. When he lifted his hand, my circulation returned and a sudden calmness came over me; a release of all tension…

"Cameron," I whispered.

His hand was back squeezing my thigh. "It's sir."

He was using pain to control me. *Master me.*

"Sir," I uttered through clenched teeth.

His hand lifted but left this heady fevered flush, a tingling between my thighs, a throbbing in my clit. I let out a long, soft sigh and Cameron gave me one of his mega-watt smiles, seemingly taking delight in making me dizzy and breathless.

The senator's envious gaze narrowed on me.

Cameron beamed him a smile. "Talking of feisty and yet responsive to the lick of a riding crop, how are those race horses of yours?"

"Profitable." The senator grinned and took a bite of trout.

The waiter topped up his glass. When the bottle moved to mine, Cameron placed his hand over the rim. "No more for her, thank you. She has to be up early." He threw him a *now fuck off* smile.

The waiter scurried away with my second glass of champagne still in the bottle.

I frowned at Cameron and whispered, "Aren't they meant to leave the champagne by the table?"

"My permission for you to speak has been withdrawn." Cameron's tone was stern as was his glare. "Understand?"

I shrank back.

The senator clinked his champagne flute against Cameron's. "Cole, it's unlike you to glean such a slow result." His gaze fell on me. "Let me take it from here."

CHAPTER ELEVEN

CAMERON PEERED OVER HIS CHAMPAGNE GLASS. "THIS ONE belongs to the assistant director."

Trying not to gape at that, I sat up straight.

"Perhaps we can negotiate?" said the senator.

Cameron placed his knife and fork together on his plate and leaned back, indicating no with a slight shake of his head.

Senator DeLuca folded his arms. "Surely an exception can be made?"

Cameron's grip was back on my thigh, and despite me communicating with all the subconscious skills I could draw on that he could very well snap my bone he didn't seem to notice.

"How is your father?" asked Cameron.

"Good. He sends his regards," he said. "I'd very much like to make this happen."

Cameron went to answer when his gaze caught something across the room. His hand lifted. I did my best not to react to the pain as blood surged back into the tissue Cameron had been cutting off.

Richard stormed toward us.

In seconds he appeared at our table looking flustered. He threw a glare at Cameron and blinked several times when he saw me. It felt wonderful to see him.

"Richard Booth." The senator rose to greet him. "My old friend." He patted his arm with affection.

"Marcello," said Richard, proffering his hand.

The senator shook it and leaned over and hugged him. "So glad you could join us."

"Actually, I was just passing."

Cameron's face lit up with amusement. "Come join us."

"I'm parked illegally." Richard shrugged. "Sorry, let's do dinner tomorrow night perhaps." His glare darted back to me. "Winston's in the car."

"Winston's his dog," I told the senator.

Cameron grinned up at Richard.

"It's the heat," said Richard.

He really did seem flustered.

"Winston hates the heat," he added. "I leave the air-con on for him when I'm not home."

I wonder what his bill must be like.

"Mia," snapped Richard.

I rested my knife and fork on my plate.

"Shall we go over those numbers?" he said.

"Numbers?" I said, and then realized. "Yes please."

"She hasn't finished her meal," said Cameron. "You work her too hard."

"Maybe not hard enough," offered the senator.

Richard gestured to a waiter. "Can we get this to go, please."

The server reached over for my plate, quickly removing it.

I picked up Cameron's champagne glass and snuck in another sip, throwing him a delighted smile that his game was over.

Cameron ignored me, keeping his focus on Richard's reaction, his hand returning to my thigh. He leaned toward Richard, keeping his voice low. "I was sharing with Senator DeLuca the challenge we're having with taming this one."

Richard looked incredulous at him.

I poked Cameron's ribs. "I'll have you know I'm a free spirit."

"I'd very much like to help with this," said the senator. "In fact I insist."

Cameron seemingly held back on a chuckle, his grip tightening. Bracing for another agonizing squeeze, I froze.

"Mia, now, please." Richard nodded his approval when I rose. "So, I know a great place," he stuttered. "The Ivy. Lots of celebs. You'll love it, Marcello. How long are you in town?"

The senator's gaze found me again. "A few days."

I smiled at him, relieved this debacle was over.

"Perfect," said Richard. "We won't be taking up too much of your visit." He clicked his fingers. "Mia."

Cameron stepped out and I eased past him. Richard blinked several times at the hem of my dress and shot me a disapproving frown. He recovered quickly, gesturing goodbye to the senator and Cameron.

Richard led me out.

"What about my food?" I said.

Richard gave a nod of thanks to the maitre d' and pulled me out onto the curb. For goodness sake, Cameron had pulled me in here and now Richard pulled me out. I felt like a rag doll.

"Get in," snapped Richard, pointing to the open top silver BMW. He slipped several notes to the valet, and from the young man's expression it must have been a lot. Richard leaped into the driver's side.

I settled into the luxurious cream leather seat and offered a thank you to the valet for shutting my door. The car took off and my head jolted back against the headrest.

"Put your seatbelt on," said Richard.

Winston sat on the backseat, happily panting away. Reaching back, I scratched his head and he licked my hand. "Hey Winston."

"Seatbelt," said Richard again.

I faced the front and pulled the strap round. "I thought you had a Jeep."

"Please take your hair out of those ridiculous ponytails." He threw me a look. "Could your dress be any shorter?" He turned the music on and Pearl Jam's *Just Breathe* blared out of the sound system.

I wondered how much Cameron would hate me if I told on him.

Richard turned the music down. "Didn't we have a discussion about you calling me?"

"Cameron told me there wasn't time."

Richard snapped his head round to look at me. "What do you mean?"

"When he picked me up. He told me we could call you from the car. He changed his mind."

"You should have told me you were having dinner with him."

"He just turned up." I slunk in my seat. "Are you the assistant director?"

He sped up, taking a corner wide. "Of Enthrall, yes. Why?" Richard threw me a sideways glance.

Cameron had told the senator whatever it was he wanted belonged to the assistant director. They'd been talking about me, I knew it. Especially since Cameron's grip tightened on my thigh when he'd spoken those words.

"Hair, Mia," said Richard.

I pulled out each hair tie and clutched them.

Richard held out his hand and I placed the ties into his palm. He threw them out of the car. Within twenty minutes we were driving along the Pacific Coast Highway.

"Where are we going?" I said.

"I'm thinking."

"Driving helps you to think?"

"Quiet helps me think."

I slid lower and gazed out at the blur of scenery. To our right the hills rose up into the darkness, and to our left luxury homes overlooked the ocean. Beyond them the sea shimmered beneath the moon. Off in the distance sprawling mountains loomed large, making me wonder what lay on the other side. I hoped Richard wouldn't leave me stranded somewhere.

"I'm sorry," I said to appease him.

He ran his hand through his hair. "Don't do it again."

I wanted to tell him that Cameron had been very persuasive, bullying me into it really, but thought better of it. Richard's gaze drifted to my legs and he shook his head in what looked like disbelief.

"You have double standards," I broke the silence.

"Next time you enter a dragon's lair," he said, "don't wear that."

"What is that supposed to mean?"

"It means you do as you're told." He shoved the car into fifth.

We drove for what seemed a lifetime. The music was a welcome distraction.

My instinct not to wear this had been right. I tried to pull it down but there was nothing really to pull down. Now out of the ponytails, my hair was out of control. I twisted it around my hand and held onto it.

We sped past a sign announcing we were in Point Dume Rivera.

Richard pulled the car up before a large brass gate and buzzed it open. I wondered who lived here and questioned if they'd mind us visiting so late. A little way up the driveway loomed an elegant Spanish home with a tiled roof, its stucco finish providing a Mediterranean air complimented by the high arching windows, and all of this overlooked by tall, lush palm trees.

Once parked, we made our way to the front door. Winston trotted beside us. I bent low to pat his head. Gingerly, I followed Richard inside, hoping whoever we were meeting weren't put off by my slutty attire.

"Make yourself at home." Richard threw his car keys onto a side table in the entryway.

"Is this your place?"

"Help yourself to a drink. I have to make a quick call." He made his way across the living room toward a large screen door, unlocked it, and stepped out.

The low lighting, expensive decor, and soft beige walls leant a colonial style. The room was spacious and yet cozy and the several beautifully carved far eastern pieces of furniture made the place homey. It smelled of fresh air and ocean.

I followed him, admiring the pool twinkling in the moonlight and the well-tended garden. Even the lighting out here had been well thought out. I wondered if Richard had used an interior designer or if this was his taste.

I knelt to dip my hand into the water, immersing it in the warmth of the heated pool. Winston nuzzled up beside me and sniffed the water.

Richard glared at his BlackBerry and screamed into it, "What the fuck, Cameron! What the fucking, fuckerty, fuck!" He threw his phone amongst the bushes. When he turned and saw me, he jolted back and his expression softened. "Well, that took care of that bit of business."

I wondered how Cameron might react when he got that message, though after the pain he'd inflicted on my thigh I couldn't help but feel gratitude to Richard.

"You have a pool," I said, making conversation.

Richard looked incredulous. "Let's take you home."

"Can I swim?"

"Sure, how about next week…"

I unzipped my dress and pulled it up and over my head. The tiny piece of material didn't take long to extract myself from. "You have a lovely home," I told him, and threw my dress over the back of a lounger. "Thank you for the dress by the way."

"What?" He ran his hand through his hair, his wide-eyed gaze taking in my body. "I'm beginning to sound like you." His brow furrowed.

"The dress for the party."

"I would never get you anything that short. And what party?"

"Chrysalis's." I knelt and reached for the straps of my shoes. "The one you had me send invites out for. Cameron told me you've changed your mind and I can go now."

The inviting water glistened in the moonlight. After Cameron had used me as bait to tease a senator, and what with Richard whisking me back to his home without my consent, I deserved this.

Still wearing my underwear, I dived in. It felt refreshing and I spun around several times, savoring the sensation of floating, treading water, wondering how long Richard's anger might last.

He stormed inside.

Winston stayed, guarding the edge of the pool. The water felt cleansing. Having not swam in what felt like years, the last time being while in college, this felt heavenly. I dived underwater and swam a full length along the bottom.

When I came up for air, I saw Richard leaning against one of the stone pillars that lined the length of the pool.

He sipped liquor from a tumbler. "I need a cigarette."

"I didn't know you smoked?" I called up.

"I don't." He downed the rest of the liquor and shook his head, and threw the glass high. It landed amongst the base of one of the palm trees. He neared the far end of the pool, his dark stare locked on me.

He gave a nod as though some realization had found its way to him. Then he pulled his t-shirt up and over his head and stripped off the rest of his clothes, throwing them onto a lounger.

I averted my gaze from his nakedness. Those taut muscles revealed how much he worked out. That erection betrayed his lust. He didn't seem in the least bit fazed about stripping off in front of me. He waded toward me causing the water to slosh around us; the only sound.

Treading water and wary, I swam backwards.

He paused a few feet away.

"You have a lovely home," I said.

"You already told me that."

"Can you see the ocean from here?"

"Mia, can I kiss you?"

"Yes."

He was upon me, cupping my face, kissing me passionately, forcefully, capturing my mouth in his as I melted in his arms. Eyes closed, I went with him, my tongue caressing his, our lips brushing together. His erection nudged against me. I hoped he'd be gentle when he entered me, take his time and not hurt me too much. He ran his fingertips through my scalp, slowly, scrunching my locks in his hands.

Here, under the night sky, floating in a pool warmed by the sun in his strong hold, I felt safe for the first time.

Off came my bra and panties, his hands making quick work of removing them. He pushed me backwards and pressed against me, his cock digging into my stomach, sending shivers of anticipation throughout my body. Our kiss grew more frenzied, desperate. He nuzzled into my neck and planted wet kisses there, his fingers finding my left nipple and pinching it, sending surges of pleasure downward where it lingered leisurely between my thighs.

Richard rested his forehead against mine and paused, his breath heavy, needy. "Mia, I…" He stroked my face, the seconds dissolving as a dull throb echoed throughout my body. "I have no idea what just came over me." He pushed away, swimming to the other side.

I wanted him to know these feelings we shared were so right, so loving. That I was ready for what would be my first time, here, with him.

I felt like I'd lost him.

Richard stretched out his arms on either side of the pool edge. His face filled with confusion.

"What is it?" I called over.

He broke my gaze, his trembling throat hinting he was holding back on his emotions. I felt terrible seeing him this way and hated myself for causing this.

"Forgive me," he said, his tone soothing, reassuring.

"There's nothing to forgive," I said, confused. "Did I do something wrong?"

"Of course not." He rested his hand over his chest and blinked at me in surprise. "You could never do anything wrong."

My heart ached with his rejection.

Winston licked Richard's ear.

Richard flinched and broke out of his trance. "Hey buddy," he said, "You always know what to say."

My confidence dissipated as my embarrassment rose.

Richard beamed an enigmatic smile my way to lessen the tension. "Mia Lauren is naked in my pool. I'm one lucky guy."

So why had he stopped kissing me?

He peered up at the sky. "Do you miss looking at the stars? I do. All this smog. You can't quite believe it until you live here."

He was right. It was hard to tell the clouds from the smog. But I didn't give a damn about that right now.

Richard returned his attention to Winston, patting his head. He kissed the end of his nose, saying, *"You ask what is our policy?"* Richard's English accent sounded flawless. *"I will say: It is to wage war, by sea, land and air, with all our might and with all the strength that God can give us; to wage war against a monstrous tyranny, never surpassed in the dark and lamentable catalogue of human crime. That is our policy. You ask, what is our aim? I can answer in one word: victory."*

"What was that?" I said, astonished.

Richard beamed a smile. "To annoy my father I majored in history." He peered over at Winston. "Didn't I, Sir?" He winked at me. "I wrote my dissertation on Churchill."

"You named your dog after Sir Winston Churchill?"

"Shush." Richard covered his dog's ears. "Winston doesn't know he's not him. He thinks he's giving a speech in the House of Commons first thing in the morning." He scratched Winston's chin. "Yes, you are, sir."

"Why Churchill?" I wondered why he'd not chosen an American president.

"Churchill was the man I wished my father could have been."

"You don't like your father?"

He gave a shrug. "That speech rallied the British to prepare for World War II. His words led a country to victory."

I swooned at Richard's worldliness. "I've never been to England. Cameron says it's very cold."

"Bloody cold."

"You should really try talking to your dad," I said. "Before it's too late. I'd give anything to be able to talk to mine again."

He gave a look of sympathy.

"I miss him every day," I said. "Even though he wasn't always nice. So I get it." I pointed to him. "No matter how many disagreements you've had, he's still your dad." I gazed up at the dusky sky. "I'd give anything for another hug from mine."

He gave a sigh. "Would you do me the most amazing favor?"

"Sure."

Though Cameron had asked me the same question tonight and that hadn't gone too well.

Richard wrinkled his nose. "Help me find my phone."

We laughed our way through the brush, searching for his BlackBerry. Despite our nakedness, I felt comfortable with Richard. After all, he'd stopped at a kiss. With his house phone in one hand dialing his cell and his flashlight in the other, we soon tracked it down.

"Let's get you dressed. I'll take you home," he said. "I've heard your boss is a stickler for timeliness."

"He is. I'd hate to cross him."

Richard kissed my forehead. "I can't ever see that happening."

I fought this urge to fall into his arms and barely won.

Richard drove me home.

CHAPTER TWELVE

S TANDING BEFORE THE COFFEEMAKER, I TOOK MY TIME MAKING
Richard's morning drink, a little nervous over having to face
him again.

My mind lingered on our kiss last night. He'd been so gentle-
manly. I hoped his resistance to go any further wasn't because he
didn't find me attractive. It made me feel a little ugly.

On the way home he'd reassured me it had everything to do with
being my boss, and he even declined to come into my apartment this
time, stating he had a long drive back. He left right after seeing me
safely to my door. I wondered how he might be with me today. We still
had to talk about what happened over that strange dinner date with
Cameron and his friend, the spooky senator. Maybe Richard could
persuade Cameron to stop whisking me off into dangerous scenarios.

Despite the excitement of being around Dr. Cole, he made me feel
like his plaything. Had Richard not interrupted us in the dungeon, I
wondered how far things would have gone. Though something told
me he'd timed Richard's arrival perfectly. As though taking pleasure
from stirring Richard up. There was something so seductive about
Cameron. He made my mind go all fuzzy, and when he turned on
that dark charm he made me go all weak at the knees too. No wonder
Penny had warned me to stay out of his way...

"Mia?"

Lotte broke my fantasizing.

She and Penny sat behind me at the coffee table.

"Everything okay?" asked Lotte.

"Oh yes," I said. "Want some more coffee?"

"No thank you," she said. "You're a little quiet this morning."

"Still waking up." I pointed to the brewing coffee. "Need one of these."

Lotte continued her conversation with Penny. I'd managed to hear some of it, though not all. My mind was too busy wondering. It felt good to have caught a glimpse of Richard's place and see how normal he really was. It was probably the same for Lotte and Penny. Despite their work here they did pretty much what the rest of us did, shopped at Ralphs, went out to dinner with friends, and even whiled away hours in book stores.

My eavesdropping revealed they even went to Costco.

Lotte chatted away. "You should have seen him," she said. "It was priceless Richard. This guy in the car behind us sees another car taking the parking spot he'd set his hopes on and he leaps out and starts screaming at this old lady who took it."

"What is it with road rage these days?" said Penny.

"So Richard tells me to stay in the car," said Lotte. "He gets out and strolls up to this guy who's going crazy on this old woman. Richard calmly says to the guy, "This is not a war zone. There are no bullets flying over our heads. This is Costco. A store. Why don't you take a breath, put things into perspective, and go and fill your basket with items you're lucky you can afford."

Penny looked horrified. "The guy could have had a gun."

"I had a car full of frozen stuff." Lotte laughed. "I was more worried about it melting. Richard can take care of himself."

Penny leaned forwards. "Go on."

"The guy swung a punch at him."

I spun round to look at them, clearly no longer eavesdropping.

"Richard placed the guy in a chokehold," said Lotte. "Meanwhile, the old woman's wandered off to go get her shopping basket with no concern for the gentleman who saved her from the egomaniac."

Penny roared with laughter.

Lotte waved her hand through the air. "Anyway, the guy apologized to Richard and trotted back to his car to find another space."

"Let's hope you don't bump into him during a shopping trip," said Penny.

It wasn't so much that Richard had stepped up to help a stranger that amazed me, but the fact he shopped at Costco. It sounded so ordinary.

"So you guys got everything we need for the party?" Penny asked her.

"Yes. Catering's booked so we're set," said Lotte.

"Did you ever find someone to housesit your friend's condo in Malibu?" said Penny.

My ears pricked up again. Though having poured sugar into Richard's coffee, I no longer had an excuse to be in here. I headed toward the door with Richard's drink.

"It's impossible," said Lotte. "You'd think with the low rent and view of the ocean you'd get a bunch of applicants."

"Bet it's that damn fish tank that's putting everyone off," said Penny.

And I was out, heading into Richard's office and wondering about this ocean front condo.

I paused at his door.

After a few deep breaths, I made my way in.

Richard was typing away on his keyboard. He leaped up from his seat and trotted past me and closed the door. "Good morning."

I placed his coffee on the coaster. "Hi."

He nodded, his head bobbing away as though so were his thoughts. I wondered if easing past him and leaving would be considered rude.

"Last night…" he began.

"You mean when Cameron tried to ship me off to Italy? Or you, me, and Winston searching for your phone?"

"Senator DeLuca's from Sicily. Trust me, I'd be more worried about him. His head would probably explode." He smiled at his own joke. "I was talking about our kiss."

A thrill slithered up my spine.

"As I told you last night," he said. "That was out of character for me. I'm sorry."

"I liked it."

"It certainly felt different." His brow furrowed. "Different in a good way. Mia, I just don't think that it should happen again. It's imperative we keep our working relationship professional and um…well, that's it really."

"You and me—"

"Mia, there is no you and me."

My heart sank. "I absolutely agree. What happened last night was a once in a lifetime occurrence." I really did sound mature even though I hated myself for not sharing my true feelings. "It was my fault."

"Well, I wouldn't go that far." Richard cocked his head. "Then we're back to normal?"

"Normal? I'd never associate that word with Richard Booth." I gave a wry smile. "I'm excited about going to the party. Lotte's going to help with my outfit."

He strolled over to his desk and picked up his mug. "I'm not sure it's something you're quite ready for."

"But—"

"That will be all, thank you." He gave one of his *this conversation is over* looks.

I headed out with a tightness in my chest. Had I really thought last night might lead to something? I cursed my naivety, this self-limiting trait never failing to let me down. I returned to my desk, wondering if he might change his mind about the party.

Lotte stepped out of the staff hallway and made her way towards me. "Mia, Monsieur Trourville will be here in less than an hour." She sat on the edge. "If he asks why you're not wearing his gift tell him to speak with me. I don't want this to be something that makes either of you uncomfortable. He's very sensitive."

"Of course," I said. "I was going to thank him and tell him Richard thought it best—"

She waved off that idea. "Say nothing. Direct him to me on the matter. I know how to deal with him."

My gaze drifted to the elevator.

"I'll tell you what," said Lotte. "I'll be here to greet him too."

I liked this plan. I twisted my mouth and held her gaze.

"What's wrong?" she said.

"I'm sorry for eavesdropping. But your friend's condo?"

"You don't want anything to do with that. It's a headache. There's a bloody great big fish tank in the sitting room and you'll be expected to feed these tropical fish and keep them alive while he's out of town."

"How long for?"

"Six months. Maybe longer."

"Is the rent high?"

"It's Malibu, Mia, so yes."

I sat back. "It was just a thought."

"I'll tell you what, why don't I speak with him later and see if he can come down on the rent?"

"Really?" I said. "That would be fantastic."

"Can't promise anything but I'll do my best."

"What kind of fish are they?"

"One of them is an Asian Arowana," she said. "At least I think that's what it's called."

I gave a nod, having no idea what one of those looked like and hoping it wasn't a piranha. She walked back through the door and headed down the staff hallway.

I Googled Asian Arowana.

My heart sank as I read the first article.

Asian Arowana's were virtually extinct and according to the news article a man in Seattle had faced federal charges for selling one to a federal officer thinking he was a dealer.

Damn.

There goes my beachfront dream home.

The idea hit me to Google Richard Booth. I typed in his name and read the list of articles. None of them were about Richard. In fact there was nothing pertaining to him at all. Not even a facebook page. There wasn't even anything about Enthrall. I navigated back to the Asian Arowana article and asked myself just how much I wanted to get out of that studio.

With half an hour before I had to face the monsieur, I had enough time to grab a coffee, add some milk, and quick foot it back to my desk.

Scanning over the diary, I noticed a new name that hadn't been there yesterday. Peering closer, I read that somebody called Courtney had a 10:15 with Richard. He'd written in pencil in his scratchy handwriting.

A wave of jealousy hit me. Her appointment was five minutes away.

I reminded myself I merely held the position of Richard's secretary and despite last night's kiss we were still on formal ground. He'd reaffirmed that very issue within the hour and I'd agreed with him a relationship was out of the question. Not that I'd had any choice in the matter. The last thing I needed was for Richard to become uncomfortable with his secretary's crush on him.

Obsession.

I had to act casual around him. Uncaring even. As though he was just another staff member and not the hot, god-like being who strolled around like he owned the place.

It really was time I got a boyfriend. Perhaps Bailey would come out with me this weekend. A night of clubbing would put me straight.

Who the hell was Courtney?

I'd met quite a few of Enthrall's clients and all of them had been escorted by the girls into the dungeon. Which meant that Richard would do the same for Courtney.

Sipping my drink, my gaze swept from the clock to the elevator and back again as I tried to reassure myself she was just a client, proof of which lay in her name being in the diary.

It also dawned on me I had no idea what really went on during a session, and despite having a fleeting taste of Cameron's technique, I wasn't sure if any of the mistresses or even Richard were bold enough to have sex with a client.

With that thought threatening to melt my brain and soak my panties, the elevator announced it was about to spit out a client. Funnily enough, I hoped it was the monsieur.

She was pretty.

I could see that from here as I rose to greet the young lady named Courtney, or who I assumed was Courtney. She walked slowly, demurely, her sensual gait reflecting a woman of the world and her petite frame begging for a man to protect her, wrap his arms around her.

Maybe a man like Richard.

The staff door opened and my head snapped round to see him standing there, his face lighting up. They embraced and it was one of those hugs you share with a best friend or, heaven forbid, a lover. Where was that in-character demeanor of masterdom Richard should be holding, like the one Lotte always held for Monsieur Trouville?

"Let me introduce my secretary," said Richard, but his gaze didn't find me. "This is Ms. Lauren."

Courtney barely gave me a passing glance.

He gestured to the elevator. "Ready?"

She blushed wildly, her hand resting on her chest. "Yes."

"Mia, the elevator," said Richard.

Head down, and hating these unfamiliar emotions raging in my chest, I turned the key and slid open the gate. I called the elevator and stared inside when the doors opened, unable to look at them.

"This is closure," he whispered to her. "It's a good day."

"The monsieur has an appointment too," I said, nervous of them clashing.

"We have more than one room." Richard's thin smile warned me to cease speaking.

Courtney looked horrified. "Somebody else will be down there at the same time?"

"Our room will be locked," said Richard. "Like always."

She gripped the gate, her knuckles white.

I wondered how angry Richard would be if I advised her to reschedule after she'd thought this through. Surely she wasn't ready for whatever lay in the bowels of this place, where pain was just another way of passing the time. Surely she'd have more fun on a shopping trip to Bloomingdales? Or lunch with her friends? Maybe therapy should be her first consideration?

"Thank you, Mia." Richard gestured for me to step back. "We'll start slow," he whispered to her. "No surprises."

My stomach churned and I found myself hating her, this rich girl wasting her daddy's money in ways he surely had no idea about, and she was wearing a wedding ring, for goodness sake.

I turned away, choking back tears and wanting neither Richard or Courtney to see them. The sound of the elevator descending, taking Richard away from me, brought a gut wrenching ache.

My gaze drifted to my screensaver. The Japanese koi pond Richard had set for me, having known how much I loved the garden, now brought sadness. I remembered him sitting in my chair, the way he'd moved the mouse to reset it. The way he caught me staring, his mouth turning up at the edges in playful amusement.

I'd taken for granted swimming in his pool last night, not savored every precious second as I should have. I wiped away another rogue tear.

The entryway elevator rumbled and I readied myself for the challenge of greeting the monsieur and having to tactfully avoid the subject of why I'd declined his gift. Lotte was expected any second but he was early again. Probably hoping for a lesser punishment from his mistress, no doubt.

Nonchalantly, he strolled toward me.

He looked startled. "Mon Amie. You look... belle comme le jour!"

Blinking several times, I tried to understand what he was saying. He'd mistaken my flushed cheeks for arousal, these shudders of emotion I'd failed to suppress, these heavy breaths of distress. I calmed at the thought; we see what we want to see.

I gestured a wave of thanks to him for the gift I'd not seen since Richard had confiscated it, and elegantly slid through the staffroom door, managing to stifle back sobs until I made it to the spa.

Where I shrank onto the wooden bench before the Buddha, biting on my hand to quiet my sobs. The thought of Richard sharing his affection with Courtney brought a surge of pain in my chest and I clutched the bench, hating myself for even thinking a romance between us was possible.

Lotte soon found me. "Mia, what's going on?"

My lips trembled and it was too hard to speak.

"What did the monsieur say to you?" She sat beside me.

"He thought I had those things in."

"That explains his good mood." She brushed a stray hair out of my face. "Did he upset you?"

"No."

"Then why are you crying?" She held my shoulders. "You're very flushed. You're not wearing them, are you?"

"No." Wiping my tears away felt like a losing battle.

"Mia?"

"Can I ask you something?"

"Of course."

"When you take your clients into the dungeons..."

"Yes."

"Um..."

"You're wondering if we have sex with them?"

I shot her a surprised look.

"I read between the lines," she said. "It's part of being a little older and a little wiser."

With my hand pressed against my chest, I scrunched my shirt up into a ball. She caressed my back, allowing the silence to have its way.

"I won't tell anyone," I muttered.

"The whole point of domination is holding onto our power. If we have sex with them then we relinquish our control. We never give up our power." She lowered her gaze. "You're asking particularly about Richard?"

"Yes."

"Master Richard is quite loveable. It's his reciprocation that's uncertain." She took my hand and squeezed it.

"I went to his house last night."

"He has exquisite taste, doesn't he?"

I shot her a look.

"We're merely friends, Mia. We've known each other a long time."

"Please don't tell him."

"Listen, my darling. If you're looking for love here, you will find it, but not the romance kind. The stick with you through thick and thin, kind. The kind that accepts you for what you are and doesn't judge you, kind."

I hated being so transparent.

"You've thrilled my client." She arched a perfect brow. "Keep this up and you'll get a promotion."

"I could never do what you do."

"Come on." She guided me to my feet.

We strolled down the hallway, my hand in hers, my heart racing with fear she was taking me back to parade me in front of the monsieur for his twisted pleasure. Instead, she led me into Richard's office.

We stood before the three photographs framed on the wall.

"What do you see?" she said.

I stepped closer, my face inches from the photos this time. I moved on to the second, and finally the last, realizing they were all shots of Richard.

Lotte stood beside me. "To understand just how far Richard is beyond saving you merely have to look at those."

"When were they taken?"

"Last year. That's new." She pointed to the one with the shark. "He changes them out every once in a while. He has more at home."

"More?"

"There's something beautiful about a broken man, don't you think? Maybe it's some unspoken promise he'll become more than he is because of it."

Studying her as she looked at the photographs, I tried to make sense of her words. I didn't like the sound of them.

"What happened to him?" I said softly.

"More pain than most of us face in a lifetime."

"What kind?"

"The private kind."

"Please don't tell Richard I asked what you do down there?"

"Of course. And we won't let him know we were in here either," she said. "You're our Mia."

My gaze found the photos again and I wondered how I'd missed it.

"I must get back to the monsieur," said Lotte. "I'll tell him you were overcome with pleasure. He'll like that." She winked at me and reached out, easing a lock of hair behind my shoulder. "Nothing good can come from falling in love with a man who's incapable of loving you back."

I'd totally embarrassed myself.

She kissed my forehead. "Mistress Scarlet would like a word with you."

Lotte left, a delicate waft of perfume trailing behind her.

My gaze roamed over Richard's neatly organized desk, his collection of contradicting ornaments, the Buddha, those crystal champagne flutes, those thumb screws, as well as the leather sofa I'd never seen him sit on.

Having never experienced these feelings flittering in my chest before, I wondered if it was too late for me.

CHAPTER THIRTEEN

MISTRESS SCARLET'S OFFICE REMINDED ME OF A FRENCH coffee shop.

It was all bright colors and big flashy prints of Parisian streets. Everything in here screamed of well-travelled and worldly. There was a chocolate colored couch in the corner, with several blue and brown chenille throws strewn over it and tasseled pillows lined along the seat. Beside it rested a spanking bench; I'd seen one similar in the dungeon.

I dragged my gaze from it.

Her heady perfume of jasmine and roses reached me from where she sat behind the desk. Remembering how she'd watched Cameron play with me in the dungeon, it was hard to keep eye contact with her. She still scared the shit out of me. I knew I'd done something wrong. And from her sternness I was about to get read the riot act.

I went to sit.

"No," she said. "You're not staying."

This probably had something to do with me hanging out with Cameron and Richard last night. I searched for the words that might offer my point of view without getting either of them in trouble. I bet they were scared of her too.

"I like you, Mia," she said. "In fact, I like you an awful lot."

"Oh."

"That's why I wanted to talk with you."

"Okay."

"Do you like working here?"

"Yes."

"Do you want to stay working here?"

My heart missed a beat. "Yes."

"I'll make this short. What I'm about to tell you must go no further." She sat up straight. "Can you promise me this? That our conversation will go no further?"

"Yes."

She held my gaze as though gauging my honesty. "Your well-being is extremely important," she lowered her glare, "to us 'girls'."

Thanks for sharing that with them, Richard.

"The director hired you because of your innocence," she said.

"Oh."

"It's an appealing quality that brings a great deal of pleasure to our clients."

My mouth felt dry.

"That, along with your blossoming sexuality, is extremely desirable." She lowered her gaze. "Dangerously so to you."

I swallowed hard.

"We, that is the girls, want to protect you, Mia."

"I know you watch out for me," I said. "I appreciate it."

"Do you trust me?"

"Yes, Scarlet."

She opened a drawer and lifted out a small blue shiny gift bag. "The girls and I have gotten you a little something." She raised her hand. "Much thought and deliberation went into it. We believe it may just save you."

I wondered for a second if it was pepper spray, but then again I was a fast learner. "You bought me a toy?" I said.

"We need to lesson that…need."

My cheeks flushed wildly.

"Turn this on full and rest it on your clitoris." She glanced at her watch. "Report back to me once you're done."

"What? When?"

"Now."

"Now?"

"Sweet Mia, you're walking around a BDSM club oozing enough innocent sexual magnetism to make our most seasoned clients come in their pants." She handed me the bag. "I'm doing this for them as much as I am you."

I clutched the bag to my chest. "Can I take it home?"

"No. Keep it in your desk and use it frequently, please." She widened her eyes. "Use Richard's office. He's with a client. He has a lock on his door."

I hesitated.

"Mia, be a good girl." She emphasized with a pointed finger. "Ensure you have two orgasms before you return to me." She shooed me out. "Take your time. No one will disturb you."

"This is all very clinical."

"Do you require my assistance?"

"No."

"Unlike Monsieur Trouville, I will know whether you have utilized this gift. We'll have some tea afterwards."

"Can I use it later?"

"No."

"How about the spa?"

"Shall I whip you while you're using it?" She gave a wry smile. "I'm sure we'd both enjoy that."

I hurried out of there with the bag in hand, my cheeks burning up.

Once inside Richard's office, I locked the door. No way was I using this thing. And certainly not in here. With the gift out of the bag, I studied the oval silver vibrator which was apparently called a magic friend according to the box.

I plopped down onto the leather sofa, defeated.

Maybe Scarlet had a point? If I took my need for Richard down a notch it might be easier to stop fantasizing about him. Although I rarely touched myself down there, something told me Scarlet knew a thing or two about this stuff. She probably knew everything there was to know about sex. There was something reassuring about being around a woman like that. I'd never want to disappoint her. Or Lotte. Having sent me into Scarlet's office, Lotte must have known about this.

I ripped open the box. At least this would make it look like I'd followed through on Scarlet's command. My heart thundered in my chest as though she stood before me now, tapping her whip and waiting for me to perform. Waiting for me to come.

After closing the blinds and checking the door once again to ensure it really was locked, I made my way back to the couch. At least she'd think I'd gone through with it.

Curiously, I flicked on the oval vibrator.

And adjusted the buzz.

My crazy muse provoked me.

After easing my panties down over my hips and leaning back on the couch, I took in a long soothing breath. I hiked my skirt up around my waist and spread my legs, exposing myself. This felt deliciously naughty. I mused further that I'd been ordered to do it. Had no choice really. With this thought in mind and totally turned on by it, I unbuttoned my blouse slowly and tugged my bra cup down.

The vibe met my nipple gently, pounding its delicate flesh—

Oh God, that's good.

Both nipples responded, teased by the vibe, their buds raised and demanding more of the toy. My pussy clenched with the thrill of it and the promise of impending pleasure, which I was holding back with this sensuous self-tease of denial.

"Oh please," I begged.

When the vibe met my clit it sent a jolt of white hot pleasure into it. A luscious charge. My thoughts drifted...

This was *his* office.

Richard's touch down there bringing this exact same pleasure. His fingers caressing my thighs, spreading them wider. Like I did for him now. With my one hand holding the vibe and teasing it over my clit and the other tweaking my nipples, giving them equal attention, I imagined it was Richard's hands that were pushing me closer.

On my back lying along the couch, my legs opened wide for Richard...

His hands moving languidly over my body, exploring, as though discovering me for the first time, roaming across my belly, around to my backside and squeezing me into him.

His tongue encircling the hardened nipples, working alongside his firm steady fingers that tweaked them punishingly. Alternating from one to the other and refusing to let up. My sigh meeting his mouth. His lips easing mine open. His tongue finding mine and tangling until he'd gained control, forcing me to submit. This delicious arousal soaking my swollen clit that throbbed beneath his tongue as he sucked, licked and flicked my clitoris, catapulting me into oblivion.

Directing the pulsing vibe, I ran it up and down and over my clit, riding this maddening bliss and imagining Richard's face buried between my thighs, his tongue exploring farther, lavishing affection.

He knew I needed this. Needed him. Why was he denying me?

"Richard," I whispered.

My body went rigid as tremors wracked through me. I was captured by this fever pitch of pleasure as my breath was snatched away.

"Yes, oh yessss..."

I collapsed, panting breathlessly, cheeks flushed. Catching my breath and feeling tingly- good all over, I rode out the last of my release and savored it.

It felt wonderful to be surrounded by Richard's things, and Scarlet's permission for me to be in here had made it okay. If this exercise had truly been construed to lesson my need, it had failed. All I could think of was *him*.

I let out the softest sigh of obsession.

Knowing I was going to have to face Mistress Scarlet soon, and with her strict orders hanging over me, I fired up my new magic friend again.

There was certainly something to be said for being a 'good girl.'

CHAPTER FOURTEEN

"E PIC?"

"Yes," I answered Mistress Scarlet. "It was epic."

Was she really wanting me to go into detail about my bonding experience with her gift?

"Here." Amused, she handed me a mug filled to the brim with hot tea, her stare scrutinizing me. The way her expression softened hinted she saw what she wanted in the way of proof.

Warming my hands around the mug, I breathed in the fragrance of citrus fruit. *Mmmm, delicious.* It reminded me of...*Cameron?*

Scarlet stepped closer. "Mia?"

"You told me the gift was from you, from the girls?"

She lifted my chin with a perfectly manicured fingertip. "Run along now. See Richard's client out."

I took my tea with me and headed out, wondering if that toy had really come from the girls. Had I just willingly succumbed to Cameron's punishment of pleasure for challenging him during dinner last night? His psychological hooks were embedded deep in my psyche. His persuasion, his dark dominance over me, had succeeded yet again. I was trapped somewhere between arousal and defiance.

There was no time to mull over my suspicion. I'd been away from my desk too long. Courtney's session had ended and Richard was escorting her out. From her expression, even here behind my desk, I could see all her tension had gone and in its place a happiness difficult to define. Courtney's cheeks were flushed, her face peaceful, bliss radiating. I wondered what Richard had done to her.

The exit elevator carried her away and out of Enthrall.

Richard turned on his heel and strolled toward me. "Where were you?"

"Well, I was—"

"It's best you choose your words carefully." He gave a shrug. "Talk about the weather. Their journey here. That kind of thing. Don't speak to my clients about anything other than that, please."

"She looked terrified," I said.

He acknowledged I'd read her right with merely a nod and his gaze flitted to my desk. He saw my drink and picked it up, sniffed, and took a sip. "Earl Grey?"

"Yes."

He shot me a look. "Since when have you been drinking Earl Grey?"

"Scarlet made it for me."

"I see. And by I see I mean I don't miss a thing, Mia. Nothing. I know everything that goes on in this place. Every detail. Every finite minutia that goes down."

My cheeks blushed wildly as my thoughts dragged me back along the hallway and into his office and back onto that couch…

"Don't do it again," he said.

I went to tell him he didn't know, couldn't know, and then stopped myself, not wanting to give it away.

"I certainly don't remember giving you my permission to do it," he said, walking off toward the staff hallway.

God, that was hot.

He was bluffing and he was damn good at it.

"Courtney needs a real therapist," I called after him.

He spun around and peered at me.

"Professional help," I added.

"She has it. Here."

I arched a brow.

"My office please," he snapped. "Now!"

I followed him down the hallway. Surely I had a point.

Richard leaned back against the front of his desk. There was something altogether eerie about his stance. Mainly because it reminded me of the day I'd asked for my job back, or as he'd succinctly put it *if you could call it that.*

Within the hour I'd enjoyed a mind-blowing fantasy about Richard. The kind never to be shared, the kind I hoped he couldn't read from my face.

"Whenever you're ready," he said.

"What?"

"The correct term is 'excuse me.' 'What' is something an errant teenager says to their parents." He gestured. "You wanted to share your insight?"

"Courtney looked terrified."

"Her expression reflected her emotions."

"She didn't look like she wanted to go down there."

"That's because you suggested another man would be sharing the same space."

I swallowed hard, my inner voice telling me to shut up. My mouth ignored my brain. "What did you do to her?"

"We completed a round of therapy."

So we're calling it therapy now?

I frowned. "We?"

Richard pointed to the wall. "That's a doorway. Each office has one. They all lead to the dungeon. Courtney is Cameron's client."

I stared at the wallpaper, hardly able to believe the flawless pattern camouflaged a door.

"What I'm about to share with you is confidential," said Richard. "Courtney suffered severe abuse as a child. Having been married for fifteen years and unable to conceive she sought out alternative therapy."

"She's infertile?"

"She had an aversion to sex." Richard shrugged. "We cured her."

"What did you do?"

"Firstly, working alongside her husband, we desensitized her to touch." He gestured downward. "Lotte escorted her husband through the ground entrance."

"Why didn't she come through that way?"

"As the submissive they rise in the first elevator, thus accepting the challenge to face change, and as they descend in the second elevator they give themselves permission to surrender." He gestured to his head. "It's subliminal of course."

"If she was so badly abused aren't you making it worse?"

"She did ask to come here, Mia."

"Maybe she needs a different therapist."

"Fifteen years of conventional therapy with no resolution proves talking didn't work. Not for her anyway." He raised a shoulder. "Her husband's a construction worker. They needed a little guidance."

"Did she say it helped?"

"This was her final session. The series of treatments helped, yes."

"How do you know?"

Richard folded his arms. "She's pregnant with her husband's child."

It still didn't seem right.

Richard stood in that familiar stance he liked to hold to intimidate whoever was in the room with him.

I placed my hands on my hips. "Then she shouldn't be drinking alcohol."

His stare narrowed. "That look on her face is the expression you'll see on all our clients when they leave. That's exhilaration." He arched an eyebrow. "Different kind of intoxication."

All he had to do to seduce me was stand there. I fought off this dreamy trance, this hypnotic enthrallment that was Richard Booth: dominant, master, enigma.

My gaze drifted over to the photographs. "What happened to you?"

"How do you mean?"

"Why do you do this? You told me you were once a stockbroker."

"Yes."

"But not one now."

"Evidently." He broke the tension with a smile.

"Why this kind of work?"

"I like it."

"Why?"

"Did you change your occupation?" He rolled his eyes. "I'm not sure if you've switched to interrogator or attempted psychiatrist."

"Is Cameron your psychiatrist?"

Richard's gaze fell upon the photo of him rock climbing. "Want to see how he does it?"

My mind raced with what he meant.

Richard strolled toward the wall and gestured to it. "We often elude the truth because of the pain it causes us." He pushed against the wall and the door popped open.

"I should be getting back."

He nudged the door wider. "Down you go."

"Not after last time." My cheeks blushed.

"Have you not learned you can trust me?"

"You knew I'd say something, didn't you? About Courtney?"

He took my hand and guided me over the threshold. Together we descended wooden steps. The walls, painted a soft beige, gave off a comforting hue from lights set in the floor.

Perhaps Cameron now had another client and was whipping the poor man or woman within an inch of their life. I wasn't sure if I wanted to see this. I should have kept my mouth shut. Instead, we found him crossed legged, meditating in an empty room. Richard guided me in and stepped back, putting some distance between us, leaning casually against the wall. Cameron stretched out of the lotus position and elegantly rose.

"Dr. Cole," said Richard. "We were discussing your expertise. Mia would like a demonstration."

The air in here was too thick to breathe. Counting how many

steps it would take to reach the door, I faced that direction. Richard closed the door.

Cameron had shown his true strength last night during dinner, when he'd gripped my leg and squeezed all the blood out of it. I dared to think what he might try here.

I headed for the door.

Richard cut me off. "That's a normal response."

I peered up at him. "Please, let me out."

"Mia," said Cameron, his voice low, soothing. Luring.

Richard gestured for me to turn around. "We won't touch you. I promise. Nor will there be anything sexual during this session."

Session?

My mouth went dry.

Cameron observed us both with a critical intensity.

My thoughts drifted back to last night, the way Cameron had sliced his knife through his steak, blood tinged juices oozing. There was something dangerous about his precision. He'd have made a good surgeon, but no, he'd chosen psychiatry and was now using his unnerving expertise to dissect me.

"We believe you may have a better understanding of what we do if you get to spend a few minutes with us. Down here," said Cameron.

Oh fuck.

"You're always fantasizing about what we do," he said. "And what kind of people we are. How about we put that mystery to bed."

"You won't touch me?" I glanced at Richard.

"We'll just talk," said Cameron. "You have our word."

"About what?" I said.

"Let's start with this room," said Cameron. "How do you find it?"

I felt lightheaded. "Empty."

"So we have no choice except to go within," he said.

My hands trembled. "Have I done something wrong?"

"Of course you would think that," said Cameron. "You have low self-esteem. Gauged by your level of confidence, you also have abandonment issues."

"Abandonment?"

"Your parents abandoned you."

"They died. They didn't abandon me."

Cameron folded his arms.

I wondered if this kind of body language was used to intimidate. They were both standing in this pose. I tried to read Cameron but his gaze held the ground, his thoughts seemingly far away. There came a real desire to please them both and make them drop this posture reflecting I'd disappointed them.

I hated the silence. "Anyway, I'm over all that now."

Richard's expression remained impassive.

"That's good to hear," said Cameron. "May I approach?" He motioned slowly with a raised hand. "At no time will I touch you."

I gave a nod of permission.

He closed the gap between us. "Let's have some fun. You can ask Richard any question you like. Let's say you get five or six of them. In exchange, I'll ask you ten questions. I know you're dying to know more about him. This is a perfect opportunity. However, you don't ask him anything about his life before he came to work at Enthrall. Understand?"

I blushed. How far would I be able to go with this and not faint with embarrassment.

"Mia, you go first," said Cameron.

This was ridiculous, like schoolgirl silly, like no way was I doing this.

"Ask him," said Cameron sternly.

"Do you have a girlfriend?" I said quickly, startled by Cameron's austereness.

"No," said Richard, his smile infectious. "I've already told you that."

I was relieved to see Cameron's face relax.

"My turn," he said. "What's your first memory?"

I twisted my mouth trying to remember. "Sitting on the sofa at home."

Cameron gestured toward Richard.

"Do you have a boyfriend?" I said with a smile.

"No," said Richard and shared an amused glance with Cameron.

"What is your favorite childhood memory?" said Cameron.

"Um…" I reached way, way back trying to remember.

"What do you hear?" he whispered.

"There's a dog barking. I think it's a Rottweiler," I said. "How did you know?"

"You glanced left. Your brain accessed a sound it remembered." He stepped closer. "Let's reach for that happy memory."

I pressed my hand to my chest. "A birthday party. Mine."

"Ask Richard a question," said Cameron.

I came back into the room feeling decidedly shaken. Had that birthday really been the happiest day? Even though, there on the couch, my father had lain in a drunken stupor.

I shot a glance at Cameron and Richard, trying to think of the next question, having lost count of where we were.

"Hint," said Cameron. "Ask an open-ended one."

"Oh, right," I said. "Do you like your secretary?" I beamed at him, realizing that wasn't an open-ended question, but all this made me nervous and thinking straight was a challenge.

"Very much so," said Richard.

I went to pursue that line of questioning when Cameron stepped in front of my line of sight. "The day your father died," he said. "Your step-mother took you to the funeral home. Do you remember?"

"She did," I answered. "How did you know?"

"She needed you there. You were the strong one." He again gestured to Richard.

This back and forwards made me lightheaded and a strange mixture of emotions washed over me. Peering over at Richard and hearing his voice made me feel safe and those moments were helping in-between Cameron's probing.

I felt brave, saying, "When we kissed last night did you like it?"

"Yes," said Richard. "Very much."

I'd asked yet another close ended question, my mind too addled with these foreign feelings rising within to focus properly. "Why did you push away from me?"

"Because it felt... so good," said Richard. "I care deeply about you."

Cameron fixed his gaze on Richard and they swapped unspoken words, it seemed. Richard merely nodded, sharing this silent communication with his friend. I tried to make out what this shared look might mean.

"Our kiss made me want to take you right there in the pool," said Richard. "But I consider myself a gentleman."

I smiled back at him, seeing a look I'd never seen on Richard before. He held my gaze with affection. Something shifted inside me as though these new memories dared to push the others out.

Cameron nodded approvingly. "What color dress are you wearing?"

I frowned at him, amazed he knew...

My step-mother and I were sitting on an old, stained sofa in the funeral home.

"Blue," I muttered.

The funeral director discussed with my step-mother which coffin might best suit our needs. Lorraine asked for the least expensive.

My lips trembled.

"Share that thought with us, Mia?" said Cameron.

"I don't remember the funeral." I fought back the sting of tears. "I think Lorraine decided it was best for me not to go. I wanted to go."

"What else do you remember?" he said.

"Lorraine was angry. Isn't that the first stage of grief?"

"Did she cry?" he said.

"I don't think so..."

Cameron looked thoughtful, his gaze finding Richard's again and another unspoken moment passed between them. Could close friends really communicate merely with a look and read each other's thoughts?

"What's your happiest memory?" said Cameron, breaking my trance.

My gaze shot to Richard and I realized that swimming in his pool had to be it. Along with that kiss. The way his hands had swept over me, caressing. The promise of getting closer to that all elusive love.

"What do you see?" said Cameron.

"Stars." I wanted to say Richard's face but felt too embarrassed. "That is, we can't see the stars because of the smog."

Richard flashed the biggest smile.

"We're not talking about your childhood anymore, are we?" said Cameron.

"No. I don't like it back there."

"Ah," whispered Cameron. "There it is."

"What?" I bit my lip. "I mean excuse me?"

"Tell me about your father."

"When I was growing up he worked as an administrator in exports and imports. After he left my mom he moved to L.A. and worked in a wine store in Pasadena." I looked over at Richard and he gave an encouraging smile. "My dad divorced my mom because of her drug habit."

If either Cameron or Richard were judging me they didn't show it. I assumed they were used to hearing all sorts of things here.

"You're an only child?" asked Cameron.

"Yes."

"How was your dad around you?" he said.

"Didn't really have a lot of time for me to be honest."

"How did that make you feel?" he said.

"Didn't know any different." I raised my hand in defense. "I've never done drugs. Ever."

"You chose to stay with your mom?"

"Didn't want to. I begged my dad to let me go with him. He told me mom needed me. So I stayed in Charlotte."

"You weren't responsible for her death," said Cameron.

"I should have been there." I twisted my mouth in shame. "She overdosed on cocaine."

"Where were you?"

"School." I lowered my gaze. "I'd always been able to read her before. Get a feel for when she was going to treat herself to the 'good stuff,' as she called it. It was the only thing that made her happy."

"You found her body?"

I gave a shrug. "Still did my homework that night."

"You still did your homework?"

"There were so many people in the house. Neighbors, cops, and other relatives. It was my excuse not to have to talk with any of them. Couldn't stand the way they looked at me."

"You came to live with your father."

"I moved to California to be with him and his second wife Lorraine. I felt guilty because I'd wanted it so badly. The only way to get it was for my mom to die."

Cameron nodded as though somehow he understood it all, all the angst, all the suffering, all the pain. *All the regret.*

"Every first Sunday in the month I go to IHOP," I said. "The one on Ventura, in Sherman Oaks. My dad and I used to eat there every Sunday." I smiled. "He always ordered the same thing. Even now I wait to get the same booth we used to sit in. I even order the exact same thing he used to eat. Same thing every time. Coffee, a plate of waffles, and a side order of grits. I never eat the grits."

"Why every first Sunday?"

I shrugged; wasn't going to share with them it was all I could afford.

Ignoring the silence Cameron was using to encourage me to go on, I held his gaze to let him know I was done.

"Your childhood pain," he said. "It has a hold on you. Your life is a journey and you're starting out with a squeaky wheel."

I swapped a glance between Richard and Cameron. "I thought it didn't matter anymore."

"That's what you told yourself," said Cameron.

"You think S & M will help me get over it?" I said.

"I didn't say that." Cameron gave a gentle smile. "What I do believe, Mia, is that it's time for you to forgive yourself."

CHAPTER FIFTEEN

I SAT ON THE BENCH WATCHING THE KOI SWIM AROUND EACH other, making hypnotic ripples in the pond, several of them coming up for air. We had something in common, it seemed.

Within this very hour my life had been turned upside down, when Richard had guided me into that dungeon via the coolest secret stairwell I'd ever seen, I'd expected to find Cameron waiting for us, wielding some form of leather paraphernalia. Or even wanting to talk about that toy.

I'd not expected this...

With what had felt like a party game, Cameron had cracked my psyche wide open, allowing me to see my life differently for the first time. Turns out I'd been dragging a whole lot of baggage around with me and didn't even know it. Which probably resulted in my sketchy trust issues. Apparently, I'd always been a member of the fucked-up crowd.

Those ivy strewn high walls on either side of the garden separated us from the world. I wondered how many people out there went about their daily lives telling themselves the knot inside their stomach was normal, like the one I had inside me now. I caressed this nagging ache, the one I thought I'd gotten used to.

It felt good to be outside and lose myself in the distraction of this well-tended garden that was a lush-green haven. I wasn't any good with naming flowers and only recognized that spray of daisies growing along the wall to my right. My mom had loved daisies though we'd only ever had the plastic kind. Something Richard would scoff at, no doubt. Still, money was tight, needed for everyday essentials like high-end cocaine for mom's dirty little secret.

I'd found her stash once. Luckily she caught me right before taking my first lick of the stuff. At seven years old that wouldn't have ended well.

I didn't want to think about that old life now, not when the promise of love loomed on the horizon. Richard's bossiness was so alluring, so protecting, and so addictive.

Every morning I couldn't wait to get to work just to be near him.

Cameron strolled toward me, his dark sunglasses making him hard to read. I rose to greet him and he gestured he wanted me to sit.

"Lunch." He lifted the brown paper bag and handed me the Perrier water. "Hope you like sparkling."

"Thank you, Cameron."

"You can thank Richard." Cameron joined me on the bench and handed me the bag. "It's a chicken salad wrap. It's from a deli down the road. They make everything fresh. Richard drove out especially to get it for you."

"Ooh, thank you." I peeked inside.

For me.

We both stared at the pond and for the first time in my life the silence didn't feel awkward.

He crossed a long leg over the other. "I really should come out here more often."

That silence returned once more as though proving to itself as much as me that all its power had gone.

"Five hundred dollars for your thoughts," said Cameron.

I giggled. "It's a penny for your thoughts."

He twisted his mouth. "In my estimation if the saying dates back to the middle ages and we take inflation into consideration—"

"That's silly."

"What can I tell you? I'm good with numbers."

He had a knack for making those around him feel comfortable, that is of course when he felt inclined, and I forgave him for what he'd done to me in Chez Polidor, using me to arouse Senator Deluca's penchant for punishment.

"How are you feeling?" asked Cameron.

"Do you think I need therapy?" I said.

"Do you think you need therapy?"

"I seem to have managed so far."

He turned to better look at me. "I quite agree."

"Do you always know what to say?"

"Pretty much." Cameron peered over his sunglasses. "So you and Richard kissed last night." He gave a nod. "I approve."

"Nothing happened."

He arched a quizzical brow. "Trust me, something happened."

"No, we didn't…you know."

"I wasn't sure if it was possible for anyone to reach into that heart. Evidently it is."

"How do you know?"

He eased his sunglasses up and rested them on his head. "Know what?"

"That I'm in love with Richard."

He peered under dark lashes. "I wasn't talking about you."

Though I stared at the pond I didn't see it, not really, my mind was too busy racing with the possibility Richard may feel the same way about me.

"Richard's calmer," said Cameron. "That was the first thing I noticed. You'd only been here a day. Of course he flew into a blind rage when he realized he had feelings for you."

"Why?"

Cameron glanced at me. "He was pushing you away."

"Did Richard tell you this?"

"That's confidential."

"Like us now?"

"Exactly."

"Last night, in Richard's pool, he looked horrified that we'd kissed."

"You read him wrong."

"I don't understand. Aren't people meant to be happy when they realize they like someone and that person likes them back?"

"Remember, we're dealing with Richard Booth Sh—" He shook his head. "Shall we keep talking?"

"Something bad happened to him, didn't it?"

"Bad happens to all of us."

"Yes, but it really does depend what that thing is."

He pursed his lips and I knew what that meant. I looked away, respecting his wish not to continue discussing it.

"Hopefully by now you've come to understand Enthrall is more than it first appears," he said.

"People who don't respond to conventional therapy use this place as a last resort."

"And some visit purely for pleasure, or pain, or both."

"Does Richard…"

Cameron leaned forward and rested his elbows on his knees. "It's a lifestyle choice. Some people choose to drink every day despite what it does to their liver, some smoke, some overeat." He shrugged. "Inevitably we all use a crutch."

I tried to think what mine might be. Yes, I liked the occasional drink, half the time I forgot to eat lunch, and, well, I'd never smoked.

Cameron leaned back to better look at me. "When I took you into the dungeon I had no idea you were still a virgin." He caressed his brow. "I'm kicking myself for doing that to you. After that daring performance in Richard's office you had me convinced you had a thing for kinky."

I bit my lip and blushed.

"Yeah, that doesn't help either," he said.

"What was that thing you did to me in the restaurant?"

"Can you be more specific?"

"When you squeezed my thigh."

"Oh, that. I released endorphins into your blood stream."

"By causing pain?" I sunk lower, burning with embarrassment but fascinated at the same time.

"It's what we do here," he said. "We control with pain. Bring pleasure with pain. Balance pleasure with pain."

He was mesmerizing.

"We banish pain with pain."

I tried to understand how that might work.

"So you don't hate me?" I said.

"Never." He stretched his arms out wide across the back of the bench. "Pain leads to the secretion of endorphins which in turn leads to euphoria."

"That's why it made me relax?"

He flashed a smile. "Amongst other things."

I broke his gaze, not daring to admit another part of me liked it too. "How did you know I wouldn't scream?"

"I profiled you," he said matter-of-factly without even a flicker of an eyelash.

My stare stayed on him, trying to see if he'd caught the weight of what he'd revealed.

"You're submissive," he said. "Which makes you a perfect fit for Enthrall. There are more than enough dominants in this place. You provide a form of repose. Perfectly so, in fact." His eyes locked with mine.

"Do you like dominating me?" I said.

"Nothing brings me more pleasure." The corner of his mouth turned up. "If you were my submissive you'd be sitting on the ground right now with your head on my lap. I'd be running my fingers through your hair."

Invisible sparks flew out of my chest; the tingly *what just happened there* kind.

"But potentially you're Richard's," he said.

"What about the ants?"

He looked amused. "I like feistiness. It's a trait I take pleasure in vanquishing in my submissive. Richard, however, desires someone more malleable. Sexually that is."

"Are you saying this to help me or warn me?"

"Trust me, submissives are honored. You'd be spoiled rotten. Encouraged to reach empowerment. Given every opportunity to fulfill your potential on every level. We encourage our women to flourish."

"So I'd be allowed to be me?"

"Goodness, yes." His gaze swept the garden and settled on the pond. "Do you like these little suckers?"

I swallowed, hard. "They're very relaxing to watch."

"From what I hear it looks like you'll have a few fish of your own soon. Along with a new address."

My head snapped round to look at him.

"Lotte's friend needs a house sitter and apparently you're about to become Malibu's newest resident."

"Really?" Excitement flipped in my stomach.

"Your rent's going to be really low. Something ridiculous. Turns out Lotte's quite the negotiator." He stood and stretched. "We'll have a welcome home party for you. Let's see if we can freak out Richard with some more normal." He chuckled. "It'll be fun to watch him squirm."

Cameron made me laugh.

"Mia, some things in life are best taken slow." He pulled his sunglasses back on.

I tried to read his face but the sun shone in my eyes.

"For the record," he said. "I'd never ship you off to Sicily. Or for that matter let anyone touch you." He beamed a mega-watt smile. "That's our privilege." He nudged his sunglasses farther up his nose. "You'll need help moving. I'll get the girls on it."

I hadn't even considered the need to pack. I let out a long sigh and watched him stroll back down the pathway toward the main building.

Reaching for my phone, I saw I'd missed a call from Lorraine. I dialed her back, making a mental note not to bring up my new home until all the details were set.

"How's my girl?" Lorraine's voice sounded extra husky.

"Did you just have a cigarette?"

"Jeez, Mia, I'm thousands of miles away and you're still on my case."

"Sorry. How are you feeling?"

"No more nausea, thank goodness."

"I'm so relieved."

"Me too. And I even managed to go to Mass last night."

"Wonderful," I said. "How's Aunt Amy?"

"Big sis is coming through for me as always," she said. "She might be able to get me some work up here. She has a friend who's a waitress at this Bistro called *Pastis*. Apparently the tips are huge."

"You feel okay to go back to work?"

"I'm not dead yet," she said, her laugh screeching down the phone.

"You know what I mean."

"I do. We went wig shopping today and Bobbi bought me this lush brunette thing." She sounded excited. "It's taken ten years off me."

"Send a photo."

"I'll get Bobbi to. I'm crap with this phone. I'm so sorry sweetheart, I forgot to ask how everything is with you?"

The fish eyed me as though edging me on to tell her I'd met someone. Though that certain someone was Mr. Elusive. Even after what Cameron had just revealed it seemed that Richard had no intention of following up on those feelings.

"You still there?" said Lorraine.

"Oh yes. Nothing new here." I gave the fish a glare.

"This is a little delicate for me to bring up, Mia."

"What's wrong?"

"Well, I forwarded that payment you sent me to the insurance company. The check was returned to me this morning in the post."

Paper ruffled in the background and I sensed she was looking at it as we spoke.

"What do you mean?" I said.

"They didn't cash it."

"Did you call them?"

"Yes," she said, 'But they went on about special grants and considerations and stuff like that. Quite frankly they lost me. Would you give them a call?"

"Of course," I said. "I'll call them as soon as I get home. What exactly did they say?"

"It didn't make any sense. Something about my account being closed."

This couldn't be happening. Had I messed up? I had been a little distracted lately. Ignoring this gut wrenching fear, I ran through a mental checklist of the last few payments I'd made. I'd only been late once but the billing department had given me an extra week to get the payment to them. Which I'd done.

"Please don't let it worry you, dear," said Lorraine. "It's probably me."

"I'll look into it. I have the money."

"I've heard of insurance companies cutting you off. I hope to God they don't do that to me."

"Please don't worry yourself over this. I've got it."

"You're such a good daughter, Mia. I don't deserve you."

"Nonsense. I'm the lucky one."

"Don't let L.A. ruin my sweet, beautiful Mia." She kissed into the phone and hung up.

I stared at my cell knowing I could never share with her my place of employment, or even the fact that the man who I worked for, the man who consumed my every waking thought, specialized in ruination.

And I'd fallen head over heels in love with him.

CHAPTER SIXTEEN

A WARM BUBBLE BATH AWAITED ME.

I'd taken Cameron's words to heart. *"It's time to forgive yourself,"* and had even promised to try and be a little kinder to myself.

I decided to enjoy some luxuries that I'd never allowed myself before, such as taking this bath. I never made the time, I suppose. Firstly, I needed to get this call to Blue West Medical Insurance out of the way. I sat on the edge of my bed with my iPhone pressed to my ear, on hold with yet another adjuster who'd passed me along to yet another department. My bath water was getting cold.

"Ms. Lauren?" came a friendly female voice on the line.

"Yes," I said, fearing the call might drop and I'd have to start over.

"I'm Karen Allen. Sorry for the wait. I have your mother's claim here," she said, her voice peppy. "Looks like the bills are all paid up."

"That's just it," I said. "You returned my last check. I mean the one my step-mom sent in."

"She overpaid on the account," said Karen.

"I have a copy of the main bill right here. I still owe you guys thirty-four thousand dollars." My throat tightened, having never before spoken the amount out loud.

"Ms. Lauren, you're all paid up."

"No, the last payment was only for six hundred dollars. You know, as part of that payment plan you set me up on."

"The balance on the account is at zero," said Karen firmly.

I could hear her clicking away on a keyboard.

This was getting frustrating. Clearly she was not getting the issue.

"Mrs. Lorraine Granger is my step-mom's name," I clarified. "We don't have the same last name."

"I'm looking at her account as we speak," her tone tensed.

"The last four of her social security number is 4406. Can you check we have the right—"

"Have the same one here."

"I don't understand," I said. "Who paid off my bill?"

"Your step-mother's account qualified for a special grant via one of our Cedars patrons," said Karen.

"Who was that?"

"They remain anonymous. It's our policy."

"Someone at Cedars paid off my entire step-mother's medical bill?"

"The funds came from one of our patrons here at Cedars, yes."

"Shouldn't they ask my permission first?"

Quiet filled the few seconds it took me to catch my breath.

"Your mother is a very lucky lady," said Karen. "Her entire debt is wiped clean. That really is something to be happy about."

"Can you send me that in writing?"

"The letter is on its way, Ms. Lauren."

Lying back on my bed, I stared up at the ceiling trying to come to terms with the fact I was now free from all debt.

And now if I really wanted to I could leave Enthrall.

That was the last thing I'd ever want to do. Not now, not after I'd found somewhere I really felt like I belonged, was accepted for who I was. Had potentially found the *one* there.

I rolled over onto my stomach and hugged my pillow. Wave after wave of relief consumed me that this ordeal was over; this far reaching responsibility of getting the best care for my step-mom was lifted.

Who, I wondered, had paid off my entire debt at Cedars? Was Richard a patron? He was certainly rich enough. How would I ever be able to ask him if it had been him?

Seriously, one chicken wrap and a bottle of Perrier and my imagination takes off on its own to crazy-land.

My bath would be a great way to celebrate.

Steam filled the bathroom and the scent of vanilla wafted. My robe slipped from my shoulders and fell to the floor. Spending time around Richard made me feel sexy and so adventurous, and right now I wished I'd brought that toy home from work.

Reaching low, gently easing apart my folds, I once again discovered my clit, feeling it swell beneath my touch as I imagined these were Richard's fingers flicking away, bringing lustrous sensations over my entire body.

Richard had admitted he liked our kiss but something told me he would never be mine, could never be mine. I'd never be worthy of a man like him. Though somehow knowing this made it easier to want him. Safer to fantasize about a lifestyle so forbidden.

My orgasm building, my eyelids fluttering shut…

My thoughts drifting, I wondered if I could ever live a life where I succumbed each day to a man's desire to control me? Possess me? My pussy throbbed, feeling so hot and wet with the thought of that man being Richard. Him mastering me, disciplining me, sending me over the edge…

Like my fingers did now, quickening, bringing me closer, those memories flooding back of him spanking me in the dungeon. That dark red walled playroom that promised hours of punishing pleasure—

I wished these were Richard's fingers, his masterful touch working me into frenzy. Nothing, no matter how much I tried, could I mimic the way he had touched me here, pleasuring me like this. His expertise was something I yearned for more than anything.

Coming hard, consumed with thoughts of being bound and gagged and used merely for his pleasure, I found release with the longest moan and shattered into a thousand pieces.

I collapsed in a heap on the floor.

Easing into the warmth of the bath, soothing my tired limbs, I began to understand what it meant to lavish pure physical attention upon myself, wallow in the luxury of self-devotion. My self-loathing was slipping away. It felt like I was truly seeing myself for the very first time. All tension left my body and this deep ache in my heart lifted. I drifted off to sleep—

Only to be jolted awake by the ring of the doorbell.

Drying off and scrambling for my robe, I made my way to the front door. It was Bailey and I gestured for her to come in quickly before someone caught a glimpse of my damp robe, which clung to my limbs, leaving nothing to the imagination.

She stepped in. "Do you have a minute?"

"Of course," I said.

"You were taking a shower? Sorry."

"A bath."

"You never take baths."

"I know—"

"Tara's seeing someone else." Her face crinkled and tears flowed. "We just had the most terrible argument."

I guided her toward the armchair where she plopped down into it, defeated.

I lowered myself to the floor to sit before Bailey and gave her knee a reassuring squeeze. "What happened?"

She wiped her nose. "Tara had her heart set on Australia. It was all she talked about. I'd come to terms with losing her. I know she's not going now but she's spending more and more time in Venice."

"Are you guys still having sex?" I don't know why I asked that. It kind of came out.

"Yes," said Bailey. "She's been a lot more experimental too."

I wondered if I'd started a line of questioning I wasn't prepared for.

"Why?" she said.

"Well it means there's still something special between you. Have you asked Tara if she really is seeing someone else?"

"Yes." Bailey sniffed. "She denies it."

"Well then."

"I feel terrible. I've been scouring her facebook page for evidence. And her phone. Breeching her trust and acting like an obsessive girlfriend."

"Love can be hard," I said, with no experience to back that up.

"Women have a feel for these things."

"Tara adores you," I said. "She's independent and that's what you love about her."

"I don't know if I can cope with losing her again."

"You didn't lose her."

"No, but I kind of came to terms with the whole Australia thing."

I gave a nod, acknowledging she had a point.

She wiped her nose with a tissue she'd pulled from her sleeve. "How are things with you?"

"Good."

"Did you really do that thing? Flash your boss?"

I blushed wildly, holding back on telling her about the Cameron and Mia double act in Richard's office. I hid my face in my hands.

Bailey looked astonished. "You really showed your boss your pussy? Whoa, Mia."

I peeked through my fingers.

"Mia Lauren, you go girl."

"You're not disgusted with me?"

"I know why you did it. How did Richard react? Go on, spill?"

"He left the room."

"Oh."

"And then he gave me my job back."

"Did he talk to you about it?"

"Yes, he was very nice about it."

"What did he say?"

"That it was brave."

"I'll say. He's probably biding his time until he can get his pervy claws into you." Bailey watched my reaction. "Has he made a pass already?"

"No."

"Mia, what happened?"

"He spanked me."

"What! Seriously?"

"It was kind of hot actually."

"Are you kidding me?" She sat up. "You could sue him for that."

"I kind of liked it."

"Why did he spank you?"

"I did something wrong. Well he thought I did, anyway."

"You know that's not right?" She glared. "I mean, what kind of work environment is it for goodness sake?"

If she knew about the dungeon escapade with Cameron, Bailey would probably stomp down to Enthrall and confront them both.

"It's all very professional," I said. "The spanking thing was a one off."

"You've lost your marbles."

I burst out laughing. "I really do love it there, Bailey."

She looked conflicted. "Well, as long as you're happy."

"Oh Bailey." I hugged my knees into my chest. "I can't remember ever being this happy."

"Don't let him spank you again, okay?"

Just the thought of it sent me reeling. I was more worried he may never spank me again. Wouldn't tell her that though.

A tap at the door snapped our attention toward it.

Bailey leaped out of the chair and took a peek out of the window. "It's Tara."

I pushed myself to my feet.

Tara stepped inside and waited for Bailey to close the door behind her.

"I thought I'd find you here," said Tara.

"We're so glad you're here," I wanted her to know.

Tara folded her arms. "So it's all right for you to have a friend," she pointed to me, "but the minute I go surfing you freak out?"

My shoulders slumped and I felt sorry for Bailey.

"We've been friends for years," said Bailey. "Mia and I go way back. We're only friends."

Tara's accusatory stare held my surprised one.

"I told her how much you love her, Tara," I said.

"Mia, I can see your nipples through that thing," she said.

Wrapping my arms around myself I said. "I was taking a bath."

"Alone?" seethed Tara.

"Yes, alone," I snapped. "Just didn't dry off probably."

She looked deflated and her focus fell back on Bailey. "I'm freaking out that we're over. We're not, are we?"

"I hope not," said Bailey. "I'm sorry for being so possessive. I never got over this Australia thing. I put on a brave face because you were so excited about it and I didn't want to cramp your sense of adventure. It's what I love about you." Her tears fell.

"Oh, babe," said Tara. "I'm not going anywhere."

I slumped into the armchair, feeling the day's adventures finally catching up.

Tara and Bailey canoodled, looking so cute together, making up in record time.

"Yay," I said, cheering them on.

They finally broke apart.

Tara came over to me. "So you got your job back?"

I brought my legs up onto the chair and tucked them under me. "I did. Thank you for that sound advice." I rolled my eyes.

"To be honest I didn't think you'd go through with it," said Tara. "I mean really, it's very sluts gone wild."

"Hey." My legs dropped from beneath me and I sat up defensively. "You're the one who suggested it."

"Don't get me wrong." Tara held up her hand. "I'm happy you got your job back."

I cupped my face in my hands.

"Didn't you do something similar to get the job?" said Bailey, coming to my defense.

"During my interview with the dominatrix's," she said. "Not in front of the guys."

"Like that's any better," said Bailey.

"I kind of feel it's all forgotten now," I said, hoping it was true.

Tara looked mischievous. "Just wish I could have been there when you got your job back."

Bailey thumped her arm.

Tara laughed and jumped back to avoid another punch. "I know I'm not the only one fantasizing about what went on in that room." She arched a brow.

"Hey," said Bailey. "She's my best friend, remember."

"Mia, you're my new hero," said Tara. "Hey, this must be a first for a BDSM club."

"How do you mean?" said Bailey.

"A virgin in their midst," said Tara.

"Leave her alone," snapped Bailey, giving her the stink-eye so that I wouldn't have to.

Slumping back in the seat, there came a feeling that Tara knew what had really unfolded in Richard's office on that day I'd asked for my job back.

Something told me Tara still had friends at Enthrall.

CHAPTER SEVENTEEN

"WELL? WHAT DO YOU THINK?" ASKED LOTTE.

This was really happening.

We were standing in the living room of 3777 Bailbard Road, Malibu. This was my new beach condo.

We were surrounded by unpacked boxes and the suitcases Bailey and Tara had leant me for the move. I'd taken a leap of faith and given notice on my studio apartment and packed up my life and moved without ever seeing this place.

"Trust me," Lotte had told me, "you'll love it."

And she was right. I'd fallen in love with the bright, spacious living room as soon as I'd stepped inside. Directly in front of us stretched out a glass fronted doorway leading out onto a balcony, and beyond that an ocean vista. It wasn't just the view that took my breath away. This place had dark stained hardwood floors with Persian rugs strewn here and there, adding a sophisticated accent as well as tying all the other pieces together. There was a plush cream colored couch and next to that an armchair easy to sink into. An enormous Samsung flat screen TV hung on the wall. I felt giddy with excitement.

Against the left wall rested a fish tank. Six tropical fish swam the full length of their blue lit world only to turn again to begin their journey to the other end. Thankfully there were no Asian Arowana's amongst them.

I'd given up my low rented studio and would be hard pushed to find anything as cheap with the way rent prices were going. "Who is this person?" I said. "What if they realize how much they miss it here and want to come back?"

"You're fine. They won't."

"I'm not doing anything illegal am I?" I feared this run of good luck might be too good to be true.

"No." Lotte continued the tour and guided me into the generously sized bedroom with its king sized bed. This room also overlooked the ocean. I stared out at the view, trying to come to terms with this really happening and questioning whether I was worth this kind of luxury.

A tug on my arm pulled my attention.

Lotte, who was as equally thrilled it seemed, had the bathroom to show me. In the middle sat an enormous porcelain tub with clawed feet. It reminded me of a photo from a high-end magazine like Vogue. The kind I flipped through at the supermarket but never bought.

"Of course you can always shower," said Lotte.

There was an oversized showerhead inside the glass fronted, granite tiled cubicle. The toilet and sink looked costly too. Plush new towels hung on a designer rack.

"It's heated," said Lotte, pointing to it.

"The towel rack is heated?" I shot her a look.

"It gets pretty chilly in winter. You'll be glad of it."

Disconcerted with all this luxury and terrified I'd somehow mess it up, I followed after Lotte. Next came the airy kitchen with its cream colored cabinets and central marble isle. This place had been newly furnished, I was sure of it. Everything looked flawless. I couldn't understand how the owner wouldn't want to live here.

This was a first for me in so many ways, and until now I'd never felt the urge to hug an appliance. The grand stainless steel fridge loomed large, fitting snugly between two glass fronted cupboards.

"This is your welcome home gift." Lotte pointed to the deluxe fridge. "It has smart cooling technology. It's from all of us."

That was all it took. Unable to fight back tears that had been building for the last half hour, all I could do was swipe at them, losing a fighting battle.

Lotte wrapped her arm around me. "There, there, sweetheart. You'll get used to it. Change is never easy."

"It's the most beautiful fridge I've ever seen." I turned to her. "I can't believe it."

"Believe it. Now do you have a paper bag?"

I looked around for one. "Why?"

She peered across the room. "Behind that door over there is a cupboard. In there is a washer and dryer. I'm terrified you're going to hyperventilate and you'll have to breathe into a bag so you don't faint."

Having had to drag my washing over to my old apartment's Laundromat, Lotte had been wise to break that little nugget of info slowly. For goodness sake I probably made her think I lived in a cave.

She took my hand and guided me back to the living room and over to the fish tank. "Remember, you're doing the owner a favor." Her gaze widened. "Keep those little suckers alive and everything will be fine."

On the coffee table rested the instructions Lotte had gone over with me about how to maintain the tank. It all seemed easy enough, especially since the fish received a visit once a week from the pet store owner who apparently would change out the water. All I had to do was feed them several times a day.

Within half an hour Penny and Scarlet had arrived. They, like Lotte, were dressed in jeans and t-shirts. Still, they couldn't pull off ordinary. They were far too pretty for that. Scarlet even wore Ugg boots, a far cry from her usual leather and lace. As promised they'd brought wine and pizza as well as delivering on their offer to help me unpack.

We split up, each taking a box to a room, and began what would have otherwise been an arduous task. Time slipped by as I hung my clothes up in the walk-in closet, musing how it reminded me of my entire studio.

I owed Lotte so much for making this happen for me.

Bailey and Tara arrived an hour later. I introduced Bailey to the girls, though Tara had needed no introduction and chatted away with them, catching up on all she'd been doing lately and everyone shared with her what she'd missed at Enthrall.

Watching them all interact, their shared respect for each other, the way they fondly listened to each other's stories, there came a feeling this might be the closest I'd ever come to having a family.

Lotte, Penny, and Scarlet all bubbled with happiness for me and shared with Bailey how much they loved having me around. Apparently many of the clients were fond of me too. Even Monsieur Trourville had developed a soft spot, sans Venus balls.

For the first time in my life I'd found a purpose. I belonged somewhere.

The unpacking resumed and we made great headway with getting the place straight. Bailey took me aside to speak with me privately. She couldn't believe my good luck either. I reassured her I was merely doing a friend of Lotte's a favor. We strolled over to examine the tank, eyeing the fish as they eyed us back, unfazed with all the activity.

"You're not becoming a dominatrix are you?" she said.

"Hardly."

Her gaze swept the room. "How much is your rent?"

"Four hundred a month." I pointed to the tank. "This guy needs someone to watch those."

Bailey folded her arms. "Why have a fish tank if you don't intend to enjoy it?"

"He had to go out of town on business."

"For a year?"

I stared at the small blue one with its pale white stripes. "I might give them names."

"Be careful."

"I've got a couple of books to read on them."

"I'm not talking about the fish," she whispered. "If any part of your brain is saying this is too good to be true it's probably right."

"Be happy for me."

She pointed a finger. "Never, ever do anything you don't want to. Promise me."

"Of course."

"One minute you're flashing your boss your cooch, the next…"

"This has nothing to do with that."

I wanted to enjoy today. Richard would be here any minute and so would Cameron. I was so excited to show them the place and share this amazing streak of luck. For the first time in my life I felt the desire to invite friends over, maybe even Richard. Maybe I'd even learn to cook.

Bailey tapped my arm. "I'm sorry. I'm pissing on your parade and you don't deserve it. I love you so much and don't want anything bad to happen to you."

I wrapped my arms around her and gave her the biggest hug.

"Hey," it was Tara's voice. "How about we make this a group hug?"

They both wrapped their arms around me.

"You guys are going to make me cry," I said.

"This place oozes with positive energy," said Tara, stepping back. "The feng shui rocks."

"You're going to love it here," said Bailey.

Looking around at all this luxury and realizing it was mine, my stomach did a flip again.

The ocean breeze felt cleansing. A wonderful change from the valley's stuffiness.

With the boxes unpacked and most of the pizza gone we all huddled in the kitchen, our conversation flowing with the wine. Several bottles of Chardonnay lay empty on the counter top.

An hour or so later, Cameron and Richard arrived, bringing with them dessert in a large white box from the Cheesecake Factory. They too wore jeans and t-shirts and as predicted still looked stylish in their casual clothes. From Richard's sticking up hair they'd driven here in one of their open top cars.

"I love open top cars," I told them, bringing a smile to Richard's face.

He ran his fingers through his golden locks to flatten them, beaming at me.

Cameron placed the dessert box on the counter. After washing his hands, Richard opened the dessert box and dipped a finger into the creamy white topping. Lotte smacked his hand, hard, causing Richard to burst into laughter, playfully sucking off the icing. Lotte served the cheesecake to each of us. There came a silent pause as we tucked into the delicious sweet dish, the sound of forks hitting the plates. The sighs of happiness coming from everyone.

Richard stole a spoonful of cheesecake off my plate, eating it with a mischievous grin. My heart threatened to leap out of my chest and splash right into my glass of wine.

"Look at my fridge," I burst out, trying to save myself from this embarrassing blush.

Richard looked horrified. "Oh no. Whatever happened to the other one from your old apartment? Let's go get it back."

"No," I said, throwing a glance at Bailey to make sure her feelings weren't hurt.

"Don't look at me," she said. "I'm as happy to see that thing go as you are."

"Look." I grabbed a cup and held it beneath the ice dispenser. "Watch this."

Ice clinked into the cup and I giggled my delight.

Laughter roared from around me. Yet again I blushed wildly, but from everyone's smiles they found my glee endearing.

Bailey threw me a *Richard's kind of cute look,* but not discreetly enough.

He caught it and his face shifted to unreadable. "I'm going to check out the view." He ambled out, taking his glass of wine with him.

"Thank you so much for my amazing gift," I said. "If ever you need me to work overtime let me know."

"Don't be ridiculous," said Cameron. "We bought it from Costco. They virtually gave it away."

Costco?

Hadn't Richard and Lotte visited Costco together over a few weeks ago? Surely that was well before Lotte's friend had asked her to find someone to live here? I peered over at Lotte. Her gaze remained on the tile.

"I'm going to take another peek at the view too," I said, feeling decidedly more confident than usual as the carbs mixed with the wine and relaxed me.

Richard stood on the balcony, resting his elbows on the rail and staring out at the ocean.

"Isn't the view amazing?" I said.

He turned and leaned back against the railing. "Spectacular."

"I'm so grateful. I have to pinch myself."

"You've got the place looking great."

"You've been here before?"

"No." He took a sip of wine. "Apparently the bathtub's something else."

"Do you want to see?"

I led him through the living room. A burst of laughter came from the kitchen and it eased my guilt over leaving my guests to entertain themselves. It felt nice to take another peek at this room.

Richard strolled around the tub, his gaze meeting mine. "Decisions…decisions…bath or shower? I'm tempted to take one now."

I feigned shock.

He set his wine down on the marble counter near the sink. "We should get back."

"I feel safe," I said.

"I don't."

Something passed between us, an invisible spark, and he took hold of my wrists and shoved me back against the wall, pulling my arms up above my head. He held them there, his firm body pressing mine. This yielding pose and the strength he'd used to get me into it made me go lax in his grip, weaken, my core tightening in anticipation of where he was taking this, taking me.

His lips came dangerously close. "Mia, the things I want to do to you."

A flurry of thrills shot up my spine.

He let go and took a step back, his stare breaking from mine. "Stay away from me. Promise you will."

"I won't."

Confusion marred his face.

"You don't want to kiss me?" I said.

"You know I do. More than anything. It's complicated."

"How?"

"With me there are no surprises," he said. "You know what it is I do. What I am. I will never give up BDSM. You and me, we're not compatible."

Right now I was willing to try anything to feel his hands upon me again, feel his affection, his touch. I wanted him to know this. How bad could what he got up to in that dungeon really be?

"We could start slow," I said, remembering Cameron's words and trying them out on Richard.

He blinked through dark blond lashes. "You realize what it is I want to do to you?"

"Yes."

With the window closed, this room lacked the air we both needed so desperately. From the way his chest rose and fell he too must have felt short of breath.

He raised his chin in defiance. "Say it."

"You want to dominate me."

"Subjugate you." He stepped closer. "Control you. Conquer you." His left hand rested against my chest and he eased me back against the wall again and pressed hard. "Fuck you."

Oh please.

He looked hesitant. "Mia, I have never taken on an untrained submissive."

"What does that mean?"

"They've always come to me primed."

"Primed?"

"Already trained."

"By who?" I sucked in my breath. "Cameron?"

Richard stepped closer and brushed a stray hair out of my eyes.

"I want it to be you," I said softly.

"You deserve someone better than me."

"Don't I get a say?"

"Right up until the moment you agree to become my submissive. Then all choice is lost." He narrowed his gaze. "You wouldn't want that. Would you?"

My legs felt weak. I breathed a sigh of sadness when his hand fell once more to his side, threatening never to touch me again.

"You and I are miles apart," he said.

"Are you trying to convince yourself? Or me?"

"What is our common ground?"

"You don't think I'm good enough for you?" My voice broke with emotion. "Is that it?"

"Other way round." He looked intently. "You are innocence incarnate."

I broke his gaze, my heart aching with the thought I'd failed him, failed me.

My inner musing told me to stay strong, tell him want I really wanted, needed. Him, it had only ever been him.

My words flowed from an unfamiliar place. "I'm returning to the balcony. If you find the strength to face what we both know, that there's real chemistry between us, join me. Ask me out on a date. I may even say yes." I picked up his glass of wine and strolled off with it, leaving him standing there. I headed across the living room and out onto the balcony.

Facing the breeze, I let it wash over me, inhaling the freshest air. This place offered a new start. The promise of fulfillment close enough to touch...

If I dared to reach out to it.

After several minutes of savoring the view, I regretted my

outburst, letting him know my true feelings. I downed the rest of the wine, taking pleasure from knowing his lips had brushed where mine were now on the glass. The softest sigh escaped me.

I turned around—

Richard leaned against the balcony doorjamb. "Start slow?" His alluring blue gaze burning fiercely into mine.

"Slow."

"Are you sure this is something you want?" he whispered. "I'm not good at compromise."

"I know."

"What do you have in mind?" he said.

"Chrysalis's party tomorrow night. Let me go with you."

He twisted his mouth as though mulling over it.

"Pick me up tomorrow at six," I said.

Richard stepped onto the balcony. "You do realize I'm the dominant." He towered over me, emphasizing his point. "An issue you would be wise not to forget."

Damn, that turned me on.

I stretched out my arms to either side and clutched the handrail. "Your irises dilate when I push back."

Don't push back. Cameron warned he prefers malleable.

Could I be this woman? Could I fall at Richard's feet and become his sex slave? What was I willing to give up in order to become his lover? His submissive.

Everything.

I'd do anything.

He shifted closer. "What else do you see?"

"That you want this as much as I do."

"Some things are inevitable." His expression softened, his face now serene. "I have so much to show you."

"I want that."

"Mia." He narrowed his gaze, his intensity returning. "Are you truly ready for such blinding pleasure?"

A flurry of what felt like butterflies burst out of my chest. Tingles of excitement caused me to shiver, and an exquisite ache in my belly settled low. In the deepest depths of my soul I felt ready for this, for him.

"It's a good thing we're not alone," he said.

"Not that it matters," I said. "I only ever see you."

Richard's frown dissolved and he ran his fingers through his golden locks.

"I'll see you tomorrow then," I whispered breathlessly, melting in the wake of his stunning smile.

CHAPTER EIGHTEEN

I 'D NEVER FELT MORE BEAUTIFUL.

Nor had I ever dressed so provocatively. Tonight was Chrysalis's party at an undisclosed location and Richard was due to pick me up at any moment. I stole another few moments to check my dramatic make-up of highlighted smoky eyes, shimmery petal lips, and softly emphasized cheekbones. I fluffed my hair, choosing to wear it down and let spiraling curls float over my shoulders.

Taking in my mirrored reflection I was amazed at how sophisticated a black corset made me appear, the way my breasts curved beneath the lacey top. That, and the high-top stockings with sheer garter belt and matching lace panties. I'd even found the Manolo Blahniks that Cameron had bought for me went perfectly.

Lotte had advised me wearing anything else would make me stand out and I didn't want that. She'd leant me her long, velvet hooded cape; perfect for hiding within until we arrived at our destination.

My black and gold mask added the mystery Chrysalis's party called for. All guests were expected to wear one. I headed into my living room to place it on top of my clutch purse so as not to forget it.

My new home was going to take some getting used to. I still had to pinch myself in disbelief that I lived here and wondered how much longer I'd continue walking around the place reverently. That cream colored couch would have to be sat on at some point.

There was wine in the fridge. I was tempted to crack open a bottle right now and drink a glass or two to calm my nerves. Still, Richard would not approve of taking a lush to what was essentially one of the most important nights of the year for his clients. Members were flying in from all over the world to partake in what I'd been told was a lavish extravaganza. I couldn't wait to see the grand house that hosted the event, after Lotte had teased me about her adventures there in years past. She'd warned me to avoid the bedrooms. Guests got up to all kind of things in those apparently, and I wasn't sure how I felt about everyone ending up in the pool naked at the end of the evening.

After thirty minutes of Richard's non-appearance, my concern for his safety increased. I opened my purse and pulled out my iPhone.

Damn, I'd missed a call from him.

Though he'd not left a voice message, he had texted:

Richard: "Mia, please forgive me. Next year perhaps. Go do something fun."

I slumped onto the sofa.

What the hell.

Hadn't last night's soiree on the balcony meant anything to him? I'd thought we'd agreed I could handle anything he wanted to throw at me. Collapsing back, I felt defeated, embarrassed even. Surely he knew how excited I had been about going tonight. I'd gone all out putting my outfit together and getting all dressed up for a party I now wasn't going to.

I texted him back.

Mia: "What made you change your mind?" I backspaced, deleting it.

Instead, feeing annoyed with Richard and assuming he wouldn't change his mind, I texted Lotte. After-all I was a member of staff and as entitled to go to this party as anyone.

Mia: "Hey Lotte. Cape looks great! Thank you. Can't wait to see you. What's the address again?"

Resting my iPhone on my lap, I eyed the flat screen TV. This would be yet another evening in for me and that wasn't such a bad thing. Though being rebuffed by Richard again was.

My iPhone pinged.

Lotte: "What happened?"

Mia: "All good."

The remote looked easy enough to use. Cameron had mentioned something about HBO and Showtime being available. I'd not had time to check that out until now.

Thanks for that Richard, my inner muse cursed him. *Grrrr. I don't need protecting. I need seducing.*

Lotte: "The Manor, Linda Flora Drive, Bel Air."

A jolt of excitement hit me.

Now I knew how an operative with the CIA felt when they closed in on their subject. Only I was in hot pursuit of Richard Booth and my evening plans had reverted nicely.

Lotte: "Drive safe. Roads twisty."

Mia: "Got it."

Lotte: "You remember the password?"

Password?

Lotte: "Avonscroft."

Mia: "Thank you!"

Lotte: "See you soon."

Mia: "Can't wait."

Lotte: "Make sure Richard meets you in the foyer."

Mia: "Got it."

Lotte: "Do not walk through the house alone."

Mia: "Okay."

I grabbed my purse and mask and pulled around my shoulders the long, black cape and headed out.

Using my phone's GPS I navigated my Mini onto Ventura, off toward Bel Air, suppressing this nagging feeling I wasn't ready for this. Still, I'd promised myself I'd try new things and stretch out of my comfort zone and this was a good way to begin this leaf turning, life changing decision.

Thanks to Lotte's warning I drove carefully up the steep, curvy roads of Bel Air, and within the hour my navigator had delivered me to my destination.

The manor rose majestically on the top of a hill.

This was the largest house I'd ever seen, even paling in comparison to the Sullivan's and I'd thought their place in Brentwood was huge. They had valet parking. My car must have looked ridiculous sandwiched between the silver Mercedes and the blue BMW. Using my rearview mirror I checked my make-up and placed my mask on.

This was the most exciting party I'd ever attended.

Head high, I handed the valet my keys, amazed he didn't react to my ride or even flinch when he climbed in. Though he looked squished in the driver's seat. He steered my car off to park it somewhere more convenient. I tucked my valet ticket into my purse.

I was glad for this cape and pulled it snug around me. Despite it covering everything I felt decidedly naked beneath it as the reality of what I was actually doing became more vivid with being here. At the front door I waited for a couple to enter before me.

Piped in from invisible speakers, the music's throbbing bass invited guests into the imperious foyer. Smoke pumped out from hidden vapor machines, creating a mysterious atmosphere. The entryway was softly bathed in golden yellow lighting.

Peering down at my phone, I went to text Richard.

A tux wearing bouncer appeared out of the mist, his physique more like a pro-football player than a security guard. His sternness was a warning not to proceed any farther.

"I'm a guest," I said.

He folded his arms, his posture defensive.

"Avonscroft." I held his gaze.

"Turn off your phone," he said. "Or I'll confiscate it."

After following his order, I dropped it back into my purse.

He stepped aside and I held my breath until there was distance between us and I was out of his sight. This man-made fog surrounded me, a blanket of whiteness making it difficult to gauge which way to go. Before me swept a large staircase fanning out to either side and I knew well enough not to begin my search up there, heeding Lotte's warning. If I could find one of the girls they'd know where I could find Richard.

Laughter caught my attention. An elegant thirty-something masked couple, strolling arm in arm, headed west. From their confident stride they knew where they were going. The fog crawled its way down the hallway, seducing me into the unknown, beckoning me to follow. Halfway down, the woman turned and peered back through her butterfly mask. She offered the softest smile, tilting her head. They disappeared through a doorway. The placard to the left of the entrance announced this as the Harrington Suite. With a quick glance back, I braved to take a peek beyond the door.

Taking a moment for my eyes to adjust, I blinked into the dimness. A crowd had gathered before me and blocked my view of the room. A high stucco ceiling with its low hung crystal chandeliers bathed everything in a balmy light, and red velvet drapes swept either side, indicating this was a ballroom. Making my way as stealthily as possible, I tiptoed left of the gathering.

The music flooding in sounded familiar: *Enigma.*

All air left the room and my feet felt unsteady beneath me—

There, in the center, rested a dark wooden table. Leaning over one side of it was a masked brunette, wearing only a bodice and no panties. She stretched out her hands before her for balance, her spine a perfect curve, her wrists held tightly by a smartly dressed masked man standing on the other side. Despite her mask she looked relaxed, as though unaware of her audience. Their gazes fixed on her, on all three of them.

The brunette was being taken from behind by a masked man, his shirt open and pants off, revealing a sculpted musculature. He kept his rhythm slow, steady, as his full length disappeared inside her, only to pull all the way out before slamming into her again. And again.

He was taking her hard.

This dark, evoking scene unraveling like a shadowy dream...

The air crackled with an electrifying atmosphere, fusing each and every person watching. A silent rousing, a burning within each stare feasting upon this never-ending sex scene. This wasn't real, this couldn't be real. My mind searched for understanding of what unfolded in this elegant suite.

The brunette moved with the grace of a dancer as she was elegantly flipped onto her back by the two men. She lay facing up on the table. Her hands were recaptured behind her by the one who had held her before. The other man who had taken her from behind was now standing between her legs. He eased her thighs apart and spread her legs wide open to completely expose her. When he seemed content that the on-lookers had seen her pussy well, having scanned the many masked faces of the audience just to be sure, he used his hand to pleasure her there. Fingering her leisurely, he easily brought her to ecstasy. He leaned in low and buried his face into her shiny wet cleft, licking away at her clit, his tongue expertly darting over that small nub. She arched her back, her moans of pleasure mingling with the music, an unfamiliar ballad that was a perfect backdrop to this lust-filled scene.

Hushed murmurs of approval came from the room.

It was hard not to imagine you were her, that woman laying there being pampered so provocatively. I fought with this desire to stay, my core tightening with anticipation of what else I might see. What else they might do. My gaze glided over the masked witnesses to these three and their uncommon pleasure, searching for Richard, Cameron, or even the girls.

I shouldn't be in here. Yet my feet remained rigid and stuck to the floor, my gaze meeting that of the masked beauty as she turned her head to the side. Her eyelids fluttered, her lips pouted in wanton ecstasy. Her moaning filled the ballroom, and the whispers of the man holding her wrists demanded her complete submission, which she gave willingly. Her orgasm snatched her breath, seizing her, taking her higher still.

Her soft sighs of bliss were shared with us all.

Turning slowly, my own arousal disorientating me, I reached the doorway, pressing my hand against my chest to calm my racing heart. I stepped out into the hallway and found myself once more engulfed in billowing smoke.

Feeling my way along the wall…

"What do we have here?" a male voice called out.

A short, plump man wearing a toga neared me. He wore a leaf crown like a Roman emperor. Beside him stood the guard I'd met at the door.

"I'm looking for someone," I murmured.

Toga lowered, his gaze and it slid over to the Harrington Suite.

My words failed me and I shook my head, *no*.

"Take it off," he said, gesturing. "Now."

I removed my mask.

"Who are you?" he said angrily.

"Mia."

"Come with me." His voice was low, threatening.

The guard grabbed my arm, his ironclad grip cutting off my circulation. In seconds we'd entered a study, a lavishly decorated office. Bookcases went all the way to the ceiling, the vast, neatly lined compendiums an impressive collection of knowledge. Leather and dark wood gave the room an overly masculine flair. A long chain hung from the ceiling in the center. I'd seen something similar back at Enthrall, but here it looked out of place.

My gaze froze upon it.

"Find the director. Now," snapped Toga to the guard.

There was some relief when the bouncer disappeared, though the thought of what kind of trouble I was in terrified me.

"What website do you work for?" said Toga.

"I'm a guest." I hesitated, nervous to mention Richard's name.

"I know everyone here," he said. "You, I don't know."

I hugged my cape tighter, regretting coming here without Richard's permission and cursing my desire to try something new. I vowed never to disobey him again. Even my thoughts leaned toward submissive. This place had a way of silencing you.

"What are you wearing beneath that?" he snapped. "Jeans?"

I shook my head, wanting the guard to come back.

"Show me," he demanded.

Hoping to calm his glare, I separated my cape and flung it over my shoulders, daring to reveal my corseted attire. His annoyed expression changed to one of astonishment.

The door opened wide, held by the guard, and in strode a tall, masked man wearing a perfectly fitted tuxedo, his gait confident, his deep brown glare on me.

"Cameron?" I took a step toward him, reassured he'd tell Toga I wasn't an intruder.

Cameron drank me in.

Slowly.

Desirously.

Tension tightened in my throat like a vice.

"Director," said Toga, breaking the silence. "You know her?"

Director?

I tried to read Toga's face to see if he'd misspoken.

"Yes," said Cameron, hissing the *s* like a snake.

"She's with you?" clarified Toga.

Cameron gave a nod and gave a thin smile that didn't reach his eyes.

"I caught her enjoying the Harrington Suite," said Toga.

"Really?" said Cameron.

"A lamb to the slaughter?" asked Toga.

Cameron tilted his head. "Not tonight, Dominic."

"Pity," he said. "Our guests would have enjoyed her."

Cameron held out his hand. "Ms. Lauren."

It sounded so devastatingly formal, so unwelcoming, and yet I took his hand, allowing Cameron to guide me out and away from the beady eyes of Toga and his disconcerting talk of slaughtering lambs. We made our way farther down the hallway and I remained quiet, no longer trusting myself to understand the etiquette of this place, glancing back to make sure Toga wasn't following.

After checking we were out of anyone's line of sight, Cameron let go and leaned against the wall as though he too was affected by Toga's creepiness. Even with a mask on I could see Cameron looked fazed. He let out a long sigh through pursed lips.

"Hi," I said, trying to judge if he was upset.

"What the *fuck*, Mia."

"I was looking for Richard."

He ripped off his mask. "In the Harrington Suite?"

I widened my eyes when I thought of it.

"What did you expect?" he said. "Chess?"

"Is Richard here?"

He rolled his eyes.

"You're the director?"

"Yes."

"Why didn't you tell me?"

"Why would it matter?"

"You run Chrysalis?" I said. "This place?"

Cameron hesitated and his gaze reached into my soul, burning through with an intensity I'd never felt before.

I crumpled my cape around me.

"Well now you know," he said.

I stepped back from him. "You organize all of this?"

"With Richard's help."

I broke his gaze. Richard had warned me what went on here was far more serious than what happened at Enthrall, but I'd not believed it, not really.

"This is my fault," said Cameron. "I teased you about coming here for my own amusement. You aren't ready."

"I thought it would be all right."

"This environment is highly-charged. You can't wander around like you're at fucking Disneyland. Especially dressed like that." His hand shot toward my corset. "Richard will be furious."

I bolted, unsteady on six inch heels, the cape billowing behind me, having no idea where I was going or how I'd get out of here without being taken down by a bouncer.

But it was Cameron who caught me. Reaching around my waist,

lifting me and slamming me back against the wall. All air left my lungs as I was stunned into silence.

"Enough," he said.

I stilled, grateful that oxygen had finally found its way back into my lungs. Panicked, I struggled again.

"Calm down," he said, fixing me with a stormy stare.

Breathing way too fast, my legs almost gave way.

He held me there. "You're not going anywhere unaccompanied. Am I clear?"

I tried to push him off.

He leaned against me, his grip tightening. "You make it worse when you fight me."

I grasped his arms, feeling his muscles taut beneath his jacket. My fingernails embedded in his flesh.

"Give me a moment," he said, his head down, his hands trembling with rage.

"I'm sorry."

"Silence."

Shaking in his arms, I tried to read his face and make out what he was thinking. Grasp what was happening.

"This is a dangerous place," he said, his tone severe, deathly cold. "There are people here whose predilections threaten you in every conceivable way. Do. You. Understand?"

"Yes."

"If they so much as lay their eyes on you they'll devour you." His grip tightened. "Like I want to right now."

My sudden gasp made him shudder.

"You are the most beautiful creature I've ever seen and until now I've been able to give you up to Richard." He slowed his breathing. "Until now."

"Oh, Cameron."

"Stop fucking moving."

Weakening, I gave myself over to him.

"I need a moment to think," he said, holding me firmly against the wall and pressing his body against me, his face full of passion, his erection hard and ready, digging in and threatening to find its way into me. His breathing was frantic. The no going back kind. Gripping my wrists on either side of me, burying his face into my neck, he nuzzled into my curling locks.

Stunned with how much his power alighted my desire, blood roaring through my ears, my clit pulsed with pleasure. His cologne reached me, and the scent of sex and danger heightened my arousal. A moan escaped my lips, an aching to be free and yet also taken by him, but I fought this conflicting urge to surrender. He thrust up against me again, ablaze, growing harder still. My cheeks blushed brightly, the burning spreading to where his lips kissed my throat. This was a scorching heat of passion, and his breathing fell heavy and labored upon my chest.

"You liked what you saw in the Harrington suite," he said huskily.

"Yes."

His grip tightened around my wrists. "And you like this."

"Yes."

It was impossible to think straight, think rationally. Clouds of mist wrapped around us, enveloping us, shielding us, edging us on.

"Dr. Cole," I made his name the softest plea.

He squeezed his eyes shut.

Cameron was impossible to fight, too strong to push off, and I had no choice but to soften in his arms.

Submit.

Gradually, his hold lightened and his sternness dissipated. "Very calmly." He chose his words carefully, as though beneath each one lay a landmine. "We are going to head out into the garden. Get some air. Find Richard."

I gave a nod.

He let go and stepped back. "This never happened."

"No."

"Say it."

"This never happened," I said breathlessly.

He gave a nod of acceptance. "You okay?"

"Yes."

He gave my corset a tug to straighten it. "I must warn you."

"What?"

"You may not like what you see."

"What do you mean?"

Cameron ran his fingers through his dark black hair. "Richard's not alone."

CHAPTER NINETEEN

MY WRISTS SMARTED WHERE CAMERON HAD HELD THEM. I surrendered to him now as he pulled me along the longest hallway that must have stretched the entire length of the house. Daring to glimpse at the occasional gathering we past, I feared catching someone else in the throes of passion. I wasn't sure if heading away from the front door was a good idea.

When we stepped out into the cool night air, there came a wave of panic for what I might see. My gaze scanned the crowd, hoping not to see Richard in the arms of another woman.

Cameron's grip refused to ease up. I teetered behind him, balancing on these high heels he'd bought me, their straps digging in and making me wonder why anyone would have a thing for pain.

Masked, well-dressed men and scantily clad women had gathered here and there, and much to my relief no one was having sex, though it was dark back here. The only light came from the pool that was lit from beneath and bathed in a deep red. Around me wine glasses clinked and conversations were heard over the music. Ripples of laughter proved everyone was having a good time.

Everyone except me, who was trying to keep up with Mr. Intensity here, and by the look of things Richard wasn't enjoying himself either.

There he sat with his legs soaking in the pool, his jacket off and shoved behind him, his pants rolled up to his knees and his legs dangling in the water. His mask lay discarded beside him. Sipping from a tumbler, he ignored the two pretty naked women swimming close by, kicking his legs forwards and backwards through the water.

"Let me do the talking," said Cameron, yanking me toward him.

Richard looked our way and his narrowed stare fell on me and then settled on Cameron with a glare. Cameron pulled me beside him to the edge.

"Richard, I want to explain—" A tug on my arm, Cameron's way of reminding me he wanted to handle this.

"Dominic found her," said Cameron. "Luckily he sent for me. He assumed she was press."

Richard cringed and shot me a wary look.

The naked women stopped swimming and trod water, eavesdropping. Cameron waved them off, his hand a commanding sweep through the air. They responded immediately, swimming to the edge of the pool and climbing out. Both of them strolled unabashedly toward two loungers where their towels and clothes awaited them.

What kind of power did these two rogues have anyway?

"Didn't you get my text?" said Richard. "The one telling you not to come?"

This had gone from the best evening of my life to the worst and I turned to leave, trying to get out of Cameron's grasp.

He held my hand tight, his attention focused on Richard. "She was found coming out of the Harrington Suite."

Oh, I'd forgotten about that. I'd been so mesmerized by Richard's frown my mind had sought refuge by going blank.

Richard crunched on a chunk of ice. "You see what we are, Mia?"

I gripped Cameron's hand and leaned into him.

"We are hedonistic," said Richard. "Want a tour?" He pulled his legs out of the water and stood. "Bet you'd like that." He bowed low to grab his jacket, whisking it up.

"Take her home," said Cameron.

"And ruin her fun?' said Richard. "Let's go back to the Harrington."

"You can't drive. You've had too much to drink," Cameron warned him.

"I don't really want to see anymore," I muttered.

"What was that?" said Richard.

Recoiling, I hid behind Cameron.

"What exactly did you see?" Richard flashed a devilish smile. "I'm dying to know."

I tugged on Cameron's hand for him to let me go and he glared back at me.

"I have a great idea," said Richard. "I'll have Dominic show her the dungeons. If you like the ones at Enthrall, you'll love these."

Cameron pulled me toward him. "You drive. Take Richard home. Talk. Open up." He looked over at Richard. "That goes for both of you."

I was grateful my way out loomed close.

Richard went to speak again.

"Shut the fuck up," snapped Cameron. "You're scaring her."

"Why else would she be here?" slurred Richard.

"I came to find you," I told him.

Richard looked surprised. "Please warn her off me."

Cameron glanced around us to check our conversation was still private. "Time to go home, buddy."

Richard rummaged in his jacket pocket and removed a valet ticket. "Think you can drive a jeep?"

"What about my car?" I said.

"I'll take care of it." Cameron lifted my chin with his fingertip. "We will discuss this tomorrow." His gaze swept over the crowd. "You will never talk to anyone about what you've seen here. You do not phone anyone. You do not text anyone. Am I clear?"

"Yes," I said.

Richard chuckled and ambled toward us barefoot, his shoes and socks in his left hand.

"Mia, if I find out you have told anyone about this house I will spank you," added Cameron with a glint of amusement. "With a paddle. Do. You. Understand?"

"I'd say *no* if I were you." Richard burst out laughing and grabbed me out of Cameron's grip. "You've been a very naughty girl. Maybe I'll spank you."

Cameron called after us. "Stop freaking her out. She's had enough scares tonight."

Richard cringed, mouthing my way, "Sorry."

For the first time I felt my shoulders ease lower, my heart soften, and my legs find their stride again. We made our way through the same door I'd come through with Cameron, down the long hallway, and past the Harrington Suite.

Richard paused before it to ease his socks back on and slid into shoes. He studied the door as he grabbed my hand again.

I tried to pull my hand out of his.

"Couldn't resist." He led me onwards down the hallway.

We soon neared the guard who'd accosted me earlier. Though he was too busy respectfully bowing towards Richard to notice me.

Within minutes the valet had brought Richard's Rubicon round. He jumped into the passenger side and I hoisted myself up into the driver's. With a quick adjustment of the seat and familiarizing myself with the dashboard, along with a tweak of the rearview, I had the car rolling away from the grand house and heading down the driveway.

"Yeah." Richard motioned toward the gear stick. "That low hum right there is the car's way of asking you politely to switch up gears."

"Sorry." I shifted it into second.

"More of scream, really," he mused. "Third would be good about now."

Within a minute or so I really felt I had the hang of it.

I sensed his stare.

The revelation that Richard might have instigated any part of what I'd stumbled upon here tonight stunned me into silence. I too stole glances his way, trying to believe this sweet young man would approve of any of it. His upper-class demeanor clashed with what Cameron had told me. He seemed so proper. They both did.

If Richard was impressed with the way I drove his car he didn't say. He merely rested his feet on the dashboard, taking in the view along the Pacific Coast Highway.

I was relieved when I parked the Rubicon in Richard's driveway, and from his wry smile I'd impressed him with my ability to get us back in one piece. He hopped out and trotted around to my side, opening the door wide and reaching for my waist, lifting me safely to the ground. He grabbed his jacket from the backseat and ambled toward the front door.

I had no way of getting home unless of course I borrowed one of his cars. Richard held the front door open for me, his furrowed brow revealing he too mulled over what to do with me.

Feeling a little lost, I followed him into the living room and onward into the kitchen. He knelt and patted Winston, and then topped up his water bowl.

State of the art appliances were all black including his oven, refrigerator, microwave and coffeemaker, offset only slightly by the central granite counter. There was so much room in here it seemed wasted on one man. Still, by the way he moved around he was comfortable here. He opened the fridge and took out two bottles of water and handed me one.

He screwed off the cap and handed me his and switched them out. He had this sexy way about him, as well as thinking of the other person, and it made me wonder if he'd ever been married. He was so dreamy to be around and I was so excited to be back here, alone with him at last.

"You'll sleep in my bed tonight," he said, taking a swig and then raising the bottle. "I'll take the couch."

Trying to show I didn't care about that decision, I took a sip of water.

Richard had this air of confidence that never let up, and I imagined him holding this very same look right before he took one of his daring leaps off a tall building, trusting in the parachute strapped to his back, or when he climbed a rock face without a safety harness.

"I drank too much. Didn't seem that anyone noticed though."

His gaze swept over me. "You look stunning. FYI, running around Chrysalis like that is ill-advised. You're likely to get caught up in all sorts of dangerous shenanigans." He shook his head as though his imagination provided a glimpse.

I was again reminded all I had on was this corset, stockings, suspender belt and thong.

"You were the most beautiful woman there," he said. "Do you have any idea how breathtaking you are?" He raised the bottle again. "I can blame the booze tomorrow and deny everything."

I broke his gaze and bit my lip.

"Now that," he raised the bottle my way, "just makes you look all the more beautiful." He smiled to himself. "Vulnerable."

I stared down at Winston, though he wasn't doing much, merely sniffing around his bowl.

Richard loosened his necktie, raising his chin to ease it off. "Not quite sure what you said to Cameron tonight. I've never seen him addled." He peered over at me. "What did you do to him?"

My face flushed as the memory returned of him holding me against the wall.

"You don't have to tell me," he said. "That's private between you both."

"Nothing," I said. "He found me and brought me to you."

"You'd aroused him, Mia." He arched an eyebrow. "We notice these things."

My face burned like fire.

"Or you can tell me?" he said.

"He talked to me."

"Did," he hesitated. "Did he kiss you?"

"No. He told me…"

"What?"

"I belong to you."

"Do you want to belong to me?"

"Yes." I focused on Winston.

"Can I kiss you?"

"Why not just kiss me?"

"Because you're my secretary." He placed his water on the counter and neared me. "You didn't answer."

"Thought I was your executive assistant."

"I demoted you after disobeying me tonight." He raised my chin with his thumb, the intensity of his gaze burning through me. His mouth found mine, his teeth nipping my bottom lip, his tongue tangling forcefully, masterfully, with mine. There came a thrill deep in my belly. He scrunched locks of my hair in his hands, his fingers caressing my scalp. His cologne reminded me of an ocean breeze, that and fresh linen, and his alluring scent made it easy to soften in his arms.

Those women in the pool had been flirting with him, their playful splashing an attempt to garner his attention, and yet Richard had ignored them, instead staring into the water and sipping his drink.

When he bit my lip I shuddered.

"Can I make love to you?" he whispered.

"Yes," I said. "But not in front of Winston."

"No, not in front of Winston." He took my hand and instead of leading me to the bedroom he led me out onto the patio, past the softly lit swimming pool and down to the end of the garden.

There, almost hidden from view, lay a stone pathway. We made our way along it, the sound of crashing waves louder now. In a tree shaded area overlooked by palms were two loungers. And though the ocean could not be seen from here the waves sounded close.

Richard pulled me into another kiss, his hands cupping my face. He unbuttoned his shirt and threw it down, his stare never leaving mine. Taking his time, he stroked my throat, then moved lower until reaching the top of my corset. That same finger traced the curve of my breasts. He eased down the left cup, his mouth taking my nipple, sucking hard, sending shockwaves of pleasure between my thighs. Weak from his affection, I reached out and grabbed hold of his forearms, trying not to tumble backward. He wrapped a strong arm around my waist and pulled me into him. His other hand moved to my other nipple, his insistent tongue encircling there now and sending out shivers of pleasure.

Gently he guided me back onto the nearest lounger so that I lay along it, and he eased down my panties, sliding them over my hips and quickly removing them. He threw them close to where his shirt lay. His kisses traveled softly, trailing lower, planting more on my inner thighs, his teeth nipping as he went…

Fearing I might scream with these unbound feelings, I bit my hand, knowing I was close to being taken.

When his tongue reached me, encircling there, I bucked in response. I threw my head back, blinded by pleasure, the sensations so overwhelming they tore a moan from me as his tongue possessed that most sacred part. I grabbed locks of his hair and tightened my fist against his scalp.

I refused to dwell on how well this man knew the female form, how well he knew the art of pleasuring, nudging me ever closer to the edge of bliss…

This was really happening.

His head bobbed between my thighs and his hands found my nipples again, pinching them with an expert touch. My orgasm erupted, stealing my breath, making me shudder against him. Then his never ending strokes sent me over again.

I was lost, forgotten, no longer here, these curling waves we couldn't see threatening to lap at our feet at any moment. Drown us, drown me, but I had already been swept off into the deep.

At last, opening my eyes, I stared beyond the low hanging branches at the few visible stars. Richard's kisses began the slow journey upwards, reaching my lips once more and kissing me ferociously, sharing my own taste upon my lips and tongue, sending shivers.

"You taste amazing," he whispered, nibbling my earlobe, sending erotic spasms into my body.

Mastering my mouth with his again, passion exploded within, forcing me into a spin. All I knew was him.

Then stillness.

He held me against him, cherished in the quiet with nothing but the sound of rustling palm leaves caught in the breeze and crashing waves. He rolled me onto my side and hugged me into him and we spooned together in the warmest embrace.

"Aren't we going to make love?" I whispered.

"Shush, my sweet Mia."

Safe in his arms, I drifted off.

When the softest morning light dared to find us, I felt Richard shift away and climb off the lounger. He sat on the edge, his bareback curled, his feet on the ground, his elbows resting on his knees, and he stayed like this for a while, deep in thought.

Richard turned slightly to glance back at me. "Hi."

"Hi." I reached out to caress his back, tracing my fingertips over the faintest white scars.

Tara had told me that Cameron had struck Richard until he'd bled. I wondered if these marks were from that. Had Richard really asked Cameron to hurt him in this way? More alarming, Cameron had appeased him by doing it.

Richard took my hand and kissed my palm. "Mia," his tone was solemn. "You know how fond of you I am."

"Fond?"

"I've fallen...I really like you."

I curled my fingers around his. "I feel the same way."

"Still." He stood up, his dark gaze once more resting upon me. "In all honesty, I don't want your first time to be with a man like me."

I sat up, trying to find the words to placate him.

He shrugged and ambled off toward the house.

CHAPTER TWENTY

I N THE LIGHT OF THE EARLY MORNING, WEARING A CORSET AND stockings felt odd.

Last night, back in my beach front condo, I'd felt like the ultimate vixen. Yet here, now, lying on Richard's lounger, alone, all my confidence dissipated. Regret lingered for daring to gatecrash Chrysalis's party and later, finding my way back here to be with the only man I'd ever loved, yet my virginity remained intact.

Fuckerty fuck, fuck, fuck, my inner musing sounded like Richard.

Maybe Richard was just being kind and in reality felt nothing. Perhaps I'd made everything up in my head about there being something special between us, having misread him. Naivety stood in the way of my happiness yet again.

Searching for and quickly finding my panties, I slipped them on, swept up my discarded strappy shoes, and began the trek up the pathway. Through the open sliding doorway I walked in, following the noise of a television.

I found Richard in his bachelor den. He sat on a chocolate colored couch, his legs out in front of him with his bare feet resting on the coffee table. He still wore his dress shirt from last night as well as boxer shorts, though not much else. He directed an X-box controller at a large flat screen TV. Coming round to face him, I was alarmed to see him wearing a scuba mask. The snorkel hung by his right ear. Winston sat beside him, panting.

"Lara Croft's kicking ass." Richard returned his attention to the screen, deftly moving the controller and making Lara Croft swim the full length of a dark blue lagoon.

"Why are you wearing that?" I said.

"They're prescription. Can't find my glasses." Richard peered down at Winston. "Go find my glasses, Winston. Fetch." They stared at each other. Winston panted away, his tail wagging. Richard looked back at me. "See what I'm up against?"

Upon a shelf to the left rested Super Bowl memorabilia, a New York Giants helmet right beside a football, both of them signed. This cozy room looked lived in and I wondered if Richard had his friends round on lazy Sunday afternoons to watch the game. I imagined them eating snacks and drinking beer in here and screaming at their favorite team. Richard had an aversion to normal so it was unlikely.

"Can I borrow a shirt?" I said.

He pointed right and I assumed it was his bedroom. I ambled out of there in hope of finding something to wear.

Richard's bed rested low to the ground and his bedroom was modestly decorated. The stunning photo of a Nepalese temple stretched the full length of the wall behind his bed. I hoped to find another clue to who this man really was, though from his office I knew he liked order. From his neatly lined shirts he liked it here too. Stripping out of my constricting corset, I borrowed one of his blue shirts and a pair of shorts. I rummaged around his dresser for a belt. This hobo chic look wasn't perfect but at least I could breathe now. I made my way back to Richard's den.

He was still engrossed in the game and his goggles were still on. Winston lay beside him, resting his head on his paws.

I sat on the closest arm of the couch. "Would you like to talk?"

"About what?"

"Last night."

He lowered his gaze and held mine.

Despite this sinking feeling in my gut, I continued, "Cameron told us to talk about things."

"Cameron has two methods. The first is to talk, the second..." Richard tilted his head. "I prefer the latter."

"You mean when he whips you?"

Richard dropped the controller into his lap. It was hard to take him seriously with that scuba mask on.

"Hungry?" he said. "There's cereal in the cupboard."

"I feel ready to talk."

Having stepped out of my comfort zone last night and right into the center of adulthood, I felt ready to face pretty much anything. Even him.

"That's the problem," said Richard, "you and I don't talk the same language."

"What's that meant to mean?"

"See, you have no idea what I just said."

"Why are you being like this with me?"

His brow furrowed. "I warned you to stay away."

I folded my arms. "Did you pay off my step-mother's medical bills?"

His hands tightened around the controller.

I moved into his line of sight, right in front of the TV. "Did you?"

"That's very immature."

"I'm not the one wearing a mask."

"You wait. Next year this will be all the rage and I'll take the credit for starting a dazzling new trend."

"Did you pay off my debt?"

"I pay you enough as it is." He shrugged.

"You did, didn't you?"

"Well, it sounds like you have enough money now to move back to Charlotte."

"Why do you push me away like this?"

"You're in my way." He gestured. "The TV that is."

"If you really hate me this much why seduce me in dark corners and kiss me, have me not be able to think straight?"

"Mia, I'm very likely going to ruin you," his voice softened. "Hurt you."

"I can look after myself."

He raised a finger. "If it makes you feel any better it wasn't an easy decision. I've wanted to kiss you since that first morning I met you and you blocked my way."

"Then why—"

"I'll damage you."

"Well at least we'll have something in common then," I said.

He frowned at me.

"Please don't fire me," I said.

"I'm not going to fire you."

"Lotte told me all about what it means to be a submissive. She says that only empowered women are able to give themselves over to a dom completely."

His gaze shot up to meet mine. "Wow. You really did take this talking thing seriously."

"You're scared of how amazing we can be together," I said. "Cameron—"

"Don't listen to him. He'll have you tied up in knots." He beamed a smile. "As well as tied up in other ways."

"Cameron cares about you."

"Lately he's been interfering in the worst kind of way."

"He's nudging us together." I wished Cameron was here right now to lend a hand dealing with Richard's mood.

"Have you heard of the Hadron Collider?" said Richard.

"I think so, yes. Why?"

"It's the world's largest and highest energy particle accelerator beneath the Franco-Swiss border near Geneva."

I vaguely remembered seeing something about it online.

He moved his fingers around in a circle. "The Hadron allows physicists to test their theories of particle physics."

"What are you saying?"

His fingers encircled. "That's you and that's me going round and around in the opposite direction very much like those protons threatening to crash into each other. Cameron's exactly like one of those mad nuclear scientists trying to figure out if: A) It's possible to collide opposing particle beams and B) To test the hypotheses that we might accidently self-destruct on impact and, oops, cause a black hole in the universe." He shook his head. "Black holes are bad. Trust me, I know. I've had one stuck in the middle of my chest for as long as I can remember."

"Maybe I can help?"

"Or maybe you'll get sucked in and we'll never see Mia ever again."

"You underestimate me."

"Actually, it's me you underestimate."

"We're talking," I said. "This is good, right?"

He arched an eyebrow. "Mia, don't take this the wrong way but I'd really love some alone time."

And with those words he'd shut me back out.

I wasn't going to let him push me away so easily, not without a fight.

"What happened to you?" I said.

Richard shook his head as though shaking off a slap. I'd struck a nerve.

"Cameron's re-wired your brain," I said. "When you came to L.A. because you needed a change, you met up with your old friend and he led you astray."

"Careful," said Richard, "you're talking about my best friend."

"You just told me he was interfering in the worst kind of way."

"Yes, but he's also the best thing about me."

"What is that meant to mean?" I shifted closer. "This stuff he's gotten you into, it's not right."

"Actually, it's nothing but right."

"Someone hurt you," I said. "They did this to you."

"Mia." He peered up at me through his goggles. "I'm made this way." He nodded to himself. "What happened to me came along after I became established in this lifestyle."

"What happened?"

"Life. The fuck you up royally, kind. Coming here and being with Cameron saved me."

"He wants you to think that."

"You know what Cameron taught me?" He shifted to better look at me. "The most important lesson a man can learn."

"Love?"

"Pain. Learn to harness it and you'll possess true power. That's the only way to truly be in this world."

"What about love?"

"Love is vulnerability. Love destroys. Love devours. Love is the lie we tell ourselves long enough to stay with someone until we procreate."

"I don't believe that." I stepped forward, my chest heaving. "Please take off those things."

"You're my secretary. Go type me up a letter or do whatever it is you do."

"It's seven o'clock on a Sunday morning." I peered at the garden. "What about last night?"

"What about it?"

My shoulders slumped and I felt even more miserable.

Richard frowned at me. "Only one person has ever earned the privilege of knowing me."

"Cameron?" My voice cracked with emotion.

"What the hell is Lara Croft doing now?" He waved the controller. "Even cyber women are annoying."

"That's why you like to beat women?"

He snapped his head round to look at me. "Never. I've never done anything like that to a woman."

"Then what is it you do to them?"

"I make just enough of a crack in their psyche for love to find its way through." He dropped the controller.

"You deserve that too."

"I'm a lost cause."

"I don't believe that."

He stared straight ahead. "I lied when I told you I have a black hole here." He rested his hand on his heart.

I waited for him to continue, scared of his words threatening never to reach me or perhaps it was the fact they would that tore me up.

"There is nothing here." He held my gaze. "I haven't felt an emotion in six years." He rested his head back. "Now does that sound like the kind of man you want to be with?"

Unsteady on my feet, I made my way to the front door, trying to remember where I'd left my keys. There came a sinking feeling when I remembered I'd left my car at the manor. I was stranded.

Next to where Richard left his car keys sat a stack of mail and right on top of the unopened envelopes was one from Cameron. His Venice Beach address was written in the top left hand corner. With shaking hands, I fumbled with the straps of my shoes and grabbed the keys to the Rubicon.

CHAPTER TWENTY-ONE

C AMERON'S WESTSIDE HOME SAT RIGHT ON THE FRONT OF
Venice Beach's boardwalk.

These eclectic properties were apparently worth millions despite their modest size. On the other side of Cameron's gray painted home lay a promenade lined with strolling tourists, vendors selling homemade wares, as well as artists, poets, and pot heads. The place buzzed with its own unique arty flavor.

I knocked several times on his front door.

After no answer, I tried the doorknob and to my astonishment it opened.

"Hello?" I stepped inside the slim entranceway, questioning Cameron's sense of security and hoping this really was his place.

The decor leaned toward an eerie sparseness. Brick walls with their numerous black and white prints gave a mere suggestion someone had tried to make the place homey. The minimalist theme of a couple of armchairs and a leather sofa gave an airy feel. Several barstools ran along a kitchen counter, though the open-plan kitchen itself looked bare. A fridge, a coffeemaker, and a flashy microwave were the only appliances. Tucked in the corner of the countertop was a full wine rack with two long stemmed glasses beside it.

Voices carried from upstairs. I moved in that direction, hoping I'd gotten the address right.

Beyond this sitting room lay a courtyard with patio furniture in the center. Tourists ambled along the pathway on the other side of that short wall and beyond that lay the beach. I wondered why anyone would want to be so close to so many strangers wandering by. Within the courtyard, resting up against a wooden fence, were two surfboards side by side. The first was a dark blue Billabong board and next to it rested a slightly shorter one with a mermaid fading away from years of use. A surreal moment came over me as I recognized it.

"Mia?"

I spun round to see Tara standing in a doorway. She wore a skinny bikini, her hair wet and tangled from what looked like a morning of surfing.

"Tara?" I said. "What are you doing here?"

Cameron appeared behind her. He'd wrapped a plush white towel around his waist, perhaps from having just taken a shower. He looked so different from the Cameron I'd seen last night, when he'd dressed in a tux and hosted his party, or more appropriately an evening of debauchery.

I felt like a criminal. "The door was open."

"Everything all right?" said Cameron.

"You're friends?" I said.

Which was ridiculous, with Tara standing there and with her having worked at Enthrall. She'd also spent time with Cameron at my house-warming. These two looked like they really knew each other.

"It's not what you think." Her frown deepened as she took in my clothes.

Richard's shirt and shorts looked odd on me, and from the way Cameron eyed me up he thought so too. I wondered if he could see I'd been crying.

The quiet made me feel awkward, and at the same time I felt upset for Bailey.

"We're just friends," said Tara, as though reading my mind. "I come down here to surf. That's all."

My gaze took in Cameron and his bare chest, his messed up hair, and his confident air that could stun a Stingray.

"Coffee?" He edged past me and sauntered into the kitchen.

Unable to grasp this terrible revelation, I turned away from her and faced Cameron, watching him place a filter in the machine. He opened a packet of coffee and poured the grounds into the filter. With a flick of a switch, he had the machine brewing.

"How's my best friend?" he said.

I managed a nod.

"Last night?" he said. "How did it go?"

"Good." I recalled Richard and I making out on that sun lounger beneath the trees. Even though we didn't go all the way it was still pretty dreamy.

Right up until our Hadron Collider crash this morning.

Cameron arranged three mugs on the countertop. "I'm delighted to see you of course, but usually what follows a night of romance is breakfast with your beau."

I neared the other side of the counter and sat on a barstool.

Tara stood right behind me. "I am going to tell her," she said. "We only surf together. Tell her Cameron."

He leaned on the counter. "Tara and I are only friends."

"Tara, she knows you come down here all the time," I said. "Why not mention him?"

"You know Bailey," she said. "She's so sensitive. She's never going to understand why I want to spend time with a man." Tara raised her hand. "We don't do anything. We surf. Hangout."

"Eat tacos," added Cameron. "We do that."

I stared at him to see if I could validate what she was telling me.

He merely gave a nod. "I didn't know you knew about this place?"

"Where's all your stuff?" I said.

"He doesn't live here," said Tara. "He lives at the manor."

"Sometimes," he added softly.

"Chrysalis?" I spun round to face her. "Have you been there too?"

"I'm Bailey's girlfriend but I'm not shackled to her."

I looked from her to Cameron.

"We just surf," said Cameron, pouring coffee into three mugs.

"I don't want his penis going anywhere near me," said Tara.

Cameron looked amused and paused mid-pour. "I'll have you know there are many women who are rather partial to my penis."

Tara curled her lips into a smile. She grabbed one of the mugs and wrapped her hands around it. "I didn't want Bailey to give me an ultimatum and tell me it's surfing with Cameron or her."

"Maybe Bailey would want to come with you?" I said.

Tara shrugged. "Maybe."

I took the mug offered by Cameron.

He took a sip from his. "Mia, let's talk about why you're here. Not that I'm not thrilled to see you. Last night I placed you in the hands of Malibu's most eligible bachelor and right now I'm wondering why you're at my breakfast bar and not his."

My eyes stung with tears.

"Tara," said Cameron. "Go take a shower."

"What happened?" she said.

Cameron frowned at her. "Please."

Tara folded her arms.

He waved her off.

Tara turned and made her way out. Cameron's gaze followed her until she was out of sight and his intense stare slid back to me.

"Richard seemed upset this morning," I said.

Cameron came around to my side and sat on the barstool opposite. "I'm sorry to hear that."

"What did you do to him?" I said, still haunted by what Tara had told me about Cameron whipping Richard until he bled.

"Can you be more specific?"

I sucked in a sob. "You re-wired his brain."

He frowned at me.

I felt self-conscious that Tara may hear. "Richard told me he doesn't feel any emotions. At all."

"Ah." Cameron slid his mug to the side.

"I think you might have beaten all the life out of him." I braced myself for his reaction.

"That's why you've been crying?" he said calmly. "You had an argument with him?"

"A discussion. He told me what kind of hold you have on him."

"He used those words?"

"No, he made it sound like you're friends."

"We are friends, Mia. We know each other very well. I'd never hurt him."

"Did you beat him until he bled?"

Cameron reached for his mug.

Tara reappeared and made her way toward us. She'd not taken that shower. She sat on the barstool beside mine and said, "I told you that in confidence."

Cameron rolled his eyes at her.

"So you admit it?" I snapped at him.

"Don't you have milk in your coffee?" he said.

"What?" I shook myself out of my revelatory trance.

Cameron rose and rounded the counter, opening the fridge and removing a carton of skimmed milk. It seemed pretty empty in there other than that. He poured it into my drink. I hated him for dragging out this tension. His way of hoping to wriggle out of his guilt, no doubt.

"Tell her, Cameron," said Tara.

He raised his hand. "I'm handling this."

"No, I won't have her accuse you of this," she said. "When Richard came to L.A. he was drowning in grief—"

"Tara." Cameron pointed to the door. "Now."

She glared at me. "You don't know anything. You're putting pieces of the puzzle together and getting it all wrong."

"Of course I could always sling you over my shoulder, Tara," he said. "And carry you out."

Cameron and I were alone again.

His voice sounded calm, controlled. "Firstly, I never divulge personal information about clients, friends, or acquaintances. In fact, this conversation we're having now is private. What I will tell you is Richard and I are very close. We have a great deal of love and respect—"

"He told me he's not capable of love." I swiped away at my tears. "He told me he's dead inside."

"What else did he tell you?"

"Nothing. Why won't he talk to me?"

"I'd feel more comfortable discussing this with him present."

"Why did Lotte warn me not to talk to you?" I pointed an accusatory finger his way.

He looked surprised. "Those were her exact words?"

Again he'd wanted me to clarify. I wondered if this was how he manipulated his submissives.

I quickly added, "She warned me not to engage with you."

He gave a thin smile. "I'm the director of Chrysalis. As you've discovered. Maybe that's why."

That tuft of dark hair on his bare chest, along with that chiseled musculature of his torso, were a visceral reminder that this man oozed sexuality in the most alluring way. His heady cologne did nothing to ease this moment.

His body pressing me against the wall and stirring forbidden desires that had lain dormant. A dark craving erupting.

The way he stared at me now. His gaze moving to my mouth and lingering. The way he shook his head as though trying to shake off a thought.

The way he made me feel when I was around him.

Cameron lowered his gaze. "What happened between us last night was a failing on my part." He shrugged. "Though, as you're here I'm hoping it means you've forgiven me."

"Nothing happened."

He caressed the tension out of his brow. "Perhaps it is best we remember it that way."

"Please tell me why Richard's so hard to get through to." I wiped my tears with my sleeve, *his sleeve.*

"What's going on with you?"

"I don't know. I've become so anxious lately," I admitted. "I can't eat. I'm having trouble sleeping. Being around Richard makes me nervous."

Cameron pursed his lips, his expression full of sympathy. "I see." He reached over and took my hands in his. "I. Would. Never. Hurt. Richard. I would never do anything to him that he didn't really want me to do to him."

"Did he really want you to whip him that hard?"

"That's not my style."

"Then who did that to him?"

"Mia," his tone was soft and strangely comforting.

"Well he didn't do that to himself!"

He let go of my hands and broke my gaze.

He did that to himself?

Stunned, I tried to read the truth in Cameron's face and find the answers. Everyone around me seemed to know what was going on with Richard except me. Even Tara. Despite being near the ocean there hung a heaviness in the air, an invisible fog sucking up all the oxygen.

Cameron peered toward the passing tourists. "When this becomes too much I return to the hills and lose myself in the manor." He took a sip.

I slumped back onto the barstool.

"Hungry?" he said. "Want a bagel?"

"No, thank you."

"So, how did you leave Richard?"

"He was playing Tomb Raider," I said. "While wearing that ridiculous scuba mask."

Cameron's mug hit the counter and coffee splashed.

Tara reappeared. "Can I come out of hiding now?"

I ignored her and turned to Cameron. "What's wrong?"

He headed off across the room. "I'll get dressed. I'm taking you back." He stopped by the door. "Did you happen to see an oxygen tank?"

"No." I swapped a wary glance with Tara. "Why?"

"Just wondering." Cameron disappeared.

Tara sat beside me.

I thought back to my housewarming party and couldn't remember seeing anything unusual about the interaction between these two that night. Though to be honest I'd not been looking for it.

"I'll speak to Bailey," said Tara. "Please don't say anything to her."

I gave a reluctant nod.

"Your eye make-up is really heavy," she said.

Having not had the chance to remove it, I probably looked like a panda. How embarrassing. Having cried all the way here, I'd made it worse. Cameron didn't need his psychological skills to work out I was a mess.

"Did you go to the party last night?" said Tara.

"Yes."

"Really? How was it?"

My face blanched with embarrassment.

"Apparently they serve great food," she said. "Did you check out the spanking room?"

I frowned at her, wondering how she knew there was even such a thing.

"Did you see anything?" she said. "Anyone doing it?"

I took a sip of coffee.

Cameron reappeared wearing jeans and a white shirt. He grabbed his car keys and threw me a smile. "Let's go visit our friend." He waved at Tara. "See you later."

"Later," she called after him and threw me a wave goodbye.

I waved back and trotted behind Cameron. "He's not likely to try something dangerous is he?" I couldn't work out why I felt like it had been me that pushed him away. "Should I have stayed?"

"Don't ever second guess yourself," said Cameron, as he led me out on the street.

He opened his Porches' passenger car door.

I climbed in, sinking into the leather seat, the irony not lost that we were leaving behind the Rubicon. Cameron drove fast, dodging pedestrians and other cars that were driving too slow for a Sunday morning. We sped along the Pacific Coast Highway and he made small talk, gesturing to points of interest and doing anything, it seemed, to not bring up why we were heading back to Richard's so fast.

In less than twenty minutes we'd arrived.

Cameron turned off the engine and twisted in his seat to face me. "Let me talk to him."

I rubbed my fingertips over my lips nervously.

He tugged on my shirtsleeve. "This is his?"

I gave a nod.

"What happened last night?" Cameron peered over at Richard's front door.

"We cuddled under the stars." I shrugged. "Nothing really happened. Well we kissed. And stuff. In the morning he told me…"

He waited for me to continue.

"He didn't want my first time to be with someone like him," I whispered it.

Cameron sighed. "It's not you, Mia."

"I feel like I've done something wrong."

"No," he said. "He's terrified he might hurt you."

"I told him we could take it slow."

Cameron looked straight ahead. "He opened up about his lifestyle?"

"Yes."

"What did he say?"

"He can only have a relationship with someone willing to be his submissive." The words sounded scratchy coming out.

"Did you give his offer any consideration?"

"Kind of. Only he mentioned only taking on a sub who is already trained." I gave him a sideways glance.

"Ah."

"I do want to be with him. I'm not sure I can handle the pain bit though."

"Pain enhances pleasure."

I nibbled on a fingernail.

Cameron removed the keys. "Have you guys talked about what you both want from a relationship?"

"Um, no."

"S & M scares you?"

I studied his window wipers; even they looked expensive.

"Richard sensed your doubt," he said.

I let out a long sigh.

Cameron gave a nod of understanding. "Richard's worldly. He's well-travelled. He went backpacking alone around the far east when he was twenty. Richard's smart, funny, and kind. He could really be good for you. Teach you so much."

I raised an eyebrow.

"Exactly," he said. "It's not just about great sex."

My mind drifted into Richard's home, recalling those carved pieces of furniture he may have bought during his travels. As well as his walls spotted here and there with framed photos of happy foreigners, offering glimpses into their culture. I wondered at what age Richard decided he liked pain.

"What happened to you?" I said. "What was your childhood trauma?" I even amazed myself with that one. "You know, why are you a—"

He raised his hand. "I prefer to think of myself as a connoisseur of the dark arts." He broke into a smile, reacting to my train of thought. "Actually I had a very privileged childhood. I grew up in the Hamptons. My father designed boats. I was spoiled. Maybe that has something to do with it. Anyway, I attended private school and later studied medicine. See, all very normal."

"What made you leave psychiatry?"

"I never left. I have a practice."

"When do you get time to run Chrysalis?"

"I make time."

"During my interview, was Penny texting you?"

"Yes. She's my secretary at Chrysalis." He shifted in his seat. "That was my way of sitting in on your interview. I had a hectic day."

"Not an exact science."

"Yes, but look at us now," he said with amusement. "We're all bonding nicely."

"Did you hire the Mistresses?"

"Lotte and I built up Enthrall and out of that Chrysalis evolved. I took over the society that had been around for a century." Cameron ran his thumb over his key fob.

It was my turn to stare and try to read the answers from him. I wanted to know more about Chrysalis's history.

"We have a club in London," he said. "And Paris."

"You run them all?"

"I oversee the foreign houses as well, yes."

"Busy man."

He gave a crooked smile. "Richard's very stable."

"I need to know what happened to his last submissive."

He rubbed the tiredness out of his eyes. "Shall we go in?"

We exited the car and I followed Cameron to Richard's front door. He used a key on his fob to open it. Apparently he had a copy of Richard's house key.

Cameron scoured the house, calling for him.

Within a few minutes of not finding Richard anywhere, I joined Cameron beside the pool. He stood there peering down at the water with his arms folded. On the other side of the pool sat Winston, panting away in his usual unfazed self. I questioned his ability to serve as a guard dog.

Cameron's gaze swept the pool.

A scream tore from me.

Underwater in the left hand corner of the pool was the blur of a body resting on the bottom. With my heart in my throat I dived in, hitting the water with force, half hearing—

Cameron shouting, "He has a tank."

CHAPTER TWENTY-TWO

RICHARD STOOD ON THE EDGE OF THE POOL.

Hands shaking, I wondered if my heart was ever going to slow. Although all was well now, my adrenaline hadn't gotten the message and still surged through my veins, causing my legs to wobble. My wet hair clung to my head, my clothes were soaked and clinging, but I didn't care.

Richard looked unshaken. As did Cameron, who seemed to have seen this kind of behavior before from his restrained reaction. He raised the scuba mask over Richard's face and rested it on his forehead.

Water dripped off Richard and formed a puddle around his feet. "What?" he said, giving a mischievous smirk. "Am I the only one who thinks better submerged?"

"I'm going to answer *yes* on that one," said Cameron, and he stepped on Richard's left fin to help him ease his foot out then did the same with the right. "What were you thinking about down there?"

"Mia," murmured Richard.

Cameron gave a triumphant smile.

Richard broke into that boyishness of his. "Can I have my jeep back?"

I looked over at Cameron.

"Something tells me Mia's about to fall in love with my pancakes," said Cameron. "How about," he brushed sopping locks of hair out of Richard's eyes, "you go take a shower and we'll go prepare breakfast?"

Richard looked so young standing there next to Cameron. He blinked his answer and ambled barefoot around the pool.

"Hey," Cameron called after him.

Richard turned to face us.

"Aren't we forgetting something?" said Cameron.

Richard's stare settled on me. "I'm sorry if I scared you. I'm also sorry about this morning."

My gaze returned to the deep corner of the pool. Richard lowered his snorkel over his face again and beamed at us both. He ambled off.

Cameron patted his leg. "Winston."

Winston trotted past us and into the house.

"The first time I found him underwater I screamed too," said Cameron. "Like a girl."

"Does he do it a lot?"

"Only when he's close to a breakthrough."

"With what?"

Cameron wrapped his arm around me and guided me into the house. "With you of course."

My heart missed a beat right there.

There was a chasm a mile wide between Richard and I, and only Cameron had crossed it. He guided me into the guest bedroom and beyond that into the bathroom.

"I'll start breakfast." He stepped into the shower and turned on the water faucet. "I'll get you a shirt and whatever else I can find that'll work."

It didn't take me long to shower and dress in the shirt and shorts Cameron had retrieved from Richard's bedroom. I liked the idea they'd have time to talk.

Inside the kitchen it was fun to watch Cameron open the cupboard doors with the ease of someone who knew his way around. He set about making the batter and preparing a hot pan for the pancakes.

With Cameron's guidance I found the plates and cutlery and laid the table.

All of this seemed so ordinary, a far cry from last night when these men had been entertaining Hollywood's elite clientele in the epi-center of L.A.'s fetish community. I couldn't make out what was more surreal, Cameron, the director of Chrysalis, frying batter on a stove or Richard, now wearing jeans and a blue t-shirt, wandering around his house followed by a British bulldog.

"Taste." Cameron held out a bite of golden fluffy pancake on a fork.

I smacked my lips together; the deliciousness was a welcome sur-prise. "That's good."

This man knew how to cook. He went about dishing up his mas-terpiece for us onto three plates. Richard joined us.

I walked my plate over to the kitchen table and sat beside Cameron, who poured English breakfast tea into three fine china mugs. After using the syrup, I handed it to Richard and he squeezed copious amounts of thick, sweet sauce over his pancakes. He still seemed subdued but now and again broke into a grin.

"He's different at home, isn't he?" said Cameron, turning to look at Richard. "He's still moody but with a hint of charming."

Richard used his fork to point at Cameron. "And you're a bossy bastard no matter where you are."

"True," agreed Cameron. "It's not easy always being right."

Richard rolled his eyes and took a syrup soaked bite of pancake.

"How did you two meet?" Of course I knew they'd met at Harvard but wasn't sure how.

"An ex-girlfriend of mine introduced us," said Cameron. "Her roommate complained her boyfriend Richard was into some kinky stuff and they came to me for advice."

"What did you tell her?" I said.

"I didn't," said Cameron. "I found Richard and advised him about their concerns." He shrugged. "It may look like a big campus but word can spread overnight."

"What did you think of that?" I asked Richard. "I mean this guy turns up out of nowhere and starts talking about your private life?"

"I asked him what club he went to." said Richard. "Dumped the girl and joined the club."

I sat back. "And then you moved to New York?" I pointed to Richard. "And you moved to California." I peered over at Cameron.

"Worst years of my life being separated from my buddy," said Richard.

"They were actually my best," joked Cameron.

"He's the best chef I know." Richard took another a bite. "Amongst other things. This is good."

Cameron crinkled his face into a smile.

There was something comforting about their friendship, yet at the same time it was hard to understand the dynamics. My mind wandered with thoughts of what kind of things they got up to together down in that dungeon without it being considered same-play, their desire for non-sexual domination and submission impossible to grasp.

I didn't feel ready for that conversation.

Richard pushed his half eaten plate aside. "I found New York suffocating and followed him here." He gestured to Cameron. "He persuaded me to come on board full-time at Enthrall."

"My second in command," said Cameron. "Rules with an iron fist."

"Hardly," said Richard. "Still, I've never been happier."

Cameron's face lit up.

"I know those photos on your wall are of you," I said to Richard.

"There's something very therapeutic about facing off with fear," he said. "Challenging life back."

"Isn't life hard enough?" I said.

"So jaded and oh so young," said Richard playfully.

I liked this tingle curling in my chest when his held my gaze, these sparks of excitement.

"Mr. Booth, something tells me you fancy your secretary?" said Cameron in a flawless English Cockney accent.

"You might be right, sir," said Richard, matching his accent and shaking his head in amusement.

Cameron turned his laser sharp attention back on me. "We're all friends here, right?" his voice back to normal. "We can talk frankly?"

I gave another nod as did Richard.

Cameron sat back. "I've never seen you so in love with a woman, Booth."

This felt like some kind of private counseling session and I suppose in many ways it was. *Never so in love*; could these words of his carry the truth my heart pined to hear.

"Mia?" said Cameron.

"Yes."

"Well?" Cameron cupped his hand near his ear.

"Go steady on her," said Richard.

"Like hiding underwater, steady?" Cameron frowned. "Mia, you've met the man of your dreams."

"Have you ever been in love?" said Richard.

"Um, I don't think so," I said.

"That's a *no* then," said Cameron. "And for the record that's what you're feeling."

Had my stomach not felt overfull it would have done a flip, yet I'd hardly eaten.

"People go around in a state of emotional flat line," said Cameron. "Have you noticed?"

"You know the zombie metaphor is surprisingly accurate," said Richard. "Have you ever walked around a store and really looked at people. They're all in some kind of trance. I refuse to live like that."

"We live in the moment," said Cameron.

"Consciously aware," added Richard.

Cameron gave a nod. "And we choose to experience the pain that lies here." He rested his hand on his heart. "And externalize it."

"Pain also turns us on," said Richard. "It's the way we're made."

"So you feel pain but no other emotions?" I asked Richard.

"They appear to be returning," he said, throwing a crooked smile at Cameron.

"You're ready," Cameron whispered to him.

There it came again. That long stare between them. That silent way they spoke without words. That mutual nod revealing they'd shared their thoughts.

"Mia," said Richard softly. "You'll make the most exquisite submissive."

A thrill shot up my spine.

Cameron reached into his shirt pocket. "I have a prescription for you both." He held up the piece of paper for me to read.

Richard took the note. "Planetarium?"

"It's where I'm taking you now," said Cameron. "I know exactly what's ailing you both. And I know the cure."

CHAPTER TWENTY-THREE

WITHIN GRIFFITH'S OBSERVATORY PLANETARIUM, LYING on a Burberry blanket that Richard had borrowed from Cameron's car, we stared up at the three dimensional display of swirling planets.

Cameron had not only made this happen, he'd used his contacts here at the observatory to secure us a private viewing, arranging for Richard and I to have the place to ourselves. Right behind us were row upon row of plush seats, and all of them were able to recline to enable a good view of the planetary display on the ceiling. The show that Richard and I were currently enjoying from our vantage point on the floor, smack bang in the middle of the room. Wagner, according to Richard, was the classical music playing in the background as we witnessed the dramatic intergalactic dance on the curved screen above.

Richard pointed to the planets. "Saturn, Jupiter, and of course Venus." He beamed when he saw that one.

"What's that one?" I pointed.

"Pluto, demoted to a dwarf planet," he said. "Scientists argued it didn't dominate the neighborhood around its orbit enough."

I giggled.

"Dirty mind," he said with a smirk.

The breathtaking display above of twirling planets made me feel so small compared to the lush earth with its vivid blues and greens.

"How did Cameron pull this off?" I said.

"He has some of the most influential contacts in the world. Our members include politicians, celebrities, and we even have a member who's an astronaut."

"Seriously?"

"You'd be surprised." He moved in closer and wrapped his arm around me. "Research has proven the higher the IQ the more likely the individual will be drawn to our lifestyle." He raised himself up onto one elbow. Resting his head upon his other hand, his gaze locked on mine. "I want to make you happy. Make you feel safe."

"You do. I am. This is perfect."

"You're so breathtakingly beautiful, Mia. Inside and out. Once I get over this feeling I don't deserve you..."

"Oh Richard, can't you see how much I love you?"

"I don't remember having loved like this. Whatever's going on inside my heart is like nothing I've ever experienced before. It's terrifying. Trust me, I face off with fear all the time but this, this is different. Feels different." He took in a deep cleansing breath. "Feel."

Snuggling into his chest, I breathed Richard in, yearning for him despite our closeness.

"Humans are made from the stars," he whispered. "Did you know that? I truly believe that you and I come from the exact same star. That star split off a millennia ago into a thousand pieces and yet we've found each other by some remarkable twist of fate. That's why it's only now, after reuniting with you all these centuries later, that I feel whole again."

"Home," I said. "I feel like I've come home for the very first time."

He planted kiss upon kiss on my forehead. "I'll protect you. Love you. Die for you."

Looking into his ocean blue eyes, I held his gaze. "Then we'll die together."

"Not sure Cameron would approve," he said with a smile.

"We do have him to thank for this."

"He knows me better than I know myself," he said. "He's certainly making up for his rascally behavior."

"Is rascally really a word?" I said.

"It really is. I know this for a fact because it's not the first time I've called him it." He brushed a stray hair out of my eyes.

"I'm going with dastardly."

"See." He rested a fingertip between my eyes. "A higher vocabulary indicates a higher intellect, which in turns leans towards," he lowered his gaze, "BDSM."

"Don't jump off anymore high buildings, okay? Or climb without a safety harness."

"Bossing me around already." He took my hand in his and rested it over his solar plexus. Although he didn't say the words, I knew his meaning.

I caressed his cheek with the back of my curled hand. "Doctor's orders." My legs felt like jelly.

"Better get on with it then," he said.

In a flurry of activity, we undressed each other, all arms and legs, shirts and pants flying around us.

Richard reached for his discarded jeans, his hand disappearing into the back pocket. He held up a condom packet with mock discovery. "Ah-ha."

He made me smile.

"I love you, Mia."

Richard's nakedness took my breath away. His chiseled torso and his tanned skin glowed beneath these swirling lights, easily earning him Adonis status. His beauty was too much. My gaze drifted up at the solar system with its preordained orbiting motion, its hypnotic never-ending rhythm. These planets were not the only ones influenced by a gravitational pull.

Braving to look again at this perfect man, impossible to resist, I reached for him.

He watched with a fascination. "This may be one of my fantasies."

"Really?" I said, gripping his erection with both hands and moving them up and down. His cock rose majestically out of glorious blond curls, hard and long, and very thick. "Maybe it's one of mine too?"

"Really," he echoed, "and what else do you fantasize about?"

"Doing this." Kneeling before him, leaning low, I ran my tongue along the full length of him. I caressed with both hands while my tongue lapped along delicate veins.

His head fell back and he let out the softest sigh.

Sucking his fullness, filling my mouth with him, I felt him twitching with pleasure.

His top lip curled. "I like this fantasy of yours, I have to say."

Running the tip of my tongue over the head, I dipped into that dewy bead to taste him, relish him. I desperately needed to know how he'd feel inside me, down there, in the channel that rippled with yearning. Covering my teeth with my lips, I took in all of him, working his full length from base to tip, relaxing my throat to take him in all the way, even as his cock demanded to go farther. He gripped my scalp and fisted locks of my hair, controlling the pace, controlling me, and I let out the deepest sigh of gratitude.

Moaning, he thrust deeper. "Yes, Mia, like that."

Lost in this sea of passion, sucking him deeper, I wanted to tell him how complete this made me feel. How perfect it felt to have him inside my mouth, lavishing him with all the pleasure and love he deserved.

"I've waited long enough," he said, shifting away and reaching beneath the arch of my back, sweeping me toward him as his smile fell upon my throat, his lips gliding up to my earlobe and nipping, sending spasms of pleasure down into my belly and farther still. My heartbeat quickened, my breaths came faster. I surrendered, wanting nothing more than this.

He reached for my nipples, tweaking them hard with his steady fingers. Leaning in, he lapped at the pertness, suckling, elongating the bud with his expert mouth, causing my deep throated moans to echo. Moving over my other breast, he took his time, licking, nipping, causing me to shudder. His right hand lowered between my legs and cupped there between my shaking thighs, sending a shockwave of pleasure through me as he ran a fingertip along my cleft.

"You're wet for me," he said, nudging me to lay on my back.

Planting kiss upon kiss down my abdomen, rimming my navel with his tongue, his mouth darted downward. It reached my inner thighs, teasing me with his flitting tongue, threatening at any moment he'd wander farther.

Like he did now.

A groan escaped me, a cry of pleasure, then I snapped into silence as he stole my voice, my breath, my reason. Sending shivers through me, he stunned my clit with blissful circles, spearing into me, bringing me so close to my release.

"I'll tell you when you can come," he said firmly.

"Oh," I moaned. "Please."

"I can see I'm going to have to take you through orgasm training." He nibbled my clit.

My protracted moan gave my answer.

There came the rip of a condom and then he eased it on, unraveling it over his pulsing head.

"Please," I said. "Richard."

Just the sight of him, the suspense of knowing my time was imminent, sent tingles into my body, causing me to weaken, my thighs shuddering.

He raised me up and I straddled him, my thighs on either side of his legs. "We'll take it slow, baby," he whispered. "This will be easier for you." Grinding against him, I stroked my clit against his hardness, stunned by this delicious throbbing, these tingles in my tender sex. Leaning back, I gazed upwards. Secure in his arms, I felt his mouth capture a nipple again as I took in the stars moving as languidly as we were below.

"We come from the same star," I whispered.

"We do," he said, nipping at a hardened nipple.

"I need you."

He flipped me onto my back, snatching my breath away, and his hand guided my head to rest upon the blanket. Richard's full weight came over me and I wrapped my legs around his waist, taking short unsteady breaths. His lips fell upon mine again, his kiss widening my mouth, his tongue possessing me, sending shivers throughout my body. I tasted myself, his kiss sharing that sweetness and making me quiver.

My back arched when he entered me, easing inside, stretching me wide, bringing a mixture of pain and pleasure and blinding me. He thrust deep, unrelenting, his cock giving me the discipline I deserved, had yearned for the first time I'd laid eyes on him. The impossible dream of having him inside me realized.

Orbs of light flashed above but I was not really seeing them. I was too distracted by the tightness down there mingled with stunning sensations of being taken for the first time.

Richard stilled. "How are you doing?"

Breathlessly, I blinked away. "Oh, amazing."

He moved his hips in a circle.

"Oh." My fingernails dug farther into his back. "Oh...yes...don't stop. Not ever. Like never."

He smiled. "How's the view?"

I stared into his eyes. "Spectacular."

He gave a heart stopping smile.

His thrusts quickened, rewarding me, bringing me closer, threatening to throw me over the edge as his rhythm increased, relentlessly mastering my body. Digging my fingernails deeper into his flesh, I clawed my way closer and closer...

Freefalling. Tumbling beneath the planets, rolling under the stars.

"Mia," he whispered. "You may come."

Lost in a sea of pleasure, I was gone, dazzled beneath him, desire coursing through my veins. I was caught up, captured by this intoxicating mixture of danger and passion as I cried out, my orgasm exploding. I was stunned by this blinding pleasure. He bucked into me, stiffened, and then stilled.

Both of us were stolen by this moment. Stolen by each other.

CHAPTER TWENTY-FOUR

N ESTLED ON A HILL IN HACIENDA HEIGHTS IS A BUDDHIST monastery called His Lai Temple. It's where Richard brought me the very next morning.

I couldn't remember ever being happier. All I needed was to be with him.

Standing halfway up a stone stairway that led into the temple, Richard pulled me into a hug, planting kiss upon kiss on my head. I marveled at how much affection one man could give a woman. Wrapping my arms around him and snuggling into his chest, I breathed him in, breathed in the peace I'd yearned for all my life. Being with him here, like this, was better than I could have ever imagined and more than I would ever have dared dream for.

Last night in the planetarium Richard had bestowed nothing but tenderness, and those memories drew me back. I'd fallen head over heels with my mercurial lover. Peering up at Richard now, I wanted him to know how much it meant that he'd shared this place with me, knowing how important it was to him. He'd told me on the way here that this temple provided an extraordinary sanctuary. It was his all time favorite place. I couldn't wait to see it.

"You're proof of God," he said.

"You are." Taking Richard's hand, I brought it to my lips and kissed it.

"Thank you for coming with me."

We strolled up the main stairway, making our way into the grand entrance. Up high, resting along the back wall, sat three Buddha statues gazing down upon us, emanating serenity. A few other people mingled here and there chatting quietly. Richard's face softened as his gaze settled upon two Tibetan monks, their orange robes pristine, their voices low. They moved serenely, kneeling before the three Buddha's and each offering a bowl of fruit. They set them before their deity's feet.

I'd already seen evidence of Richard's interest in eastern religion from the elements he'd brought into Enthrall as well as his home. These unfolding moments felt like a gift.

Right in front of us in the center, resting upon a table, were two jars standing side-by-side, each filled with small blue plastic balls. Richard dropped two dollars through the top of the plastic box between them and removed one of them. He gestured for me to do the same.

"Inside each one is a sacred message," he said, resting it within his palm. He carried the ball over to a wooden crusher and smashed it open. Inside lay a tiny scroll which he unraveled and read. "Turns out I need to bend like a reed. What does yours say?"

It felt sad to crush the cute little ball. Have it join all those other pieces of plastic that had gone before it. Shards of blue lay discarded on the bottom.

Richard took mine from me and crushed it beneath the wooden lid. "May I?" He peeled open the cracked ball and read the message on the tiny scroll.

I tried to peek.

Richard brought his hand to his mouth, suppressing his laughter. His eyes lit up and crinkled with joy.

"What does it say?" I failed to ease it back out of his hand.

Richard laughed hysterically. "Mia, this is in Cantonese. You took it out of the wrong jar."

I burst out laughing, seeing how ridiculous that was.

"We'll keep it safe." He tucked it into his coat pocket. "There's something alluring about a mystery."

"You're a mystery."

He smiled coyly, took my hand in his as he led us down a well lit hallway.

We stepped out of the first temple only to be greeted by a sweeping stone courtyard. Up ahead stood yet another temple, only this one was larger than the first, it's design intricate. The dramatic, highly decorated tiled roof swept wide above it. It felt like we'd traveled to Asia. The fall breeze rustled leaves around us. Another monk strolled past. A few other visitors ambled by.

There, to our right, stood a fountain surrounded with even more statues and all of their expressions serene. The soothing sound of the falling water filled the courtyard. We made our way up the sweeping stairway, soon reaching the second temple.

Following Richard's lead, I took one of sticks of incense stored in a jar and we made our way over to the open candle flame to light them. Carried on a wisp of white smoke came the scent of jasmine. I closed my eyes and breathed it in.

"Say a prayer," said Richard.

"A wish."

That he'd open up to me and let me in. Give us the chance we needed for our relationship to stand any chance of surviving.

He broke my gaze.

Inside the shrine we were greeted by three more Buddha statues, only these were much grander. Reverently, we knelt upon the plush red cushions and admired the grand, golden gods.

"We're not worshiping them," whispered Richard, gesturing toward them. "These symbols are merely used to help us focus our minds, stir devotion, and elicit gratitude."

Soaking in their peace, grateful for these moments of quiet, I marveled at the kaleidoscope of Richard's life and his ability to stretch across the spectrum of human experience including extremes of pain, pleasure, and, more surprising, spirituality.

The scent of incense. The hushed silence. The reverence of others.

There were thousands of tiny perfectly aligned Buddhas set inside small alcoves in the surrounding walls, each with a personalized plaque beneath, and I wondered if they represented loved ones who'd died. We knelt for some time, my hand in his, our incense held out before us, sharing the sacredness.

Richard gestured he'd found comfort here. I had too.

We placed our still burning incense sticks just outside the shrine in what looked like a miniature black temple. Gently, we set them side by side and upright in the center of the sand. Smoke wafted along with the promise our prayers would be heard. We made our way over to the temple tea and souvenir shop where Richard found us a private corner table. We nursed our china cups of tea and continued to savor the peacefulness. Richard's shoulders were relaxed and for the first time I sensed his calmness. This place made it easy to welcome the tranquility in. Soothing lost souls who came to find refuge. It's non-judgmental aura comforted.

"Cameron brought me here three days after I arrived in L.A." Richard's gaze swept the room as though remembering.

Wrapping my fingers around my cup, warming them, I sipped my tea, refreshed by its delicate flavor.

"I have a confession," said Richard softly.

"Oh."

"My last name isn't Booth."

"You changed it?"

He offered a look of sympathy and it made me shift in my seat.

"My real name is Richard Booth Sheppard."

My mind raced with all the reasons he might have changed it, and it was hard to settle on one. Having Googled him it made sense why I'd found nothing.

"About six years ago," he said, "I was a successful stockbroker living in Manhattan. I loved my job. Loved my life. I had it all, or so I thought." He broke my gaze, taking a moment. "I worked for my father. He'd always been a whiz with numbers. He was renowned as the master when it came to finance. By the time I was twenty my father had amassed an enormous fortune. I'm talking billions." Richard paused, his expression pained. "Everyone, including my two older brothers, worshipped him. Of course what we didn't know was my father had masterminded the most elaborate insider trading scheme the financial world had ever seen."

I placed my cup on the table.

He took a sip from his. "You know what insider trading is?"

"I think so."

"Employees divulge secrets about their company. Non-public information that would greatly benefit those exploring the buying or selling of a security. Stocks, bonds, that kind of thing. The investor therefore has an advantage over other investors. When a share falls, you buy it. Lots of them. I'm talking millions of them. You can only juggle the pieces of the puzzle for so long until the single fact cannot be denied: the money's being manipulated, as are employees, along with the financial market."

I felt terrible for him. I could only imagine the shame of having a father hurt so many people.

Richard swallowed hard. "As soon as I'd heard my father had been arrested, I drove over to the city jail to see what our lawyers could do. My father was held without bail. I was permitted a few minutes with him." Richard rubbed his chest as though the pain from that day had found him again.

He gave a nod he was ready to continue. "The first thing you notice about prison is the smell. The second, the noise. The shouting. I was terrified I was going to throw up in front of my father. Even after all he had done I still wanted to do the right thing in front of him. You know what my father told me in those few minutes I had with him?"

I thirsted for the tea no longer in my cup.

"My father told me all of this was my fault. That he had done all of it for my mother and her three sons. That the pressure for us to attend the best schools and garner the best education had weighed so heavily he'd felt he had no choice." Richard paused, catching his breath. "My father was unrepentant. He delivered the burden of guilt upon me. But that wasn't the worst of it."

A heaviness settled in my chest.

"While I drove home I went over the words that would reassure Emily, my fiancé. Reassure her I'd get all the money back her family had invested in my father's business. It was all gone. Confiscated by the feds. I went over and over my speech in the car. It took three hours to get home. Traffic was heavy. After all, Wall Street had been decimated and New York was on its knees." He used the next few moments to steady himself.

"That ride in the elevator to my penthouse was the longest journey I've ever taken. I eventually managed to get the key in the door. Emily's handbag was on the sofa, as was her cell, so I knew she was home. The news was on, discussing my family's scandal in the background. It was so unlike her to leave the TV on. She hated noise. Preferred music. Classical. Incriminating photos were shown just to make sure the public had a good idea of who'd ruined their lives. One of them was of Emily and I at a fundraiser. She apparently was guilty by default. She was an attorney and had nothing to do with finance.

"Our place was vast. Situated on the upper east side of Fifth Avenue. We used to sit at the window with our coffees in the morning and stare out at the park. I liked it there." He coughed to clear his throat. "Emily was in the bath. She used to say it helped her relax. I've always preferred showers. When I found her she was immersed in red tinged water from where she'd slit her wrists." Richard stared past me though he didn't focus on anything. "Her suicide note explained everything. As I took her in my arms, begging her not to leave me, all I could think of were my father's words, telling me this was my fault. I believed him of course, as we so often do. I'd not been attentive enough to see my father was an illusionist."

I wanted to tell him it had been his father's doing and not his, but all I could muster was, "I'm so sorry."

"Within a week, I'd buried Emily, put our home up for sale, and flown to L.A. Cameron met me at the airport. I don't remember much about the flight or those first few weeks at his place. I remember this place though." His gaze roamed fondly. "Cameron let me stay with him. Insisted on it. He was worried about me. I was having a problem with forming words."

"Cameron helped you?"

"Saved me. At first he referred me to a traditional therapist. She didn't know what to do with me. The second and third therapists I went to both agreed the only treatment that would help was ECT. An electric shock to jumpstart my brain. Their second choice was a chemical straightjacket. Cameron refused to let them do that to me. He was of course reluctant at first to take me on as a client, considering we're best friends, not to mention the nature of what he practices, but I can be very persuasive. I insisted I didn't want to forget the pain. The diagnosis landed on PTSD. In the end we went for the lesser known treatment of facing the pain head on. Cameron's technique." Richard's focus returned as though he'd joined me once more within the cafe. "It worked."

"That explains why you're so close to Cameron."

"He's always there for me. Never judges me. He proved himself as a friend when I arrived homeless and without a job."

"Is that why you took the position at Enthrall?"

"I was having sessions with Cameron and was actually hanging out there so much I kind of slid into it." He shrugged. "I really am happy there. I met you there."

"Do the girls know about your story?"

"Yes. They're discreet, but you've already discovered that."

"It also explains why Cameron's so protective over you."

"The feeling is mutual."

"You never use your real name now?"

"I dropped Sheppard in hope of distancing myself from..." He gestured the rest.

Leaning forwards, I took his hands in mine, curling my fingers around his.

He squeezed my hands. "This is why I pushed you away. Not

because I don't care about you but because I would never want to expose you to my past. I've been trying to protect you. I let Emily down terribly. I'm responsible for her death. She was so fragile."

I rose and made my way around to his side and settled into his lap, wrapping my arms around his neck and hugging him.

He kissed my forehead again and again, his affection unrelenting. We stayed like this for what seemed like an eternity. It was hard to remember him not being in my life and I didn't want to go back to the time he wasn't. I planted soft kisses upon his lips.

Richard rested a finger beneath my chin and tilted it upward. "Until I met you I didn't believe I could ever feel another emotion." His eyelids fluttered. "I don't want to scare you away."

"Never. I love you." And life pre-Richard was an empty, desolate land without love.

"I'll always love you, Mia, always." He sealed his promise with a kiss. "I will never do anything to hurt you."

"I'll do anything for you," I said. "Richard Booth Sheppard."

He gave a smile. "Be happy. That is all I'll ever ask of you."

I snuggled into his neck, his steady heart beating against my chest, wanting nothing more than to stay here forever.

CHAPTER TWENTY-FIVE

I WROTE MY NAME IN PENCIL IN ENTHRALL'S APPOINTMENT BOOK and secured myself an 11:00 A.M. with Richard.

Soon he would arrive, and just as I'd done each morning since I'd begun working here I'd hand him the book. There came little doubt that in Richard's arms I'd feel safe when taken down into Enthrall's depths. Thoughts of what might unfold there caused tingles of excitement to unfurl, sending a thrill between my thighs.

"I have so much pleasure to show you."

Blushing wildly, I tucked my Frederick's of Hollywood shopping bag farther beneath the desk, barely hiding it behind the glass fronted panel. I took a moment to check email. There were several of them and all of them routine.

Half in a daze, I opened my Google browser and entered Richard Booth Sheppard. In stark contrast to last time I'd searched, there were literarily thousands of results. By merely dropping his last name he'd successfully removed himself from any listings. I clicked images. Richard stared back in numerous photos. There he was with his father, or so the tag indicated, and in another, strolling out of a restaurant after an evening of fine dining in Manhattan. In the one beneath, Richard huddled with his two older brothers, their similarities startling, their gazes upon their father hinting at happier times.

There were quite a few of him beside a pretty, smiling blonde, and as I ran the mouse over one of the photos I confirmed this was his fiancé, Emily Oren.

I clicked the link.

Baron King, a New York Times journalist who'd written the article on Richard, confirmed what I now knew. Emily's suicide note had been the only evidence keeping Richard from going to jail. The homicide detectives had quickly authenticated that Emily had indeed committed suicide, as had the on-call coroner lending his expertise on the matter. I felt terrible for Richard, losing his fiancé like that and almost being accused of her death. It must have been what sent him over the edge.

Throat dry, I read on, and a wave of guilt washed over me because I was able to have this love affair with him due to some terrible event that had wiped his life off the map.

Emily had used one of Richard's razors to cut her wrists according to Baron King, who had an indifferent way of writing, as though merely dissecting a set of experiences and not a man's spiraling life or a woman's death. Upon the screen I followed King's words, trying to grasp them. Emily had been three months pregnant when she'd taken her life.

A moan of sadness escaped my lips.

With unsteady legs, I made it through the staff room door and ran into the restroom. There, I splashed water onto my face, my chest shaking with sobs. A terrible sense of loss tugged hard and thoughts of that baby dying inside her wrenched at my insides. I imagined how Richard coped with having lost his child.

Cameron had alluded to this when he'd taken me with him to that restaurant Chez Polidor, providing a slither of insight that someone had eviscerated Richard's heart. The fact Richard might believe the blame still rested on him made me wonder how he'd carried on at all. I grabbed a paper towel from the dispenser and dapped my face, haunted by this startling realization.

I froze.

I'd left the screen up. I flew out and along the hallway, pushing the door open to the reception and almost tripped over my own feet.

Cameron sat in my chair with his stare fixed on the screen. His gaze found me. "It's best to delete your search history. That way your subject won't feel stalked."

"I know what happened."

"All of us here do our part to protect his privacy."

I gave a nod, wanting Cameron to know that was important to me too.

"We don't want a client seeing this now do we?" he said firmly.

"Emily was pregnant."

"Three months." Cameron clicked away until all evidence of my search had been closed. "Terrible ordeal."

"I'm so sorry."

His gaze found me again. "No harm done."

"Richard and I visited His Lai Temple," I said. "He told me everything."

"Good."

"His father lost all those people their money."

"That's an understatement. Edwin Sheppard crippled the financial system and left a wake of devastation." He lifted his hand off the mouse. "Did Richard tell you about the death threats against him?"

I shook my head, having not even thought of the consequences raging a war even now.

"He's safe here." Cameron glanced at the screensaver, taking in the Japanese garden that Richard had set for me. "Mia, I owe you an apology."

"I don't think you do."

"When I heard about you from Tara, I decided you'd be perfect for my patient." He tilted his head. "As you know, Richard isn't only my best friend."

I tried to remember if I'd turned the air-con on and couldn't.

"Months ago," he said, "Tara showed me a photo of her girlfriend Bailey. Mia, you were also in that photo. When Tara told me she was leaving I asked her to encourage you to apply for her position. Of course you're stunning. There's no question about that. You radiate a rare beauty. Natural and breathtaking. A striking combination. What I had also hoped for was you'd be as endearing as you looked." He peered at me beneath dark lashes. "You are. You're enigmatic. That trick you pulled when you asked for your job back in Richard's office made me believe I was some kind of genius."

"You lured me here?"

He reached into his pocket and removed a white envelope. "You've accomplished everything I could have hoped for and more. You've outdone yourself. You've achieved what the rest of us failed to do and that is rescue Richard from himself. His addiction to danger is dissipating thanks to you."

I stared at the envelope.

"I knew Richard would fall for you," he said. "But this result went far beyond my expectations."

I couldn't bear to hear anymore. My legs felt unsteady again and a surge of adrenaline gave me what I needed to run.

"At your housewarming party," said Cameron, "Bailey told me about your dream of becoming a fashion designer." He leaned forward. "In this envelope is your ticket to freedom."

"What do you mean?"

"Come here," he commanded. "Your work is done."

I stepped forward and took the envelope from him, hands shaking, heart aching.

"This check will provide enough money for you to enroll in the college of your choice. Set yourself up and live well for quite some time. Money's no issue. I come from old money. If you want more, text me. There's an endless supply." He glanced over at the screen. "I'm sure if you've Googled me too you'd have confirmed that."

I hadn't, but now I wished I had. Maybe somewhere in that search I'd have found something to enlighten me on what kind of man Cameron really was. Was this blackmail or merely his way of getting rid of me? Had I come between him and Richard, his protégé?

"Are you sending me away?" I said.

"I'm giving you your freedom. A relationship with Richard means crossing the line into our world and never looking back. This is not who you are. Quite frankly, you're not that type of girl."

My gaze found my Frederick's bag.

As did his.

He peeked inside and caught a glimpse of my corset. "Honesty with oneself is the most important factor in finding true happiness."

I gestured to the bag. "That's my answer."

"You don't have to do this."

"I don't want to leave."

"You're not even sure what it is you're leaving."

I stood my ground.

"Prove to me this is what you want," he said. "That you won't panic and desert Richard. Something tells me this relationship you have with him is about to get heavy. I don't want him hurt. And equal to that is your fulfillment. Your happiness too, Mia."

I swallowed hard, my heart and head racing in response to what he was saying.

I stepped closer to him. "Soon after my mother died I snuck into the attic to explore her personal items. You know, find out more about her from things of hers stored in a few dusty old boxes. I wanted to know her better. Understand who I was, I suppose. My mom loved to read, and amongst her collection of old books I found this one by Ayn Rand. My father had bought it for her according to the note inside. Well, I took that book and hid in my bedroom and read it under the covers with a flashlight. I was staying with a neighbor until they could get in touch with my father and ship me off to him. There was something comforting about knowing I had a piece of my mom. From the dog-eared pages, both my parents had read it."

"Atlas Shrugged?" said Cameron.

"It was hard to understand most of it. But I was determined to get what the book was about. I reasoned it might help me grasp a philosophy for living. Maybe even show me how to survive. A message from my mother from beyond the grave. Like she'd wanted me to find it."

Cameron's expression was calm. His focus never wavered, as though those intense brown eyes could read every emotion matching each word.

Shakily, I went on, "Ayn Rand made it quite clear that if you came across a child in need of help... you should let her die." A sob caught in my throat. "This was apparently not an uncommon philosophy. Even politicians have raved about how amazing *Atlas Shrugged* is and marveled at her philosophical system."

"Objectivism," said Cameron.

I took a deep steadying breath, hoping to make him understand. "Cameron, I..."

"You were *that* child."

"One week away from digging around the garbage for food."

Cameron's eyes watered though his expression remained still, focused.

I gazed down at the envelope he'd given me and ripped it in half. "When I first came here all of you were so kind to me. A kindness I've never known. My step-mother took me in because she needed me. Where others turned their backs on me you all opened your arms and welcomed me in." I moved closer, close enough to touch. "Richard paid off my debt. We're talking thousands of dollars. His kindness was unconditional." I caught my breath, trying to remain calm and let him see I could handle talking about this. "Don't push me away, Cameron. Please."

"Mia, I—"

"I know that condo I'm living in is yours. You did that for me to get me out of that studio."

He leaned his elbow on the desk and caressed his forehead. "How did you figure it out?"

"You used Lotte to entice me." I tilted my head. "I wasn't certain but now I am."

"Clever girl."

"Who's idea was the fish tank?"

"Richard's," he said. "We needed to think up a reason why you'd be asked to house sit. Do you want me to get rid of it?"

"I'm not sure I want to stay there."

"Don't be ridiculous."

"What I do know is this, I love Richard and he loves me. I belong here."

"That's a half million dollar check you ripped up."

"I don't want your money. I want Richard."

He held out his hand and I dropped the torn halves into his palm.

"Forgive me," he said. "I had to make sure you were certain. I brought you here. I'm responsible for you. For both of you."

"I've never been more certain of anything. I may still pursue my dream of becoming a fashion designer one day. For now, though, I'm happy here."

"Nice corset by the way."

"I think so." I gave a smile. "Look, I don't want my life to be vanilla. I want to have that same expression that everyone has when they leave here."

"Something tells me you will." He peered into the paper bag. "And stockings."

"Do you think Richard will like it?"

"I'm not sure who is rocking whose world."

"That'll be me rocking his."

"Bravo, Ms. Lauren, Bravo." Cameron leaned back. "And a bottle of champagne. You do know we have a no-booze rule? Giving Richard an excuse to punish you is pure ingenuity on your part."

"Maybe he'll make an exception."

"Maybe he'll use a paddle." He grinned.

I tried to suppress mine. "You're an expert when it comes to pro-filing. You knew I'd stay."

"Sometimes I'm wrong, though rarely." He brought a finger to his lips. "That'll be our secret."

The elevator pinged.

Richard headed out fast toward us. "I slept in. Someone kept me up all night." He flashed that adorable smile.

It felt wonderful to see him.

Richard frowned at me. "I woke up and you were gone."

"I hate being late," I said.

He rummaged through his satchel. "Everything okay?"

"We were discussing Ayn Rand," said Cameron.

"So early?" said Richard.

"It's ten in the morning," said Cameron, amused.

"As long as it's not Nietzsche," said Richard. "Rand was inspired by him. No wonder her philosophy was skewered."

Cameron looked over at me. "And Rand became sick in her later years and actually signed up for social security and Medicare." He pointed a finger to make his point. "So much for letting the weak die."

"I'll say," agreed Richard. "Nothing quite like life to humble you."

Cameron rose. "It really is impressive how many of those former less fortunates come back around to make a phenomenal impression on the world." He looked at me. "Everyone's worth saving."

"All very heavy before breakfast." Richard tapped Cameron's arm. "No doubt you've run six miles."

"Four."

"Only four," said Richard. "You're slipping, sir."

"I'm meeting Lotte for brunch." Cameron smiled. I'll see you two later."

Within moments he'd stepped inside the elevator and the doors shut on him, taking our conversation with him and hopefully never to be repeated.

"What was he doing here?" said Richard.

"He wanted to talk to me."

"About?"

"Us."

Richard stared at the elevator. "Well?"

"He cares for you so much he just wanted to know that I love you and I want to be with you." There, I said it, and it felt wonderful to share the truth.

"He's worse than my mother," said Richard, shaking his head. "I didn't like waking up and not seeing you there. What happened?"

"I told you. I didn't want to be late."

"I'm sure your boss would understand."

"I'll make him some coffee."

Richard waved that off. "I'll make it."

I grabbed the appointment book off the desk and followed him down the hallway and he wrapped his arm around my waist, kissing my forehead.

"What's in the Frederick's bag?" He opened the door to the coffee room, allowing me to go on ahead.

I bit my lip and handed him the diary.

He peered down at today's date. "You were having a pretty serious conversation with Cameron. What brought that on?" He walked away, keeping his back to me.

"I Googled you," I admitted.

"I Googled you too."

"Really?" My attention stayed on the glass pot.

He made his way over to the coffeemaker and rested the book aside. He set about brewing fresh beans. How strange, I could plan such a rendezvous and yet talking about it terrified me.

"I'm afraid nothing came up on you." He shook his head and smiled. "We may need to remedy that."

My face fell as thoughts of the articles flashed back to me.

"I imagine what you read about me blew your mind?" he said.

I opened the cupboard and reached in for two mugs and placed them on the counter before us.

"You read about Emily?" he said.

Brown liquid trickled and sputtered into the pot, the scent of coffee filling the air.

He ran his fingertip along the box of filters. "We hadn't decorated the nursery yet. We couldn't agree on the color scheme. She wanted yellow. I fucking hate yellow."

"I'm so sorry, Richard."

"I could have gotten used to yellow."

I cursed myself for bringing it up and questioned my ability to be any use to him, or anyone. I couldn't understand why he wanted to be with someone like me. A naive girl with little to offer. Tears stung my eyes.

He reached for my arms and pulled me into him. "See, now that's out of the way."

"You're not angry?"

"Heavens no. It's not exactly something you share on the second date." He shrugged. "Do you have any secrets you want to share?"

"No," I said, unable to think of any.

He let me go and poured coffee into the mugs. "Please cancel my 11:00 A.M." He handed the diary back.

My head jolted up and I stared into those blue eyes of his that only held mine for a second. The contents of my Frederick's bag was now redundant.

He added milk to my coffee and gave me one of the mugs. "Let's have lunch together."

"I'd like that."

He took his drink and headed out.

I clutched the diary to my chest, wondering why I'd not challenged him. Yes, he liked to be the one to lead in a relationship but I had an opinion too. I had desires to explore, and right now I felt him pushing me away again. I cursed myself for sabotaging today with my snooping.

Opening the appointment book, I ran my fingertip over where he'd put a line through my name under his 11:00 A.M. and lowered my gaze.

Richard had written my name against his 6:00 P.M. designation. Only this one he'd written in pen.

CHAPTER TWENTY-SIX

R ICHARD'S GAZE HELD MINE WITH A FIERCE INTENSITY.
Unable to wait any longer, I had headed on into his office for my 6:00 P.M. with him. I stood before his desk wearing my Frederick's corset, lace-top stockings, and thong, as well as these six-inch black heels that finished off my sexy-siren look. My hair cascaded over bare shoulders, tussled curls falling softly over the curve of my breasts. In the spa I'd taken my time doing my make-up, using black eyeliner to bold my eyes and applying eye shadow, going for a smoky effect. Mascara lengthened my lashes and plump bright red lips distanced me from the old Mia.

Richard pushed himself to his feet and made his way around to my side.

"I'm early," I said nervously.

"That's unacceptable." He looked indignant. "I made an appointment for you tonight as there's something I'd like to discuss."

Feeling awkward and disappointed he'd not mentioned my outfit, I crumbled inside.

Richard reached for a check on his desk and held it up. "Well?"

I read the signature. "I don't know why Monsieur Trourville would want to give me..."

"A thousand dollars? The memo has your name on it," he said sternly. "Something you'd like to share with me, Mia?"

"There was that time…"

Richard narrowed his gaze.

I raised my hand. "No, listen—"

"You can be assured I'm listening."

"Monsieur Trourville saw me distressed and mistook it for me wearing those thingys."

"Venus balls? Were you?"

My face flushed brightly. "No."

A ghost of a smile swept over his face. "Why were you distressed?"

"Because you took Courtney into…"

"What about it upset you?"

"It wasn't me. I wanted it to be me."

His frown deepened. "I need to decide what to do with this." He stared at the check. "You've put me in a very difficult position."

Despite wearing this corset, he'd managed to make me feel naked.

"You do realize alcohol is forbidden?" His gaze was on the open bottle of champagne that rested on the side table. The one I'd snuck in half an hour earlier. Endless bubbles rose in those two ornamental flutes I'd borrowed from his shelf.

He sighed. "They're antique."

"They're beautiful," I said. "It's a shame not to use them."

He arched an eyebrow. "They came from Winston Churchill's estate. I don't use them."

"I thought it might steady my nerves."

He really did have an obsession with Churchill. I wondered what else in his office or even home pertained to the man. There was no way I would enjoy that drink now. I'd be worried I'd drop the glass.

Something in his eyes…

A flitter of nerves burst from my chest. A smoldering need burned between my thighs and my eyelids grew heavy.

"Entering subspace so quickly?" he said. "Impressive."

My mind raced to grasp his meaning.

Richard moved away and reached for one of the glasses. "I want you aroused. Alcohol suppresses you. I will permit one final freedom." He handed me the champagne flute.

I took the glass by the stem, holding it with the reverence it deserved, and took a sip.

One final freedom.

I went for another.

He eased the glass out of my hand. "Enough."

My gaze stayed on the champagne as though it was my last ever drink.

"You must trust me," he said. "Do you?"

"Yes."

He curled his fingers and traced my chin and downward, pausing on my throat. "Your heart's racing." He gave a look of approval.

I was breathing way too fast. My breasts strained against this corset, threatening to burst out of their confinement. His fingers caressed the line of my bustier, causing my skin to tingle. A shiver of apprehension went through me as feelings flooded in that were hard to make sense of.

"It's called a frisson." He rested his hand over the exact spot where I felt the tingles.

I glanced at where his hand was. "But how...?"

"I'm your dom. It's my job to know." He looked intense. "Your safe word. Should you want me to stop, you'll say a word." He swept his hand through the air. "Choose something you'll remember."

My thoughts scattered.

He gave a smile of approval. "Venus?"

"Okay."

"Think you can remember that?"

"Yes." Though really I had no idea if I'd be able to. I hoped *stop* may also do the trick.

This wasn't the Richard I knew. He'd taken on a masterful demeanor. "Remember what I told you about the elevator?" he said. "What does it represent?"

"Surrender."

"Am I assured yours?"

"Yes."

"Do you know what enthrall means?" he said.

"Mesmerize."

"Enslave."

A stirring of desire took me over.

"It's time for your punishment." He rested his hand on the arch of my spine.

And led me out.

I found comfort in the strength of Richard's hand gripping mine. Stealing a glance at my desk, I became aware I was no longer that naive girl who had begun her journey there. A world of pleasure had always been waiting for me on the other side of this gate.

We stepped into the elevator.

Descending, there really did come the sense of surrendering.

Once out, I sauntered elegantly behind him, my pace slow and deliberate, wanting to emphasize I really was ready for this, but unsure how far he'd push me.

Punish me.

Walking through the main chamber, we soon passed the crisscrossed board that Cameron had strapped me to.

"Next time I bring you down here," he said, disrupting my thoughts as he opened a door to a smaller room, "you will wear a collar."

A rush of excitement hit me as I realized I truly was *his* submissive.

Despite being smaller, this room was similar to the one we'd left behind. The walls were painted a deep red and candles were scattered here and there, throwing shadows. Upon the central table hung fine silver chains.

We were bathed in soft red lighting. Time slowed as I took it all in.

"It's called a St. Andrew's Cross," he said, having caught me staring. "Bring back memories?"

I reveled in these unseen sparks shooting between us.

"Take off your panties," he said.

I stared down at my trembling hands.

He tucked his into his trouser pockets. "Can I be any clearer?"

My breaths were faster than they should have been, and I merely stood there as waves of lightheadedness provided a sense of unraveling.

He stepped closer. "Obey."

I slipped off my thong, allowing it to drop to my ankles, and he rescued my underwear from the floor then tucked them in his trouser pocket. With a nod, he ordered me over to the table. He took his time to roll up each shirt sleeve.

A tilt of his head. "Need I tell you again?"

I approached the table and, with both hands, gripped the edge.

This man was proud, complex, and oh so beautiful, and I was about to witness what he was capable of.

What I was capable of.

Richard pulled me back so that my buttocks shifted out a little from the table, readying me.

"I want to look at you." He arched my spine and prized my cheeks apart. "Beautiful arse, Mia." He rimmed the puckered hole with a fingertip. "One day I'll fuck you here."

My grip tightened on the edge.

He slapped my buttock. "But not today."

The dull ache between my thighs made me swoon as the sting lingered. With a firm grip, he shifted my butt higher and forced me to arch my back farther. "Part your legs. Yes, like that. Good. What is to follow has been deemed that which you deserve." He traced a fingertip along the spine of my corset and then gathered locks of hair, twisting it around his hand. "Am I clear?"

"Yes."

He raised my chin.

"Yes, sir," I said quickly.

"Better."

This yearning for him was so intense, a desire to please in any way he wanted. I was a slave to him, to his love, and willingly gave myself over.

"Wrists together," he said.

He showed a pair of handcuffs and swiftly secured my wrists within each band and snapped them shut. Shocked and excited by this confinement, my heart raced and blood thundered in my ears. He'd stepped away from my line of sight, forcing me to endure being bound and exposed while my anticipation built. Richard grabbed the bar between my handcuffs and dragged me farther down, straining my arms out in front of me and securing them to the silver chains at the end.

"This perfect ass is begging to be spanked." He slapped me hard. "All in good time." His hand slid between my thighs, caressing my cleft and exploring farther, fingering me.

Groaning, I rocked my hips against his hand.

"Did I give you permission to move?" He withdrew his fingers.

I groaned my disappointment. "No, sir."

"Lift your head." He eased those moist fingers into my mouth. "Suck."

My lips quivered as I tasted myself and a wave of pleasure flooded my groin. Another moan escaped me and I dragged my teeth along his fingers as he pulled them out of my mouth.

"This flirting with clients must cease."

I turned my head toward him to protest.

He slapped my buttock hard. "You were going to say something?"

"No, sir."

"Do not speak without permission. Understand?"

I buried my face between my arms.

"This is a cat-o-nine-tails." Richard grasped a fist of my hair and raised my head so I could see it. "Is it a suitable punishment?" he asked. "You may answer."

"Yes, sir." When I caught sight of the short multi-tailed black whip I buried my head again.

He dragged the tassels along my calves and across my thighs before tapping it over my sex and causing it to flinch. The lashes hit my buttocks in a continuous rhythm and I jolted forward to escape them. With a strong arm around my waist, he repositioned me. The strikes resumed one after the other and I gritted my teeth, the stun of the whip intense, my body quivering, my trembling fingers curling around the chains.

Forgetting time and place, this momentum bestowed flashes of insight with each lash, sending me into a trance.

It felt so good.

Standing upright now and free from the chains, yet still cuffed, I swooned from this rush of excitement making me shake uncontrollably. There was no time to savor this. I was too busy trying to keep up with him as he pulled me toward the wall, his ironclad grip forcing me to stay beside him. He positioned me to stand with my back straight against the brick. When my sore buttocks touched the coldness, I sucked in my breath.

"Hands above your head," he said.

With my handcuffed wrists held high, my arms felt the tension of this pose. Easing down the material of my corset, Richard cupped my right nipple. He rested it on top of the lace and did the same with the left. He tweaked my nipples firmly, causing shivers of pleasure.

"Oh, please," I moaned.

"Silence." He tweaked some more.

My jaw slackened, my breathing grew shallow. I pouted my pleasure and lowered my cuffed hands to reach for him.

His glare forced me to raise my arms again.

"Better," he said.

Every movement set me up for a punishment yet staying still was impossible.

"You're doing well," he said. "But there's room for improvement."

My eyelids fluttered shut.

"Open your eyes."

I was greeted by his fierce blue gaze.

"Hold your hands out." He unclipped the handcuffs and removed them, dropping them to the floor. "Hands behind your back."

Richard reached into his pocket and removed a silver clamp. He pinched my right nipple, working its pertness and closing the clasp over it. The pinch made me shudder and forced a groan from me.

"Hush."

He secured a clamp to the other nipple too and gave it a tug, shooting pleasure into my groin. I turned my head toward him wanting, needing, to be kissed.

"You have to deserve that." He turned me around so that I faced the wall and he positioned my hands out in front of me.

"Use your hands for leverage," he said, leaving my side.

With my fingers splayed on the brick, I leaned my weight against my arms and glanced back. I caught sight of the paddle.

He neared me. "Did you move without permission?"

"Yes, sir." I bit my lip, hard.

"Why?"

"To see what you were going to do, sir."

"How about I show you."

Oh...

My breaths were faster now, my legs trembling, my nipples straining against their silver captors.

"You may have noticed I don't like asking twice," he said.

I arched my back and pushed out my buttocks just as I'd done on the table. Every part of me wanted this, needed this, and there came an unfamiliar desire to fall at his feet, beg for forgiveness. Beg for more.

The whack to my butt came hard and I flew forward. He waited until I'd repositioned myself and then gave twenty or so slow gentle pats over where he'd struck me.

Another fierce strike.

"I'm waiting for you not to move." Richard ran his fingers over my butt. "I need to see you deserve your reward."

Bracing, I offered myself, wanting that slow burn of each strike that somehow made my clit deliciously pulse. The paddle came down hard and yet this time I managed not to flinch, instead remaining still, obeying. He dropped the paddle and wrapped his arm around my waist. His hand slid over my belly and down, his fingers finding me and expertly playing with that sweetest place.

"You like your reward?" he said.

"Yes."

He stopped.

"Sir."

Richard's hand slid over my buttocks, caressing the flesh and softening the sting. I let out a long moan.

"Back into position," he commanded.

It felt easier this time knowing what followed was a mind-blowing reward, if only I could remain still. Richard used the paddle again. Another strike, and another, but I so wanted my reward I buried all resistance.

He turned me around so that my back was now against the wall. My skin felt flushed and sensitive. He eased himself between me and the wall so that it was his back that met the brick and mine was against his muscular front, pulled into a hug. Richard's left hand reached for my groin and he eased apart my nether lips, exposing me. Proficiently holding me in this delicate pose, he used his right hand to bestow erotic slaps to my clit, and my cries responded to these shockwaves of bliss.

A dazzling throbbing. "Oh, please," I moaned.

"Silence, Mia."

My mewling echoed as he prolonged my indulgence by timing split-second pauses between each slap, perfectly maintaining this exquisite throb. With each one my body shuddered, anticipating the next, and the next, and the next…

Enthralled, I gave myself over completely.

Unrelenting, he continued to spank my pussy, sending seamless charges of pleasure through it, and I reveled in the sound of his slaps. The soprano sang ever higher, notes lifting and falling, dancing around us and sharing our intimacy.

Ecstasy.

The slapping ceased and his fingers took on their own rhythm, flickering faster, sending me over the edge and beyond. My orgasm shuddered through me as air snatched from my lungs, shattering me into a million pieces of nothingness.

Richard held me still until those last few shudders left me and I could breathe again, my strength barely returning to my wobbly legs. I wanted to turn and bury my head in his chest but Richard slid out from behind me, his expression of sternness not changing.

The nipple clamps came off and he guided me back over to the table where he lifted me up, my legs dangling over the side.

"You've been a good girl," he said, ripping a condom packet open. "Time to be rewarded."

Though not sure if I could take any more pleasure, my gaze fell upon Richard's cock, which was rock hard, and I yearned for it to be inside of me. He nudged me back so that I lay staring up at the ceiling and he lay upon me, grabbing my hands and easing them above my head.

My back arched when he entered me, tight and full, all the way to the hilt. The pleasure of his first thrust lessening the pain of this inner tautness. My channel tightened around his thickness and rippled with pleasure.

"You belong to me, Mia."

"Yes, sir." I wrapped my legs around him. "Yours."

He thundered above, sending delicious spasms into me and my back arched. My moans were suppressed only by his kiss.

Notes came and went, taking us with them and I closed my eyes, extracting nothing but fulfillment from having Richard master me completely. This searing pleasure rose ever higher.

"Wait for my permission," he said.

Blinded by these sensations, I tried to obey, really I did, but it was so hard to concentrate and I knew I was dangerously close. Richard perfected his pace, slamming against me, the sound of our sex slapping together.

Drenched in a wet heat, his face was focused and fierce, his pupils dilated as he took on a brutish pace.

"Sir, please let me come."

"Not yet."

I cried out, coming hard, digging my fingernails into his back and refusing to let go, refusing for this to be over. He went rigid, thrusting one final time before stilling and collapsing onto me.

We hugged like this for the longest time with neither of us willing to let go.

Eventually, the music faded.

Still inside me, Richard raised himself up. "You disobeyed." He gave a crooked smile. "Unacceptable."

"Oh."

"So many tortures of pleasure await you my darling, Mia."

I swooned. "When can we do it again?"

His lips twisted in amusement. "I've created a monster."

I reached up and ran my fingers through his hair.

Richard arched an eyebrow. "Why, Ms. Lauren, you have *the* look."

"Look?"

He beamed a heart-stopping smile. "Exhilaration."

I let out the softest sigh of realization and his lips met mine, kissing me firmly, opening my mouth wide as his tongue masterfully tangled with mine…

Claiming his submissive.

CHAPTER TWENTY-SEVEN

T HE SOUND OF ROLLING WAVES STIRRED ME AWAKE.
Dawn's arrival brought with it the freshest morning breeze
that kissed my skin awake. I lay curled up on Richard's lounger,
hidden amongst the palm trees, having fallen asleep with him on it last
night. Though he wasn't here now. I sat up, gripped by a wariness he
might have changed his mind about us. Of course this wasn't healthy but
with all I knew about Mr. Mercurial it was an easy conclusion to reach.

Still dressed in my jeans and sweater from last night, I needed to
take a shower and brush my teeth. Winston sat beside my lounger and
I assumed Richard had told him to stay and watch over me. Or maybe
Winston was getting lazier if such a thing were possible.

Memories of last night flooded in and I lay back once again, gazing
up through the palm leaves and beyond at the dusky sky. The warmth
of the early morning sun found me. A soft blush burned my cheeks as
I recalled what Richard had done to me within Enthrall's lowest room.
I had to admit the pain hadn't been that bad, and Richard had mingled
his punishment with so much pleasure it was all I could remember now.
The evening had been breathtaking.

A tingling in my chest made me catch my breath as residual sensations found their way back to me, leaving me giddy. I let out the longest
sigh.

Footsteps on the pathway signaled Richard's return and I sat up, ready to greet him. He turned the corner carrying two small bowls with silver spoons and a flask tucked under his right arm.

"Good morning." I smiled up at him.

He beamed at me. "How are you?"

I felt shy again. "Fine."

"I thought breakfast on the beach might be fun. Bring the blanket."

I'd missed him, even for such a short amount of time, and couldn't help but grin ridiculously with the thought of spending more time with him. I scooped up our blanket.

Following Richard's lead, I padded barefoot behind him and he led the way down the pathway. I was excited to see where it led. A little farther down he side-stepped, allowing me room to flick open the wooden gate.

We made our way beneath the archway of shrubs, soon finding ourselves standing on a sandy beach, and there, stretching out before us, lay a vast blue ocean. The sand was warm and smooth beneath my feet. Richard caught my expression of wonder and gave that serious regard of his and I melted all over again.

"Will this do?" he said.

"We'll make it work."

He grinned, looking so young and so innocent, the breeze ruffling his hair. It was hard to believe he had a penchant for pain, impossible to grasp this was the dominating Richard from last night. Sweeping the blanket wide, I spread it out upon the sand and we sat snuggled close to each other. It felt dreamy to have him back beside me.

"Oatmeal?" Richard handed me one of the bowls.

He rested his upon the blanket before him and reached for the flask, unscrewing the cap and pouring steaming coffee into it. The scent of fresh brewed beans wafted. He handed me the cup.

I took a sip. "You make great coffee." I gave the cup back to him and tasted my oatmeal. "This is delicious too."

"Secret family recipe." He raised his hand. "Please don't ask for it."

"Really?"

His smile reached his eyes. "Trader Joes."

"How come you're not down here all the time?"

"Believe it or not it can get kind of lonely." He shook his head. "Well, hopefully not anymore."

I reached around his waist and hugged him, resting my head on his shoulder. I breathed him in. The scent of fresh linen mixed with a waft of delicate cologne. That, and the sensation of his hand caressing my back, was a heady combination.

"We'll come down here more," he said.

"I'd like that."

He scooped a handful of sand and let it slip between his fingers. "Move in with me."

We were moving at lightning speed, actually make that warp-speed, and Richard's world was threatening to burn me up brighter than a solar flare.

"At least think about it." His fingers played with my hair. "You certainly know how to make a man's day, Ms. Lauren."

"I could say the same about you. This is the most romantic setting on the planet."

"Only if you're in love." He leaned over and kissed my cheek.

I now knew how it felt for my heart to skip a beat.

"Otherwise this place is merely a vastness," he murmured.

I wondered how many days he'd sat down here on his own with nothing but his thoughts for company.

Lotte's words came back to me. *"There's something beautiful about a broken man. Maybe it's some unspoken promise he'll become more than he is because of it."*

Although I'd not understood her words then, having not known Richard's story, I now had a sense of what she was saying. Richard's previous lifestyle of privilege and position and later his fall from the graces of New York society had softened him, made him a kinder man. He certainly seemed more approachable than the Richard I'd first met.

He pointed toward Venice Beach. "I imagine Cameron's surfing right now. Somewhere in that direction."

"Maybe Tara's with him."

"Maybe." He shifted to better look at me. "Let's talk about last night."

My face blushed and I turned my head away.

"What we did was considered tame." He played with my hair.

"Oh."

"You looked stunning. It was hard not to devour you in my office right at the start."

I could swear the waves were coming closer. "I liked it," I whispered.

He leaned in to me. "What was that?"

"I really enjoyed it."

"You're going to have to say it louder."

"You heard me just fine, sir."

"Back to sir, now. I approve."

I poked him in the ribs and he squirmed away from me, laughing.

Resting my bowl on my lap, I took the coffee from him again. "It was pretty amazing."

"And to think that's level two."

"How many levels are there?" I screeched it.

"About a hundred."

"What are you doing at level one hundred?" My throat tightened and I took a sip of coffee, hoping it would go down.

"Have you ever seen Clive Barker's Hellraiser?"

"No." And I didn't like the sound of it either.

"Before your time." He raised his hand with insistence, giving the widest grin. "It's a joke. Please don't go and Google it. Which I know you love to do."

"Why?"

"You'll throw a conniption." He pointed. "Oh look, there's a California Gull."

Following his gaze, I saw nothing.

"My mistake." He ate his oatmeal. "Yum."

"You're masterful at smoke and mirrors, *sir*."

He gave me a sideways glance. "Tell me this, Mia, how come nothing I do scares you away?"

"I think I might have fallen for you that first time I saw you at Enthrall."

"You mean that time you forbade me entry?"

"Yes. You had your hand over your eye and you looked so vulnerable."

"Pirate fetish, aye?"

He made me giggle and he laughed too.

"Seriously, Mia, the day you came into my life everything felt different. And when I say *felt* we're talking a miracle. I hadn't felt an emotion in over six years." He looked down at his hands. "I didn't believe I'd ever feel again."

Reaching out, I took his hand and held it.

He squeezed mine back. "Cameron reassured me my emotions would return but after several years I kind of lost faith."

I ran my hand up and down his back to comfort him.

"I've always had a thing for pain, but these last few years it was the only way I'd get a rise out of my feelings," he said. "Then you came into my life. I fell in love with you that first time you entered my office. You weren't afraid of me. You merely took in the room and then you took in me."

"You were nice to look at."

He flashed a smile. "It was probably your boots that sealed the deal."

"Do you think you'll always work at Enthrall?"

He narrowed his gaze. "For now."

I wondered how I'd adjust to dating a man who specialized in domination for a living. And I still had to share this news with Lorraine. I pushed that thought away.

"Does Cameron use S & M on all his clients?" I said.

"Goodness, no. He'd lose his license to practice medicine."

"Doesn't it make him dangerous, having such a deep understanding of people?" I said. "He could really manipulate someone if he wanted to."

"I suppose he manipulated us. Kind of," he agreed. "Still, Cameron's one of the nicest guys I know. He's worth a fortune and would rather spend his time with his patients."

"Or spanking clients at Chrysalis." I ate another spoonful.

"You make it sound so naughty." He pinched his tongue between his teeth.

"Cameron told me he's old money. Does that mean his family's rich?"

"He's the Cole's oldest son. The Hampton Coles. His great grandfather was Sir Thomas Cole, the tea magnet. His company makes an exquisite Earl Grey."

Of course Cameron had this air of privilege, but this news of his family came as a surprise. I wondered if Tara knew.

"He told me his father designed yachts," I said.

"He does. His father's a hard man to live up to."

There came a flash of inspiration and I felt like I'd gotten a glimpse into Cameron's psyche, which was a nice change from him rummaging around in mine. Perhaps his father's high bar of success had pushed him into a life of whips and chains.

Richard knitted his eyebrows together. "What's going on in that beautiful head of yours?"

"Why did Cameron become a psychiatrist and not go into boats?"

"Why such fascination with my friend? Something you'd like to share?"

"I'm trying to ward off any more Cameron manipulations," I said. "He's been nice to me but he's also intimidating."

"Gathering intelligence on him?" Richard feigned an appalled look. "And you're using his best friend to get to his weak spot."

"Mmmm, what is his weak spot again?"

"He doesn't have one." Richard shrugged. "That's probably why the rest of us hold him in such high regard."

"He scares me."

"He's harmless. The only thing to watch out for is his serious chase fetish."

I snapped my head round to look at him.

"He's hardwired to respond to a chase," said Richard. "Never run away from him."

My mind shot back to that evening in Chrysalis when Cameron had chased me, and then trapped me between him and the wall.

"Cameron's fetish is to chase, catch, and fuck." Richard beamed at me as though he found this amusing. "With the woman's consent of course. He'd never hurt anyone."

I turned my head away, not wanting him to see me blush. "What's your fetish?" I tried to change the subject, kind of.

"I'd have thought you'd have guessed it," he said. "I like spanking naughty girls." He arched an eyebrow. "When you trespassed into the dungeon against my orders you triggered my proclivity." He raised a shoulder. "By kissing Cameron you also stirred my jealousy. He knew I really liked you."

"Cameron knew what he was doing."

"My fixation played out just as he knew it would."

I reached out and grabbed Richard's hand.

"You okay?" he said.

"With you I am."

"You're so much more than this to me. You do realize that?" He stared off at the horizon. "I'm ready for a commitment." He brushed a strand of hair back behind my ear. "That is, of course, if you want that too."

I snuggled closer, wrapping my arm around his waist. "Yes, more than anything." Closing my eyes, I feared the words I had to share.

Richard sensed it.

Looking into his eyes, I braved to say it. "I'm not sure I could be your submissive all the time."

Richard leaned back slightly.

"I really enjoyed what happened in the dungeon," I said, "but as far as living like that every day, kneeling at your feet at breakfast and scrubbing your bathroom floor for your sexual pleasure…well…"

"Don't knock it till you've tried it." He planted a kiss to the top of my head.

A flurry of nervousness burst out of my chest.

On my look of concern, he added, "Mia, I have a housekeeper." He shook his head ruefully. "Though ever since she won that Miss World competition she's insisted on cleaning the house in the nude."

"Very funny." I poked his ribs.

He laughed and squirmed away. "Carmen's worked for me for years. She's fifty something. A grandmother."

"She better be," I said, smiling. "And not one of those super hot fifty-year-olds either."

"Look at you." He took my hand and kissed it. "I'm so happy you brought this up. We need to be open and honest with each other. This is good."

"So you would be okay with me becoming empowered?"

"Have you been talking with Cameron?"

"A little."

He caressed my back. "I'm not an egomaniac, Mia. I'd love nothing more than to watch you grow into a beautiful fully-realized woman."

I relaxed a little, reminding myself to trust and let go. Waves rolled in, bursting white foam onto the sand before pulling back again, lulling in the most perfect way. The sound was soothing, hypnotic.

Richard sighed. "So this is what heaven feels like."

Resting my head against his shoulder, I savored the peacefulness. An unfathomable calm settled within.

"I want you to know I'm financially stable." He broke the silence.

"Oh, Richard, I don't—"

"No, please listen. This is important. Although my father was corrupt my mother wasn't, obviously. She comes from a wealthy family. It's probably what intimidated my father so much. Anyway, what I'm trying to say is I'm a trust fund baby. Do you know what that is?"

"I think so."

"I inherited a large sum from my mother's estate when I turned twenty." He shook his head. "Funny thing is I didn't collect it until a few years ago. I was too proud. Which ironically kept the money safe from my father. Of course I also earn a good salary from Enthrall."

"So do I."

I didn't care about his money. I'd always taken care of myself and I loved the feeling of independence.

"Let's skinny dip." He rose and held out his hand to me.

He picked up the bowls and swept up the blanket.

I picked up the flask. "Where are you going?"

"We're not going in the ocean, Mia."

"The neighbors?"

"I don't care what they think. It's the sharks. They love this time of morning." He tilted his head for me to follow.

"But Cameron's out there!"

"I'm not the only one who lives life on the edge, apparently."

"And Tara." I stared out at the blueness as though I'd caught sight of a fin heading for Venice Beach.

Richard chuckled as he opened the gate. "Statistically it's unlikely."

I headed on through. "I think you just took all the fun out of skinny dipping."

"Well then," he said, "I'll have to think of something that will inject some fun back into it." He bit his lip and peered down at me with a glint of mischief.

CHAPTER TWENTY-EIGHT

HOW BEAUTIFUL RICHARD LOOKED IN THE MORNING sunlight. It burst through the blinds, bathing my bedroom in the softest yellow. I'd awoken to Alex Clare singing about falling leaves from somewhere far off in my condo.

Richard demurely moved around, searching for and quickly finding the clothes he'd lost in a hurry last night before making love to me throughout the night. That discarded necktie of his on the floor was a reminder of how he'd blindfolded me and then tortured me deliciously with pleasure. We'd hardly slept. Yet he looked as fresh and wide awake as always and I marveled at his ability to be like this without caffeine.

He beamed my way. "Enjoying the floorshow?"

"You're a lovely sight to wake up to," I said, stretching. "What's the time?" I leaned up onto my elbows to better see the clock on the bedside table.

He hopped into a sock. "Six. Go back to sleep. I have to visit home for a few things."

"Winston?"

"My housekeeper feeds him. I have a dog walker."

I eased up against the headboard. "Shall I come with you?"

Richard pulled on his pants. "No, I won't be long." He came round to my side of the bed and planted a kiss on my forehead.

Closing my eyes, I wallowed in his affection. He kissed my wrist and that small gesture of affection made me melt.

"I missed my IHOP visit yesterday," I said. "Maybe we can go today. Have breakfast together?"

"You don't have any cereal here?"

"It's my tradition, remember—"

"I don't have time. Sorry."

"Maybe next Sunday then?"

"Sure." He sat beside me. "I won't be in today." He picked up the clock and fumbled with it. "I was going to leave you a note."

"Are you taking the day off?" I wondered if I might get a free pass too.

He reached for my hand. "I'm going away for a week."

"New York?"

Maybe a visit to see his mother, which would be good for him and nice for his mom, too. I'd miss him terribly.

He put the clock down and twisted it to face the bed. "I'm going to be staying at Chrysalis."

All color drained from my face.

He shrugged. "We rotate. It's what we do. Four weeks at Enthrall and one at Chrysalis."

My chest felt heavy and I dared to ask him the haunting question. "Will you be..."

"It's my job, Mia. It's what I do."

I pulled my hand out of his. "Will you be having sex with people?"

"I'll be working as a senior dominant."

I scrunched up the blanket and pulled it higher. "Senior?"

"Let's discuss this some other time?"

"Maybe if you talk to Cameron he'll let you skip this week?"

He looked sympathetic. "I refuse to let him down. Anyway, Chrysalis is as much my business as it is his."

The ache in my chest tightened. "Business."

"We have high-paying clientele arriving." He glanced at his watch. "I have to go."

"Don't." I knew it sounded clingy but I couldn't bear the thought of him touching anyone other than me. Even if it was with the end of a whip.

Thoughts of Courtney came to mind. Richard would be doing a whole lot more with a greater number of clients.

I rubbed my stomach to ease the tension. "I'll come with you."

He scoffed. "I'll see you soon. We'll go to Santa Barbara for the weekend. I'll get to spoil my girl." He went to kiss me.

I pulled back.

"Don't be like this. I've been honest with you right from the start."

"Don't go," it came out as a sob.

"What we do requires concentration. Focus. Stop rubbing your stomach like I've delivered bad news." He sat up and folded his arms. "Your support would be appreciated."

"Support."

"Yes. Be mature. Accepting. Non-judgmental."

"How can I?" I snapped. "You're off to play manwhore for a week." It came out wrong.

Richard rose off the bed and let out a long, steadying breath. Casually, he strolled out. The front door opened and shut.

I was alone again.

CHAPTER TWENTY-NINE

C RYING IN ENTRHALL'S PARKING LOT YET AGAIN, I RECALLED the last time I'd been pouring my heart out here. Right after Richard had fired me.

He'd been trying to protect me from his lifestyle as well as his past. The thought of him not being in my life wrenched agonizingly at my heart and the knot in my stomach tightened.

I'd ruined everything.

Peering through my car window, I took in Enthrall. The building appeared so elegant from the outside with all that ornate brickwork sculpted along its facade. No one would guess the kind of things that went on in there. I couldn't go in until I'd gotten these tears under control. I dared not arouse suspicion about having an argument with Richard this morning.

I didn't mean that awful word I called you.

It felt like someone was trying to dig my heart out with a spoon. I grabbed my iPhone and I dialed his number. I was sent to voice mail. A lifeline within this terrible storm.

"Richard, I'm sorry," I sobbed. "I hate myself." I clamped my hand over my mouth, afraid of wailing into the phone.

I waited for him to call back. Richard had opened up his heart for the first time in years and I'd betrayed his trust. My moans filled the car again.

A ping snapped me back.

I read his response.

Richard: "*Mia, I love you. Everything is fine. We'll talk. Are you still my girl?*"

Mia: "*Yes. Do you hate me?*"

Richard: "*I only have love for you. I understand. Please be happy. Eat breakfast.*"

I'd been nothing but cruel to him and he'd responded with kindness. It was all too much. I burst out crying again.

Mia: "*I miss you.*"

Richard: "*Miss you too, my sweet Mia. More than you know. I may be off the grid soon. Don't worry. Nothing will change between us. Unless you want it to.*"

Mia: "*No.*"

Richard: "*Tell me you're okay.*"

Mia: "*Now I am.*"

My cell's low battery signal flashed on and off.

Mia: "*Cell dying.*"

Richard: "*Stepping into a meeting. Will call later. I love you!*"

Thank God, we weren't over.

A meeting? That sounded so formal. I wondered when the leather donning, whip wielding, paddle spanking bit began. *Don't go there*, I told myself. Think about how wonderful it is to wake up in his arms with nothing but the sound of waves. The ache in my chest lifted.

Not wearing any make-up this morning had been the only reasonable decision I'd made. I flipped down the sunblind and checked my face in the mirror. My cheeks were flushed and my eyes were red from tears.

I made my way into Enthrall.

Within half an hour I'd applied make-up in the restroom and disguised all sign of anything being wrong. Nursing this hot cup of coffee at my desk, I went through his emails and tried to take my mind off the bad start this morning. With Richard gone, I didn't feel like doing anything.

Perhaps Richard wouldn't mind if I took the day off, I mused. With that flash of inspiration, I pulled out my iPhone to text him. He'd get the message after his meeting. Hopefully I'd catch him before he went off the grid.

Mistress Scarlet strolled through the staff door and I hid my iPhone in the drawer.

"There you are, Mia," she said. "How are you?"

"Fine thank you," I said, "How are you?"

Scarlet was clutching a beige folder. "Richard's out of the office this week, isn't he."

"He's at Chrysalis." I tried to fake I was fine with it and studied her with the same laser sighted stare she held me with.

Her heavily massacred eyelashes blinked at me. "Mia." She stretched my name out, like a purr.

I took a sip of coffee.

"How are things really with you?" she said.

"Good."

"Hhmmm." She twisted her mouth as though readying to discuss all that had happened this morning.

Had Richard told her?

"What's your favorite movie?" she asked.

"Um…I'm not sure." I'd not seen one in months. I could certainly afford to go to the cinema now. Maybe I'd catch a movie this afternoon. Maybe I'd go shopping too and buy some sexy new underwear.

"Mine's the Matrix," she said. "There's this bit in the film—" She paused. "Have you seen it?"

"Yes."

"There's this scene where Morpheus is offering Thomas Anderson the choice of two pills. One is red and the other is blue. Do you remember?"

I gave a nod.

I'd seen the movie with Bailey. We'd watched it at her place on Netflix some time ago. I'd found the younger Keanu Reeves particularly hot in that long, black trench coat. Not surprisingly Bailey had found Trinity hotter.

"Do you know what those two pills are meant to represent?" she said.

"Making a decision?"

"The blue pill represents blissful ignorance versus the red pill that allows a person to embrace reality as it really is. The red pill brings heart wrenching, agonizing pain."

She must have seen me crying in the car.

"If given the choice, which one would you take?" she said. "Red or blue?"

"Is this about Richard?" I held my breath. "He's told me everything."

She narrowed her stare. "No."

"Cameron?"

"It pertains to you."

"Me?"

"Which pill would you take, Mia?"

My gaze drifted to the beige folder. "Have I done something wrong?"

"Red's my favorite color," she said. "I also tend to face my dragons."

"Red," I said. "I'd take the red one."

Her voice was steady and sure. "We do a background search on all of our staff. It's quite routine. It's the only way to ensure we hire responsible and honest staff."

A wave of guilt washed over me...*but you haven't done anything wrong.*

"We conduct a thorough search," she said. "We hire a private detective to round out the vast body of information we gather." She lay the folder on the desk and rested her perfectly manicured fingernails on it. "Your background search turned up something interesting. Richard and Cameron both decided it was best not to confront you with it just yet."

A wave of dizziness came over me with the thought of what they'd found.

"I thought you'd want to know. We did of course go round and around trying to make the best decision about how and when to tell you. In the end we agreed to disagree."

I took a sip of coffee to moisten my mouth.

"I can't keep this from you anymore," she said gravely. "Just can't. Cameron will be pissed but he won't fire me." She tapped the folder. "I'll be in my office. Come see me when you've read this. We knew you'd need proof when the time came."

When the time came.

Scarlet left me alone with the folder. I slid my mug to the side, careful not to spill any. My mind raced with what might be inside. Richard, Cameron, and in fact everyone here had been keeping a secret from me.

With an unsteady hand, I reached for the folder.

CHAPTER THIRTY

H IS FACE STARED BACK IN THE PHOTO.
An older version of the man I'd once known as my father. My dad who was meant to have died when I was four-
teen, yet these photos proved otherwise. His familiar strong jaw, that
thick waft of hair now salt and pepper, and those intense brown eyes.
The ones that had stared me down so many times as a child when I'd
played in the sand pit too long or made a noise when his favorite show
was on.

Standing with my back pressed up against the elevator gate, I
eventually found my breath again and took those few short steps
back to my desk and sat down. Hands trembling, I searched the file
for evidence my mom might be alive too. All I found was her death
certificate.

In one of the photos my father was wearing a sunhat, and from
the look of it he was working on a ranch. A vineyard, apparently,
from the detective's notes. Roscoe-Harvey Winery and Vineyards, in
a placed called Yountville in the Napa Valley. My father lived merely a
few hours away.

The paperwork clarified how the private investigator had tracked
him down. First following up on a lead that someone had been cash-
ing in my father's social security checks. Perhaps they thought it had

been me. The investigator had followed the trail, soon locating the man who'd evaded my life for over seven years.

In the same photo, a fortyish woman picked grapes alongside him. They were hugging. There was also a close-up of their wedding rings. My father had remarried.

Panic stuck in my throat and forced a sob out of me.

Lorraine had known about this all along. That's why she'd sold his stuff and not kept anything. That's why she'd not grieved. I needed to know why she'd not told me. Bile rose, bringing the stale taste of coffee.

My dad was alive.

And he had never once reached out to me. Surely he'd known the pain he'd caused me, the suffering of trying to make it without him? Surely he knew how much I loved and needed him? My mind raced on with all the reasons Richard had kept this from me. His own broken relationship with his father influenced his decision, no doubt.

Grabbing the file I ran for the elevator, ignoring Scarlet's invitation to sob on her shoulder. I couldn't be weak and ineffective. I needed to see my Dad.

Now.

As the elevator descended my legs gave out and I slid down the mirrored wall, landing on the floor and hugged my knees into my chest.

Still alive.

Swiping tears away, I tried to focus on driving.

Speeding toward Chrysalis, I knew Richard would have the answers I needed. How long had he known? Had he already reached out to my dad? I wouldn't stay long at Chrysalis. I needed to get on the road to Napa. Maybe Richard would come with me. What lay between here and seeing my dad felt like an eternity.

The manor loomed large on the horizon. I navigated too fast up the long driveway and leaves scraped along the right side of my window and a branch shoved my wing mirror back. Chrysalis was even more intimidating in the daylight. Parking farther down, I avoided the valet. The two men on duty were already busy greeting the arriving guests. One of the valets had a set of Louis Vitton luggage on a cart, having just removed them from the back of a BMW.

Without the fog machine came a clearer view of the foyer. It reminded me of a five-star hotel, like the Bellagio in Las Vegas. The marble flooring, low ceiling, and soft lighting made everything look expensive. They even had a pretty brunette working behind a reception desk.

Richard had told me only millionaires could afford to be here. I assumed the thirty-something woman who'd owned the BMW was one of them. She reminded me of Mrs. Sullivan. She regarded me critically.

Oh no.

Dominic stormed toward me. Gone was that toga I'd last seen him in and in its place he wore a flashy pinstriped suit.

"Why, if it isn't the director's plaything," he said.

"Can you get Richard Booth for me please?" I sucked back tears.

"What's wrong?" Dominic reached for my arm. "Let's hide you."

I pulled out of his grip. "I have to see Richard."

"Mr. Booth is in a board meeting. As is the director. Come, let's have you wait in his office."

I pulled out of his grip.

"What's that?" He stared at the beige folder. The one I was currently clutching to my chest.

He looked worried. "May I see it?"

"Please, tell Mr. Booth I need to speak with him immediately."

He held his hand out. "Give it to me."

"Is Cameron here?" My tears welled. "Dr. Cole?"

"Oh dear, please don't. We have VIP's arriving." He gave a reassuring nod to Mrs. Sullivan's look-alike. "You can't be seen sniveling." He snatched the folder.

The contents went flying. Papers glided through the air and fanned around us, showing photo after photo of my father going about his business, thriving in his new life and no longer caring about those he'd left behind. The only clue to his selfish philosophy was his Ayn Rand book.

I escaped Chrysalis.

Driving at full speed towards the 5 freeway, hands shaking, wiping tears away, I knew there could be no other way but to face this alone. My iPhone rang but I ignored it and left it inside my handbag on the passenger's seat. I didn't want to talk. No one would understand this anyway.

"Roscoe-Harvey Winery and Vineyards," I made it a chant, having left the file scattered on Chrysalis's marble tile.

A mixture of hurt and hope welled within. A sense that if I could get over this betrayal a brighter future really did lay ahead. If I'd learned anything it had to be the wisdom of allowing others to open up in their own time and give them the space they needed until they were ready to share the reason for their decisions. Thinking of Richard and all he'd taught me brought comfort.

Still…

I'd been betrayed in the worst kind of way by the one person who was meant to protect me from these kind of horrors. Anger and relief wrapped around each other and it was hard to tell one from the other.

A blue light flashed in my rearview mirror, followed by the wail of the police car's siren.

Oh no. Oh fuck.

Blood pounded in my ears. With my indicator on I navigated across three lanes and pulled to a stop on the hard shoulder. Despite wanting to hide my face in my hands, I acted like nothing was amiss. I buzzed my window down and placed both hands on the wheel and watched the officer approach. My right wing mirror was still flipped back from its collision with Chrysalis's foliage.

The cop leaned low and peered into my window. "Turn off your engine, Ma'am." He flipped open his notebook. "Driver's license and registration."

He barely glanced at my license. "Ms. Mia Lauren?"

"Yes."

"Step out of the vehicle, please."

"Why?"

"Step out and lock your vehicle, please. Bring your valuables." He glanced behind him at the speeding cars. "Careful please."

Gripping my right arm, he guided me around the back of my car and toward his patrol vehicle. Its light still flashed. Clutching my handbag into my chest I cringed; other drivers were catching this. The officer opened the rear door and gestured for me to get in. Somewhere in the far reaches of my mind I tried to remember if this was routine. Wasn't he meant to give me a ticket and send me on my way? His partner, a young officer with a kind face, turned in his seat to peer back.

"Your car will be towed," he said. "No need to worry."

His colleague climbed back into the driver's seat.

"There's nothing wrong with my car," I said. "I got the oil fixed."

They swapped a glance with each other.

"Please put your seatbelt on," said the young officer.

"Have I done something wrong?" I said.

We took off smoothly and merged into in the slow lane. The other cars on the freeway gave us a wide berth. Abandoning my Mini felt horrible, as though somehow I'd let it down.

The young officer turned and held out the contents of a yellow candy packet. "M & M?" He offered me one.

Half in a daze, I reached in and took one. "Was I speeding?"

"Yes," he said, reaching into the bag himself and popping a candy into his mouth.

Upon the central console flashed my driver's license photo. The officer driving punched a few buttons and cleared the screen. The radio crackled and he replied in short bursts of lingo.

The M & M was melting in my palm. I peered down at the small red oval of stickiness.

"Which one would you take?" Scarlet had asked. *"Red or blue?"*

I popped the candy into my mouth and sucked away on this surrealistic moment.

We sped down the other side of the freeway, heading fast in the opposite direction of Napa Valley, and my heart ached with my failure to even get out of L. A. I considered phoning Richard but then again his meeting could keep him busy for hours and I wasn't sure if I really wanted him knowing about this. Though his private detective would probably find out.

We were back on the street now, swiftly gliding through traffic and passing shops, homes, and pedestrians. We drove for too long and seemed to pass several counties, along with their police stations. This was so drawn out. I cursed myself for not taking more care with my speed. We headed into the hills.

"Ma'am," said the young officer. "May we drop you off here?"

I tried to read his expression to see if I'd heard him right. We were approaching Chrysalis. The car glided up the sprawling driveway with Chrysalis rising above the arch of the hill. This revolving nightmare promised never to cease.

Dominic and Cameron were chatting away on the front steps of the house. With my seatbelt off, I waited for the car to come to a stop and the officer to unlock my door.

I flew out of there and stomped toward Cameron. "Did you send them to arrest me?"

Cameron arched an eyebrow.

"Did you?" I said.

"Were you read your rights?" He stepped past me and headed toward the police car.

"No," I said.

"Then they didn't arrest you." He greeted the officers.

From the way Cameron spoke casually and shared a joke, he knew them well. Dominic moved toward me and I stepped back, focusing on the interaction between Cameron and the officers.

"See you Saturday." Cameron waved goodbye and on my reaction he added, "They pick up extra hours as security for me. Very reliable, as you can imagine."

The police car disappeared down the driveway. Although relieved to be no longer their passenger, my anger bubbled up and my fists tightened around my handbag, threatening to hit Cameron with it. He'd scared the hell out of me.

"Sweetheart," he said, "let's go inside."

"I need my fucking car back," I said.

Richard hurried out of the front door and he was holding my folder. "Mia, are you okay?"

"You had no right!"

"Shall we take this inside?" said Dominic.

"Come on." Cameron gestured.

"No. I'm going to Napa." I stared at the folder. "Why didn't you tell me?"

Cameron stepped closer. "Scarlet told you?"

I broke his gaze.

"Scarlet," said Cameron, sharing a stern glance with Richard.

"You should have told me," I said.

"We were waiting for the right time," said Richard.

"You had no right to snoop into my private life," I said. "Invade my privacy like this."

"Take a breath," said Cameron.

"Have you spoken to my Dad?" My lips trembled.

"No," said Cameron. "Not yet."

"Does Lorraine know?" I covered my hand over my mouth, trying to suppress my sobs. "He never died. You knew and you didn't tell me."

Richard reached out for me. "We just found out."

I stepped back.

"Try and understand," he said. "We were waiting for the right time."

"The right time for you," I said. "My father's alive. I'm not wasting another second. I'm going to see him right now."

"She right," said Cameron. "Mia, I wanted to have a session with you first. Feel out how you felt about all this. Break it to you slowly. I'm so sorry you found out this way." He clenched his jaw, the muscles working their tension.

"I need to borrow your car," I said.

"You're in no state to drive."

"I'm fine."

"You can't go alone." Cameron peered over at Dominic. "You're me tonight."

"Oh goody," said Dominic.

"Get Scarlet over here," said Cameron. "She'll take your place, Richard. It's the least she can do." He rolled his eyes. "We'll take the Benz."

"What about the guests?" said Dominic.

"I'll make an appearance later." He took a step closer to Richard. "We'll have Lotte come with us."

Richard chewed his lip thoughtfully. "Good idea."

Cameron glanced at his watch. "You sure you want to see your father today, Mia?"

"Yes."

"Doesn't Gabe Donnell have a house in Napa?" asked Cameron. "In fact I think it's not far from Yountville."

"One of many, yes," answered Richard.

"Dom, tell Gabe we're dropping in," said Cameron. "Have a car ready for us when we arrive at his place."

"Got it," said Dominic. "Any preference?"

"Make it a convertible," said Richard. "Mia loves convertibles."

In a daze, I followed them inside.

Despite all the activity, I could do nothing but think of the words I'd say to my father. I hardly caught what Richard and Cameron were saying to me or each other. Something about the arrangements for here. Something about notifying somebody about something.

Waiting was killing me.

We made our way through the manor, passing room after room. Once outside, we walked past the swimming pool that had been lit from beneath with bright red lights the night of Chrysalis's party.

Richard wrapped his arm around me and we followed Cameron and Lotte down the twisting pathway. Lotte was dressed in jeans and a sweater, a quick change from the black leather she'd been wearing twenty minutes ago.

A silver helicopter rested on a helipad.

"It's an EC145 Mercedes-Benz," said Richard. "Very safe."

I looked around for the pilot. "We're going in that?"

"Yep," he said.

He assisted me into the backseat. Inside looked just as impressive with its stitched leather seating and wood trim. This day continued to spiral into the realms of revelations and unexpected risks, leaving me speechless.

Richard pulled a blue safety belt across me and strapped me in. "Comfy?"

I gave a nod, though still not sure about all this.

Richard trotted around to the front passenger side and climbed in beside Cameron. Lotte settled next to me. Her hand reached for mine and she gave it a squeeze. She handed me a set of headphones with a mouth piece and I placed them on. Richard and Cameron already wore their headgear. I could hear Cameron's voice in my headset. He was conducting a set of checks and talking to someone in air traffic control. There were so many buttons and lights on the front panel I wondered how he'd remember them all. It all looked so complicated.

"What's this one for again?" Cameron pointed to the panel.

"He is of course joking." Richard's voice echoed inside my headphones and he turned to glance back at me. He rolled his eyes.

I willed myself not to throw up over the leather seat.

Cameron's voice came from my headphones. "As far as I can remember, you just jiggle a few gadgets and hope nothing falls off."

Lotte burst out laughing. "Will you shut up."

Cameron flicked a switch on the ceiling. "Look at this as a character building exercise."

"My character's just fine, Dr. Cole," said Lotte.

"She has a point," said Richard.

"I'm the only one who's allowed to be right," said Cameron. "Remember that memo?"

"Oh yeah," said Richard, "I remember now." He turned to look back at me again. "Seriously, he's the best pilot I know."

Cameron flicked switches on the front panel, setting off a whirring above our heads, scattering leaves around us. A swirl of dust blew outward. The engine hummed as the rotaries chopped through the air, blurring the blades.

"I usually keep my eyes shut during takeoff," said Cameron wryly.

"Thanks for that," said Richard.

Despite this adventure, there was a hole in my heart, and a knot in my gut making it hard to breathe. Feelings of betrayal welled along with that old familiar grief as pain found a home inside me again. Confusing, conflicting emotions twisted in my chest over the thought that I'd soon be reunited with my dad.

Gravity pushed me down into my seat as the helicopter rose, banking left.

The grand view of Chrysalis shrank below.

CHAPTER THIRTY-ONE

WITHIN MY HEART LAY THE POSSIBILITY OF FORGIVENESS. I couldn't wait to see my Dad again. Though there was also a stirring of something unfamiliar for the man who'd put me through so much pain. It should never have been like this. I'd never stopped him from doing anything, ever. I couldn't grasp why he'd rejected me. He might as well have been dead.

Had this been any other day, I would have raved about flying in a helicopter. It made me wonder what other skills Richard and Cameron might have. Perhaps I'd even have felt excitement for visiting the wine country for the first time.

We had made a smooth landing on Gabe Donnell's helipad in Yountville. Abe wasn't there because he was off training for Saturday's game. As one of the Baltimore Ravens' star players, he wasn't due home for a while. His house was enormous, and from the air we'd gotten a good view of both his tennis court and an Olympic-sized swimming pool. We ignored his invitation to hang out there and merely walked the short distance to a waiting convertible Lexus.

We passed vineyard after vineyard with their lush bunches of green and purple grapes strewn upon vines that sprawled on either side of us. The greenery was a refreshing change from L.A.'s dry landscape. The open top car allowed this evening breeze to find us.

Sitting in the backseat beside Lotte, I balled my hands into fists of nervousness, willing Cameron to drive faster. He focused on the road ahead, having checked the location of the winery before we'd left. He drove with confidence since he'd memorized our route. Now and again I caught his reassuring smile for me in the rearview mirror.

Richard sat beside him in the front passenger seat and occasionally shared a word or two with him but mostly stared at the view. Lotte frequently offered a look of support and it went a long way to ease this uncertainty.

A well of emotions made me sigh.

And sigh again.

Running over the words I'd use to comfort him, I vowed to reassure my dad there was no anger but only joy with our reunion.

Forgiveness.

Richard's love gave me the strength I needed to see this through.

There were so many questions. I was about to know more about my father than I ever had, and even other relatives too. Unanswered issues could be solved. I needed to know what he'd done with his life until now. I knew it wouldn't be easy for him or me, but in my heart I knew we'd survive this. The thought of his embrace, the feeling of falling into his arms again, would be forever treasured. I marveled at my ability to let the past go. I'd come to understand. I knew I would. With Richard by my side, I could face anything. And Cameron too, with his remarkable ability to communicate with anyone. He'd see to it I was understood. He'd help me say the words that would no doubt come out scrambled.

A sign announced we'd arrived at Roscoe-Harvey Winery and Vineyards. Trying to calm my pounding heart and not leap out of a moving vehicle, I rested my hand on the door handle. Cameron slowed the car and brought it to a stop halfway up the driveway. I climbed out. A ranch-style house was surrounded by a white picket fence. Old brick surrounded by a lush landscape of trees gave away this estate had been here for years. A hundred at least. There was history here, the family kind, and I wondered how my father had found this place.

A ranch hand approached. "Have you come for the wine tasting?"

"We've come to visit Mr. Lauren," Cameron told him. "Can you tell us where we'll find him?"

"You have an appointment?"

"We do," lied Richard.

The man pointed. "Over there."

Richard gave me a *well that was easy* glance.

"Mia," said Cameron softly. "This is a very delicate time—"

"I'm not wasting another second," I said, squirming out of Richard's hug.

"We'll be right here, baby, okay?" Richard, seemed lost as to what to do with his arms.

"Mia," Lotte called after me. "Go easy on him."

"Call if you need us," said Cameron.

I began the journey down the longest avenue, striding between the vines.

My mind looked for refuge, turning to the mundane, like what kind of wine these purple grapes would make. Richard loved wine. Cameron too. Maybe we'd get to taste their vintage. No doubt Cameron would want a bottle or two to take home.

I should have had them come with me.

There, ten or so feet away, stood my father. his heavy jaw clenched in concentration. He picked grapes off a vine, his sunhat pulled low. He painstakingly twisted each grape with a delicate motion, a care I couldn't remember ever seeing in him.

I took a deep, steadying breath. "Dad."

He paused, his face unreadable.

"It's me, Dad."

"*Mia*," he mouthed.

I tried to contain my excitement at this moment I'd never dreamed possible, my joy threatening to fill the air and find its freedom.

A fiftyish blonde stepped into view. "Who is it, dear?"

Her cream colored straw hat flopped over her face and she eased it up. This was the woman from the photos, her cheeks flushed from the sun, her many lines revealing years of exposure to weather.

"It's no one," said Dad. "The girl's lost." He pointed. "The winery's that way."

My mind tried to reason with the truth, my own thoughts betraying me, reassuring that he hadn't just denied he knew me.

The knot in my stomach tightened, bringing with it a wave of dizziness. Nausea threatened to spill. I reached out to the side and quickly withdrew my hand. With nothing but vines to hold onto, I feared damaging the grapes, feared ruining everything.

It was already ruined.

"She looks like a little lost waif," whispered the woman.

With a nod of agreement, my father resumed easing grapes off a low hanging vine, his attention focused once more upon his delicate work.

My legs rescued me. Taking over where I failed, they guided me back along the pathway. The journey took longer to get back. Waiting for me beside the Lexus stood Cameron, Richard, and Lotte, their faces marred with confusion.

Walking a steady path back to them, I left myself behind. That innocent version of myself. That silly girl who in my mind's eye lowered herself to her knees, clawing the dirt, her tears soaking the soil, her fingernails filthy, her wails reaching over this ranch and beyond its stupid perfect white picket fence and its hateful lies.

Its ugly betrayal.

This Mia, this new woman of the world, merely made her way calmly. I followed what Richard and Cameron had taught me about pain, forcing it into a ball to be dealt with later, manipulate it into whatever I needed it to be.

Vaguely, I felt Richard wrap his arms around me.

"Oh baby," he said, burying his face in my hair.

"What did he say?" asked Lotte.

"It's what he didn't say," said Cameron, resting his hand on my shoulder.

"What happened?" said Lotte.

"In her own time," said Cameron.

The sob refused to leave my body, preferring to settle in my throat and threaten to choke me should I move, talk, or dare breathe.

"Let's get back in," said Cameron, breaking away and opening the front passenger door.

Richard took a step forward and his stare swept the vineyard. "I'm going to talk to him."

Cameron grabbed his arm.

Richard looked heartbroken, as though losing his father all over again in that awful New York prison, thousands of miles away and so long ago.

"In you get," said Cameron.

Richard climbed into the backseat and Lotte sat beside him. The soft leather saved me from falling. Cameron sat in the driver's seat, his face still and fixed on the road ahead as though he too contemplated what to do next. He started the engine, navigating the Lexus back down the pathway.

Silence screamed louder than I'd ever known. This aching, vice-like grip around my throat stole each breath, forcing a twisting in my chest. Despite the fresh air of the convertible, I couldn't catch any air.

"*We banish pain with pain.*" Came the memory of Cameron's words.

"Make it go away," I murmured.

Cameron reached out and held my hand.

"Please," I said.

He pulled the car off the road and brought it to a stop.

"Do that thing," I said. "Take it away."

"Oh Mia, right now that would be temporary," said Cameron.

"But it will work."

"How about we shower you with affection?" said Richard. "We'll go get a drink."

Cameron ran his fingers through his hair. "I'm so sorry, Mia, I should have thought this through better."

"No," I said. "There was no other way to do this."

He stared skyward.

Caressing my chest, I feared this ache would never cease. "He doesn't want me." Cameron spun round and stared at Richard, his expression questioning. "We'll get a hotel. Stay the night. Regroup."

"Good idea." Richard looked over at Lotte. "You okay with that?"

"Absolutely."

I leaned forward, the pain suffocating. "Oh, God. It's going to kill me."

Cameron turned in his seat to face me. "Take a deep breath. We're here. We're right with you."

There was nothing but an aching, a wrenching, making me fear I might disappear inside it. I pulled my hand out of his. "Do that thing."

"Mia," soothed Cameron.

"Do it." I begged. "Please, just do it."

"Cameron," said Richard. "Help her."

Cameron gave a consolatory glance my way.

Richard wrapped his arms around my seat and around my shoulders, grabbing my arms into my body, his hands gripping my wrists, holding me pressed back.

"Hush..." soothed Richard.

Cameron's hand rested on my inner thigh just as he'd touched me in Chez Polidor. His ironclad grip tightening, bringing with it a blinding pain, more than he'd delivered in the restaurant, and a moan tore from me. Yet held firm in Richard's grip, I couldn't move.

The only place to go, forcing me within.

To surrender...

Immersed in stillness, the heaviness in my heart lifted, swept downwards toward my thigh, burning brightly in a ball of pain and light. I squeezed my eyes shut as this absolute agony released me.

Cameron's hand lifted and he eased down my skirt, returning his grip to the wheel. "Better?"

My breathing settled. "Better."

"We get to spoil you," said Richard, letting go and leaning back once more in his seat. "That's non-negotiable."

Cameron navigated the car away from the curb and back onto the road, pressing his foot on the gas and picking up speed. Calmness descended as all pain dissipated, the ache in my heart gone. I shot Cameron a look and he gave a nod of acknowledgment; he knew.

I breathed in a deep cleansing breath. "Thank you."

As we picked up speed, I allowed the breeze to blow wisps of hair across my face and into my eyes. I let go.

Windswept.

CHAPTER THIRTY-TWO

T HE BARDESSONO WITH ITS FIVE STAR EVERYTHING WAS
the classiest hotel I'd ever stayed in. Cameron's decision that
we should book rooms in Yountville had found us here. He
told us that sleeping on today's events in order to make the right
decision was crucial. So we 'regrouped' surrounded by all this rustic
luxury, not far from my father's vineyard.

The view from our dinner table was breathtaking. Stretching out
beyond our private restaurant balcony was a spectacular vista of the
sprawling wineries that were enveloped by lush greenery as far as the
eye could see. This was the place that had helped my father forget me.

The table was elegantly set with gold-rimmed plates, polished silverware, and a pristine white tablecloth that I was terrified I'd spill
something on. The Chardonnay we drank had apparently won all
kinds of awards, including a top one in France, which apparently was
a big deal.

Not that I cared.

A ball of grief was stuck in my throat. I'd hardly touched my
creamy carrot soup that Cameron had ordered for me. He knew my
appetite was dulled and this was all I'd be able to manage. I hadn't
touched my bread roll.

I just wanted to go home.

"I'm going to burn it," I murmured.

"What's that, Mia?" asked Richard, his brow furrowed.

"The baseball card," I whispered.

Richard looked across the table at Cameron. Both he and Lotte had paused mid-bite, their hands elegantly poised on their silverware. I'd watched them eat. They held their knives and forks so gracefully. Same with the way they'd sipped their water, along with that award-winning wine, dapping their mouths oh so elegantly with those starched white napkins.

"I've been holding mine wrong," I said, gesturing with my spoon to Richard's knife and fork.

"Come here." Richard pulled me up and onto his lap. "No one cares about that crap. We love you. We just want you to be okay."

I snuggled into his chest and wrapped my arms around him. "Will you teach me?" I looked over at Cameron and Lotte. "Everything you know about everything?"

Cameron gave a gentle smile. "Mia, you've taught us. Don't you see that? It's you who have brought true beauty back into our lives."

"You saved me, baby," said Richard, nestling into my neck. "Showed me how to love again."

"You've already faced so much," said Cameron. "We wish we could make this easier on you."

"Your father's scared," said Lotte. "This has nothing to do with you."

"The truth is glaring," I said. "There's no room in his new life for me. If he is scared then it's for him." My hand swept wide. "That he'll lose all this."

"When his wife finds out he faked his death and put you through all this she's going to see him for what he really is," seethed Lotte.

"Eat your halibut," said Cameron.

She raised her hand. "I'm sorry. I'm just trying to say the right words to lessen Mia's pain."

"These are unusual circumstances," said Cameron.

"What about your dad?" I asked Lotte. "What was he like?"

Her hands tightened around her knife and fork. "I love my life now."

It seemed we all had a father thing going on, and as I made eye contact with Cameron, Richard, and Lotte they knew it too.

"Mia," said Richard. "We're here for you in any way you need us."

How, I wondered, would I ever have survived this without him.

Richard raised his glass high. "To solitary trees!"

Cameron threw a smile. "I'll toast to that." He raised his glass too. "*Solitary trees, if they grow at all, grow strong.*" He winked at me. "Churchill's words."

I stretched over, reaching for my glass, and clinked it against Richard's.

"Here's another," said Richard. "Churchill was accused of being drunk in the House of Commons. He replied to his female accuser, "*I may be drunk, Miss, but in the morning I will be sober and you will still be ugly.*"

I burst out laughing. "He did not say that."

"Oh yes he did," said Richard.

"Did Richard tell you he's a descendant of Churchill?" said Lotte.

"He sure is," said Cameron. "On his mother's side. He has that same intense look of concentration. Same ears."

"You never told me I have the same ears," said Richard.

"Waiting for the right time." Cameron winked.

"Are you really?" I said, laughing.

Richard gave a nod. "Churchill's related to an American. I wonder what the Brits have to say about that?"

"And I thought you were just another fan boy," I said.

Richard feigned horror and burst out laughing.

"I'm going to take you to London next time I go," said Richard. "You'll love it."

"Oh, I would love that. Can we ride on one of those red busses?"

"A double-decker?" he said. "Sure."

"Let's get a massage in the morning?' said Lotte. "Mia, you and I will get a stone massage. My treat. Have you ever had one?"

"No," I said, "Does it hurt?"

"No, it's wonderful. They warm up these stones to get them really hot and then massage you with them up and down your body." She shook with ecstasy. "Heavenly."

"I'll try it. Thank you."

"How about we do dessert in Mia and Richard's room?" said Cameron.

"I think I'm going to go to bed," said Lotte. "It's been a long day."

"These are no ordinary profiteroles," said Cameron, eyeing the menu. "We're talking award-winning—"

"What's a profiterole?" I said.

"Really?" said Richard. "There's no way we can let Mia go another day without ever having tasted one."

I glanced back at that perfect white table cloth. Not one of us had spilt anything on it. Cameron, Richard, and Lotte always showed respect for everything around them. I knew how lucky I was to have them in my life. They were showing me so much. Every moment, every experience, with them was so exciting. I'd flown here in a helicopter, for goodness sake, and I'd never in a million years have stayed in a hotel as beautiful as this one if it weren't for them.

Cameron ordered in room service.

Richard, Cameron, and I kicked off our shoes and sat huddled on the oversized bed in our luxurious suite. We sipped champagne from crystal flutes. The bubbles rose up my nose and it felt as wonderful as it tasted. Between us rested a silver tray upon which sat a mound of chocolate profiteroles with sauce drizzled around the plate.

"So, this is your first time?" said Richard with a look of mischief, bringing one of the small pastries to my mouth with his fingers.

Cream oozed out onto my lips and deliciousness stunned my taste buds. I rolled my eyes in ecstasy. "Yeah, I see what you're doing there, Mr." I laughed.

Cameron and Richard laughed too.

"Why, I don't know what you mean," said Richard.

I fed a profiterole back to him and his face lit up with ecstasy. I fed one to Cameron too and he licked the cream off my fingers.

"You guys are way too decadent," I said. "What am I going to do with you?"

"I can think of a few things," said Richard.

I popped another profiterole into his mouth and he beamed in delight.

Cameron climbed off the bed.

"Stay," said Richard. "Please. We want you here."

"Yes, please stay," I said.

Cameron looked thoughtful. "Another profiterole? You twisted my arm." He sat back down and popped one in his mouth.

We devoured the rest of our dessert. After clearing the plate from the bed and setting down our champagne glasses, we collapsed in a post-sugar lull. Laying between Richard and Cameron, our heads aligned and resting comfortably on the super soft pillows, we stared up at ceiling. I'd never felt safer.

"We love you so much," said Richard. "You know that, right?"

"I didn't know what love was until I met you," I said.

Cameron took my hand and kissed it.

"How do people survive?" I said. "How do they get through life?"

"Like this," said Richard. "Together."

"And we shove chocolate into our faces," said Cameron. "Truckloads of it."

"I thought it was just women that loved chocolate," I said, laughing.

Richard and Cameron gasped and shook their heads in fake disapproval.

"I love you so much," I whispered. "Both of you."

"Mia, you're proof of god," murmured Richard.

He fell asleep first. My hand still held tightly in his. Soon after Cameron's eyes drifted closed, his right arm flung over my stomach. Even with them asleep I felt their unending support, their love that shone more brilliant than the stars I could see from the far left window.

My thoughts drifted...

And settled on Chrysalis and the darkest wonders within its walls. The promise of freedom yet to be discovered, harkening back to Richard's words…

"Refreshed. Revitalized. Renewed. Reborn."

THE BEGINNING…

Also from Vanessa Fewings

MAXIMUM DARE

PERVADE LONDON and PERVADE MONTEGO BAY

PERFUME GIRL

THE ENTHRALL SESSIONS:

ENTHRALL, ENTHRALL HER, ENTHRALL HIM, CAMERON'S
CONTROL, CAMERON'S CONTRACT, RICHARD'S REIGN,
ENTHRALL SECRETS, and ENTHRALL CLIMAX

&

THE ICON TRILOGY from Harlequin:
THE CHASE, THE GAME, and THE PRIZE

vanessafewings.com

About the Author

USA Today Bestselling Author Vanessa Fewings writes both contemporary romance and dark erotic suspense novels. She can be found on her Facebook Fan Page and in The Romance Lounge, Instagram, Twitter and Goodreads.

She enjoys connecting with fans all around the world.

Made in the USA
Las Vegas, NV
05 November 2021